"You're a...lawyer?" Oh no, anything but a lawyer.

She looked more closely at the card. "Ritchie Perez. Flanagan, Berrington & Perez." She looked up. "You own the firm?"

"With my two partners. We do personal injury law. Serious cases." He smiled at her, seeming to sense that her reaction was not altogether positive. "I'm not one of those ambulance chasers you see on TV in the middle of the night."

Of all the jobs he might have had, she hadn't expected this one. He didn't dress like a lawyer. And he didn't act like one either. The few lawyers she'd had dealings with weren't the sort of people who volunteered at soup kitchens, or cared about anyone except themselves. Either they ran over anything and anyone in their path just to win a case and chalk up another victory, or they took your money and made you promises that never came true. Or worse, pretended you didn't even exist.

Ritchie. A lawyer. He was wearing faded jeans and a short-sleeved polo shirt that also looked worn. Of course, now that she looked a little closer, she could tell that the shirt wasn't cheap. Did she think a lawyer would wear his expensive suit to a soup kitchen?

He had fancy degrees and a successful professional career. So it was more than just her distrust of lawyers that was making her feel uncomfortable. Yes, she still thought of herself as an artist. But the truth was she was a waitress who'd dropped out of college four years ago and had dreams that each day seemed to slip further and further away. It made her wonder why he kept asking her out and why he was so willing to help Joey. There must be dozens of rich, sophisticated women with much less baggage than she had who would be happy to go out on a date with Ritchie Perez. And she still couldn't get out of her mind the notion that she'd met him somewhere before.

ALSO BY JANE PEDEN

The Millionaire's Unexpected Proposal
    --a Miami Lawyers novel

AND COMING SOON

The Millionaire's Intriguing Offer
    --a Miami Lawyers novel

THE MILLIONAIRE'S
convenient
ARRANGEMENT
a *Miami Lawyers* novel

Jane Peden

MR. MEDIA BOOKS
ST. PETERSBURG, FLORIDA, USA

This book is a work of fiction. Names, characters, places, and incidents are either the products of the author's imagination or are used fictitiously, and any resemblance to actual persons, living or dead, businesses, locales, or events, is entirely coincidental.

Copyright © 2016 by Phyllis J. Towzey
ALL RIGHTS RESERVED

No part of this book may be used or reproduced in any manner whatsoever without written permission except in the case of brief quotations embodied in critical articles and reviews.

Published by Mr. Media Books, St. Petersburg, Florida

All rights reserved under the Pan-American and International Copyright Conventions, including the right of reproduction in whole or in part in any form.

Visit us on the web!
http://www.JanePeden.com
http://www.MrMediaBooks.com

Edited by Bev Katz Rosenbaum
Copy Editor: Rebecca Cartee, Editing by Rebecca
Cover Design by Lori Parsells, Vibrance and Vision
Cover Art by iStock

Mr. Media® is a registered trademark of Bob Andelman

Manufactured in the United States of America
10 9 8 7 6 5 4 3 2 1

ISBN: 1537627880
ISBN-13: 978-1537627885

Also available as an e-book.

To Dave, Tom and Megan, my happily ever afters

THE MILLIONAIRE'S
Convenient ARRANGEMENT

Chapter One

Ritchie Perez closed the lid on his laptop, leaned back in his expensive leather chair, and looked out the floor-to-ceiling window of his office, taking in the panoramic nighttime view of the Miami skyline. It didn't matter how many million-dollar verdicts he and his two partners brought in. Ritchie never forgot where he came from. And the years of hard work and sacrifice it had taken to get here. He'd come a long way from the salary he'd made as an Assistant State Attorney, prosecuting gang members and drug pushers. His life now was a world away from his memories of growing up in one of Miami's poorest and toughest neighborhoods.

"You want to grab a beer?" His partner Jonathon – the Berrington of Flanagan, Berrington & Perez – stuck his head in the doorway. Jonathon, unlike Ritchie, had been born with a silver spoon in his mouth. He came from a long line of blue-blood New England lawyers who didn't exactly approve of his departure from the tradition of practicing corporate and tax law. Not that Jonathon was looking for their approval. It always amazed Ritchie that Jonathon, who'd had every privilege, was the cynical one, while, he, Ritchie, was the object of his partners' good-natured jabs about his reluctance to let any good cause go unchampioned. It was the main reason he'd left the State Attorney's office and joined his two partners launching their firm six years ago.

As a prosecutor, he'd seen so many victims, and although he'd

THE MILLIONAIRE'S
Convenient ARRANGEMENT

brought justice to the criminals who hurt them, he'd wanted to do more. In their personal injury law firm, he and his partners only represented the victims of serious injuries that were the result of the grossly negligent or reckless acts of others. They had built a reputation for taking on corporations whose dishonest practices resulted in serious injury or even death to consumers. And they'd qualified for membership in the million-dollar verdict club many times over.

He realized Jonathon was still waiting for a response.

"Sorry," Ritchie said, glancing at his watch. "I'm already late for St. Theresa's." His parish sponsored a Wednesday night soup kitchen that fed the homeless and, unless there were pressing matters at the office, Ritchie tried to be there in person working the food line.

"I still don't know why sending the check isn't enough," Jonathon grumbled. He dropped a heavy file on the corner of his partner's desk.

"Tough day in court?" Ritchie grinned. Anything less than an unqualified victory left Jonathon in a bad mood. So even though they'd been certain the judge would grant the opposing attorney's motion to continue, he knew Jonathon was steamed at what amounted to just one more delay getting a major case to trial.

"You don't want to hear about it," Jonathon said, scowling. "*Especially* since the way my schedule's looking now this case is probably going to screw up our fishing trip in Bimini Christmas week."

Ritchie shrugged. "Maybe the case will settle by then."

"Yeah, maybe. Sure you won't skip the food service at St. Theresa's tonight and go wind down with me? I'm buying."

"Go hit up Sam," Ritchie suggested.

"Like that will happen," Jonathan said. "Flanagan doesn't have time to grab a beer after work anymore. Not since he went from carefree bachelor to family man."

Ritchie laughed, and headed for the locker room of the small gym they maintained for use by the three partners and their employees, to trade his suit for jeans and a t-shirt. Jonathon had decided to get in a workout and by the time Ritchie left, he appeared to be in a competition with one of the younger lawyers in their office on dueling treadmills.

If Ritchie were honest with himself, he had to admit he was a little jealous of Sam. A little more than a year ago, Sam hadn't even known he had a son. Now five-year-old JD was the pride of his life, he was reunited with Camilla– the woman he'd loved and lost, and they were happily married with a second child – six-month-old baby Sophia. Rounding out the family was Camilla's sixteen-year sister, Olivia, who had become a fixture here in the office, working part-time after school and dreaming about the day she'd go to law school and follow in Sam's footsteps.

Despite the tireless efforts of Ritchie's mom and his five sisters to fix him up with "a nice girl," he was still single at thirty-three. He was a self-confessed workaholic, and when he wasn't working, he was busy donating his time to local projects, like the soup kitchen at St. Theresa's. At least for now, the occasional casual date was about all he had time for.

As far as he was concerned, unless a person could fully commit to supporting a family, not just financially but emotionally, they had no business starting one. Single parent homes and broken marriages were, in Ritchie's opinion, one of the leading causes for kids dropping out of school and turning to drugs and gangs. Effective intervention programs were pretty much nonexistent, and the criminal justice system was a poor excuse for a safety net. He gave his own parents a lot of credit for successfully raising six children on a tight budget, in an area where teenagers were much more likely to get pregnant or arrested than they were to graduate high school.

Tonight, at St. Theresa's, he found himself standing next to a surly thirteen-year-old boy dishing mashed potatoes and vegetables onto the waiting plates.

"So what's the matter, Joey?" Ritchie asked. He'd taken an interest in the kid lately. Joey reminded him a lot of himself at that age. The kid had a sharp mind, a quick tongue, and a knack for talking his way out of trouble. At the moment, he also had a black eye, a swollen lip, and a bad attitude.

Joey jerked his shoulder toward his older sister.

"*Maria* did that to you?" Ritchie asked. Maria was the other reason Ritchie had been enjoying spending time with Joey. Joey was just a kid, but his sister was all grown up. Ritchie figured she was probably in her mid-twenties, and other than the fact that she rode herd on her little brother and seemed to spend as much time volunteering as St. Theresa's as he did, Ritchie didn't know much about her. But he liked the way her

THE MILLIONAIRE'S
Convenient ARRANGEMENT

smile lit up a room, and he wouldn't mind spending more time with her.

"Nah," Joey said. "I just got into it with some guys, you know? Back in the old neighborhood."

"So what's the beef with your sister?"

"I'm grounded." Joey glanced over as his sister walked toward them carrying a replacement tray of mashed potatoes. "Probably for the rest of my life," he muttered.

Maria waited for Ritchie to lift the empty tray, then she slid the new one smoothly into place.

"You're lucky if I let you out again before you're thirty," she said. Her dark eyes flashed, and her skin was flushed from working in the kitchen. She glanced over at Ritchie and sighed, then tapped Joey on the shoulder.

"I'll bet *he* wasn't running around getting into all kinds of trouble when he was thirteen."

"Just don't ask my mother," Ritchie said. "But if you let me buy you a cup of coffee after we're done here, I'll tell you all about my life as a reformed thirteen-year-old troublemaker."

She flashed one of those smiles that had attracted him the first time he met her, and it looked for a moment like she might say yes. He'd asked her out before on an actual date, but she'd thanked him politely and told him she was too busy. If she didn't want to go out with him, he wasn't going to press it. But hey, this was only coffee.

"I'd like to," she said, her voice sounding a bit wistful, "but I really don't have time tonight. Besides," she said, shooting a withering look at her brother, "I have to keep this one in my sight at all times."

"Bring him with you," Ritchie suggested, and saw Joey perk up.

She laughed, tossing her hair back as she took the empty tray out of Ritchie's hands. "Can't. In case you haven't heard, he's *grounded*." She turned and Ritchie watched her walk back toward the kitchen.

"Man, she always says no," Joey said. "Why do guys keep asking her out?"

"Because someday she might say yes?"

"She does, you'll be sorry you asked," Joey said, lowering his voice and checking to make sure Maria wasn't in earshot. "She's a real ball-buster."

THE MILLIONAIRE'S
Convenient ARRANGEMENT

Ritchie cuffed him on the back of his head.

"Hey!" Joey said.

"Watch how you talk about your sister," Ritchie said.

"Yeah, yeah," Joey muttered.

It was only temporary, Maria thought later that night as she helped Joey pull out the sofa bed and get the pillows and blanket out of the closet. No wonder the kid hated living here. He didn't even have his own room.

"I promise you," she said. "As soon as I get a little more money saved up, we'll get a bigger place. Someplace nicer," she promised. "And you'll have your own room again."

"Our old place was just fine," Joey said, getting into bed and turning away from her.

Maria sighed. She hadn't realized when she first came back how much the neighborhood really had changed. All she had been able to see was how cancer had turned her young, vibrant mother into a frail woman who looked so much older than her forty-one years. Alarmed, Maria had taken a leave of absence from college and moved back home. Within six months her mother was gone, and, at twenty-two, she was the only one there to take care of nine-year-old Joey. Their brother Tito certainly wouldn't be around to help. There had been a small life insurance policy, but the medical bills and the funeral expenses had used that up. Returning to school to complete her degree hadn't been an option.

Now, four years later, she was more concerned with paying the bills than finishing her art degree and pursuing the career she'd dreamed of since she was a child. And a couple months ago, she was awakened in the middle of night by the police bringing Joey home – drunk and suspected of being one of a group of kids who'd vandalized a neighborhood business. After that, she'd decided she had no choice but to move them out of that neighborhood and get him away from the "friends" who were nothing but trouble.

It wasn't the first time Joey'd had a run-in with the police. Just a week before, Maria had to beg the owner of the same vandalized store not to press charges against her brother for shoplifting. So, she'd sold the house and moved them into a one-bedroom apartment that was way too small, but at least it was in a better neighborhood. With the second mortgage her mom had taken on the house and declining property values, she'd been lucky to sell it for just about what was owed on it.

She'd taken the bedroom in the small apartment herself and set Joey up with a sofa bed in the living room because she hoped he'd soon be bringing home new friends from school. She'd pictured gangly adolescent boys hanging out in the living room eating pizza and having sleepovers, while she retreated to the bedroom and shut her door to mute the sound of their loud voices and blaring video games. But so far, Joey showed no signs of fitting into their new life, and as far as she knew he hadn't made any new friends. And keeping him away from the old ones was turning out to be a lot harder than she'd expected.

She got ready for bed, leaving the door to the living room open to discourage Joey from sneaking out after he thought she was asleep. As she lay there in the dark, she let herself imagine what it would be like to actually go out on a date with that gorgeous guy who volunteered at St. Theresa's. He always had a kind word for Joey, and he didn't get offended or pushy when she turned him down. There was something familiar about him. She'd thought so the first time he smiled at her, but if she'd met him before she was sure she'd have remembered. With his dark wavy hair, quick smile and chiseled good looks he wasn't the kind of man a woman would forget.

Thinking about Ritchie's smile made her wonder what it would be like to have his lips pressed against hers, and those strong, capable hands holding her instead of trays of food. He was probably a really good kisser, and she'd bet he knew exactly what to do with those hands. She sighed, letting her head sink deeper into her pillow, closing her eyes, and willing herself to fall asleep.

Maybe once she got ahead a little financially, moved herself and Joey into a bigger place, felt comfortable that she could actually trust Joey to stay out of trouble for more than five minutes... then, if Ritchie asked her out again, just maybe she'd say yes.

Chapter Two

How much trouble could a thirteen-year-old boy get into? That was the question on Maria's mind as she left the school, Joey in tow.

"Three days suspension? Fighting in the hallways?" She knew her voice was shrill. She couldn't help it. "I had to leave work this afternoon, which means I not only don't get paid, I don't get any tips."

Joey looked up at her, his lower lip curled defiantly. "Those guys started it."

"I don't care who started it. Somebody always starts it. Next time somebody starts it, you walk away, do you hear me?"

He shrugged, scraping the toe of his sneaker against the cement while she searched through her purse for her keys. She glanced over at Joey and sighed.

"And stop scraping your foot like that. Do you know how much I paid for those shoes?"

Joey just gave her a look like he hated her, and got in the car.

She wasn't getting through. He was tuning her out. And she was deathly afraid that no matter what she did, he was headed down the same path as Tito. Tito had just turned eighteen when he was arrested. A few months younger, and he would have been in the juvenile justice system. Instead, he'd been tried as an adult, and was serving a mandatory sentence on a drug charge. He'd sworn he hadn't been involved, that he had been picked up just because he was in the building when the drug bust went down. The lawyer their mother had hired said it helped that Tito wasn't actually a member of the gang, although he'd been on the fringes and was headed that direction. The lawyer had thought he could get him off with probation. But some hotshot young prosecutor from the State Attorney's office had had other ideas. She pressed her hand to her forehead.

She'd take Joey back to the restaurant with her. She'd already missed the lunch rush, but hopefully there would be some business from the early dinner crowd before her shift ended. It was Wednesday, so they'd spend the evening at St. Theresa's. But what would she do with him the rest of the week? Thursday, Friday, and Monday. There was no way she could miss that many shifts. She doubted her boss would want her dragging her thirteen-year-old brother along to work with her three days in a row. And she sure didn't want to lose this job. But leaving Joey at home on his own was out of the question. He'd be out the door and on a bus, headed back to the old neighborhood and looking for trouble five minutes after she left.

She was still trying to figure it out as she was serving food at St. Theresa's that evening. When one of the regulars shuffled up, she was barely able to conjure up a smile.

She jumped when she felt a strong hand close over hers.

"You look about a million miles away from here tonight." It was Ritchie.

Maria pulled her hand back, startled by the little tremor that had shot up her arm in tiny shock waves when he touched her.

"It's nothing," she said. The last thing she wanted to do was start spilling out all her troubles to the guy she'd been having secret fantasies about when she couldn't sleep.

"I'm taking you both out for coffee when we get done here."

"Sorry, Joey's —" She started to give her perfunctory answer, but Ritchie cut her off.

"I know. Joey's grounded." He looked at her steadily through those intense, dark eyes, and there was a slight smile on his lips. "Consider it house arrest. Coffee house."

She didn't say yes, and she didn't say no, but somehow they ended up in a coffee shop down the street after the food service was over. I'm doing this for Joey, she told herself. He needs a positive male influence.

Joey was slouched in an overstuffed leather chair in the corner, and the only thing influencing him at the moment was some kind of game on his phone. She'd warned him that he was grounded from texting too and if she found out different when she got the cell phone bill there'd be hell to pay.

"So I finally got you out on a date."

He hit her with that killer smile, and she clamped down the urge to smile back at him like a lovesick teenager. It hadn't been *that* long since she had a casual cup of coffee with a man she was attracted to. Well, maybe it had.

"It's not a date," she said, as primly as she could manage.

"What would you call it?" He had this sparkle in his eyes and tiny creases in the corners that only appeared when he smiled.

"Coffee. I'd call it coffee."

"It's a start. How about a real date? Tomorrow. Dinner."

She had a sudden image of what it would be like. Going out. To a nice restaurant. With an attractive man. It seemed like a lifetime ago that she had indulged in such simple pleasures.

She sighed. "I can't."

"I'm starting to think you don't like me."

"I have to look out for Joey."

"Who looks out for you?"

"I can look out for myself." She glanced over at the boy hunched over his phone, intent on his game, his leg dangling over the arm of the chair, and his unruly hair falling across a face that suddenly looked unbearably innocent and young. She sighed again. "The one thing I can't seem to do is figure out how to keep that one out of trouble."

"What's the problem?"

"How long have you got?" She nibbled on the corner of the muffin Ritchie had insisted on buying for her, and wondered if he really was interested in her troubles or just making conversation. Maybe talking about it would actually help her to figure out what to do.

"The immediate problem is a three-day suspension from school. And a kid who's definitely going to get into more trouble if I leave him on his own all day while I'm at work."

"That's easy," Ritchie shrugged. "I'll just take him to work with me."

Maria stared at him.

"Take him to work with you? Why would you do that? This is a little over the top if you're just trying to get me to go out with you."

"I like the kid. He reminds me of when I was that age." He gave her a slow grin. "And it's a small price to pay to get you to go out with me."

She found herself smiling back at him.

"I don't even know what you do."

He reached into his wallet and handed her a card.

"You're a...lawyer?" Oh no, anything but a *lawyer*.

She looked more closely at the card. "Ritchie Perez. Flanagan, Berrington & Perez." She looked up. "You *own* the firm?"

"With my two partners. We do personal injury law. Serious cases." He smiled at her, seeming to sense that her reaction was not altogether positive. "I'm not one of those ambulance chasers you see on TV in the middle of the night."

Of all the jobs he might have had, she hadn't expected this one. He didn't dress like a lawyer. And he didn't act like one either. The few lawyers she'd had dealings with weren't the sort of people who volunteered at soup kitchens, or cared about anyone except themselves. Either they ran over anything and anyone in their path just to win a case and chalk up another victory, or they took your money and made you promises that never came true. Or worse, pretended you didn't even exist.

Ritchie. A lawyer. He was wearing faded jeans and a short-sleeved polo shirt that also looked worn. Of course, now that she looked a little closer, she could tell that the shirt wasn't cheap. Did she think a lawyer would wear his expensive suit to a soup kitchen?

He had fancy degrees and a successful professional career. So it was more than just her distrust of lawyers that was making her feel uncomfortable. Yes, she still thought of herself as an artist. But the truth was she was a waitress who'd dropped out of college four years ago and had dreams that each day seemed to slip further and further away. It made her wonder why he kept asking her out and why he was so willing to help Joey. There must be dozens of rich, sophisticated women with much less baggage than she had who would be happy to go out on a date with Ritchie Perez. And she still couldn't get out of her mind the notion that she'd met him somewhere before.

"What's wrong?" He was studying her intently, and she felt herself blush.

"Nothing. I...I was just thinking that you look familiar, and wondering if maybe I'd seen your face on a billboard."

"No billboards," he said. "That's not my style. Not that there's anything wrong with it."

"Okay."

"So what do you say?" He took hold of her hand, brushed his thumb over her knuckles, and she felt her mind go blank.

"What was the question?"

"Joey. I was offering to take him into the office with me the next couple of days. Keep him busy making copies. Running errands."

It would be a lifesaver for her. Even if Ritchie was a lawyer, he seemed like a decent guy. Anyone who volunteered at St. Theresa's as much as he did probably had many good qualities that Joey would benefit from being exposed to.

"I don't know what to say."

"It's simple. Say yes."

When she still hesitated, he added, "No conditions, Maria. I'll take Joey to the office regardless of whether you go out with me." He paused, treating her to that killer grin again that made her knees go weak. "But don't expect me to stop asking."

"I'd love if you'd take Joey to work with you." She paused. "And I guess it wouldn't kill me to go out to dinner with you tomorrow."

He laughed. "That kind of enthusiasm will go to my head."

His tone was light, teasing, but the gleam in his eyes made her feel giddy inside. Like the time freshman year when her high school crush – an unattainable senior – had leaned against her locker and asked if she wanted to go grab a burger or something after school. Her mom had put a quick end to that romance, when she found out the boy was eighteen and a senior. All of which spelled trouble. But Mom wasn't around to warn her off this time. And she had a feeling it was already too late.

As she looked back at Ritchie, she couldn't help wondering what was she getting herself into?

Chapter Three

"So after one day of having Joey around your office, you think you know better than me what's going on with my own brother?" Her face was flushed, and Ritchie had a good idea it wasn't from the glass of wine she'd barely touched.

It wasn't turning out at all how he'd expected. Instead of a romantic dinner and a chance to get to know Maria better – maybe help her out with some insight into the problems she was having with Joey – she seemed to take everything he said as some sort of an insult on her "parenting" skills. And she wasn't even the kid's mother.

"Maria, the last thing I want to do is criticize you."

"Really?" She picked up the wine glass and took a healthy gulp, then set it down firmly on the table. Her dark eyes flashed indignantly. "Because you sure are doing a good job of it."

"Listen. I've had some experience with kids his age."

"Have you? Well, that's nice. I live with him. I've been taking care of him myself since he was nine."

"What about your parents?" He'd assumed Maria was just helping out at home, but he was starting to realize she might be the *only* one involved in raising Joey.

"Dad died when I was fifteen. Our mom had it really rough after that."

"I'm sorry. What happened?"

THE MILLIONAIRE'S *Convenient* ARRANGEMENT

"Massive heart attack. If there were warning signs, he never said anything. One minute he was there, and the next minute he was just...gone." She looked away from him, took another drink of her wine. When she looked back, her eyes just seemed so sad he was sorry he'd asked.

"It must have been terrible for all of you."

"I focused on my art. I graduated high school. Had a partial scholarship to Temple University in Philadelphia. The Art School there. I was so busy focusing on myself, I never noticed the changes in my brother. I let him down." There was a little crease between her eyes when she looked sad, and he had the sudden urge to kiss it away. He reached across the table and took her hand.

"Joey would have been just a little kid then. He wasn't your responsibility."

She looked up quickly, and her eyes were wet. "Joey? No, I don't mean..." She paused so long he thought she wasn't going to say anything more. Finally, she continued. "You're right, of course."

Something had closed down. Ritchie could always tell in the courtroom when a witness was holding something back, and it was no different in his personal relationships. He wondered what it was that made Maria feel so guilty for leaving her mother and her little brother and going off to college. It seemed like she was harboring serious regrets for doing something that was completely normal.

"So you went off to college," he prompted. "How did you end up back here, raising Joey?"

"My mom got cancer. She...she didn't tell me until it was pretty well advanced. Didn't want me to leave school. By the time I realized, she didn't have much time left."

"I'm so sorry. That had to be rough." He thought about his own mother, the cornerstone of their close-knit family, and couldn't imagine how hard it must have been for Maria to lose both parents in such a short period. And what a devastating blow it had to have been for Joey. But for a college student to suddenly have to leave school and take on the role of *de facto* mom to a grieving child? It must have been overwhelming.

"And there was no one else who could step in and raise Joey?"

She looked up again, sharply this time. "Joey's my responsibility."

THE MILLIONAIRE'S
Convenient ARRANGEMENT

"That seems like too much for you to take on when you weren't even out of school yet," he said, realizing even as he spoke that it was the wrong thing to say. He *admired* her for taking on raising her little brother on her own. He didn't mean it as a criticism, but she seemed to take everything he said the wrong way.

Sure enough, she bristled visibly. "What exactly do you mean by that?"

He probably should just keep his mouth shut. Or change the subject. But he really did know more than most people about all the wrong decisions a kid Joey's age could make, especially growing up in a single-parent home in one of Miami's rougher neighborhoods. Like the ones surrounding St. Theresa's parish.

"All I'm saying is, I think what you're doing is really hard. A kid Joey's age needs some structure in his life, and I don't know how you can provide that and still manage to support the two of you. If he's on his own too much, he's bound to get into trouble. I've seen it happen before." He could tell from the look on her face that was exactly what she was afraid of. But apparently she wasn't about to admit it to him.

"Easy for you to say. I'm working two jobs. You think I should hire a babysitter after school? He's thirteen."

Now she was definitely angry, but in Ritchie's opinion, angry was better than sad. He didn't think he could stand to see the sad look that had come over her when she talked about losing both her parents so tragically.

"I'm not criticizing you, Maria. Trying to raise that kid and work two jobs all by yourself is just too much for one person to handle. He's going end up in trouble."

"I'm doing just fine. I don't need your help or your advice."

He was starting to get ticked off now. People who were too proud to accept help– or even a little well-intended advice – when they needed itwere just plain foolish, as far as he was concerned.

"I think you could use a little help."

"I think I'd like to go home now."

She was so stiff as they walked out to the car; everything about her was tense. It made him wonder what it would be like to see her relaxed, to see her looking like she didn't carry the weight of the world on her shoulders."

"When's the last time you did something for yourself. Just because you knew it would make you feel better?"

"I came out on a date with you. Look how that turned out."

He had to laugh. "That bad, huh?"

"No, I love spending my whole evening arguing."

"Maybe we should try not talking for awhile," he said, angling in closer to her.

"The date's over."

"Not yet," he said and studied her as she took an instinctive step back. "Actually, it's about to get a lot better."

"I don't know what you mean," she said. Her chin pointed up defiantly, but her lower lip was trembling just slightly.

"I think you know exactly what I mean."

It was so easy to slip his arm around her narrow waist and pull her up against him. He felt her stiffen instantly.

"What do you think you're doing? If you think I have any intention of kissing you when all we've done all evening is –"

"Argue. I know. Let's try this instead," he said and pulled her closer. He was surprised how her body molded to his. He brushed his lips across hers softly once, twice, and waited until he felt her start to relax. When her arms came up around his neck and she pressed her body tighter against him, he kissed her the way those lips were meant to be kissed. He felt her go tense again for a moment and then explode with unexpected passion.

Desire slammed through him like a hot flame, and he took the kiss a lot deeper than he'd intended. He wanted her in his bed. By God, he wanted her right there on the hood of his car. His blood coursed through his veins at the thought of what it would be like to slide his hand up under that short little skirt and ... It took a conscious effort to pull back, to break his contact with that hungry mouth that yielded and demanded at the same time. He realized with a start that his hand had moved from the small of her back down to her round bottom, that in a few more moments his hand would have been under her skirt. He hadn't been so desperate for the feel of a woman's bare skin since he was a hormone-crazed teenager, and he wondered what the hell had gotten into him.

THE MILLIONAIRE'S
Convenient ARRANGEMENT

Maria was leaning back against the car, her eyes half closed, her face flushed, her heart pounding. He could tell by the way she was visibly trying to catch her breath, regain her composure, and he was grateful for the few moments it gave him to get his own breathing back under control.

When she spoke, her voice was low. "I still don't like you trying to tell me how to raise my own brother, Ritchie."

He brushed his thumb over her lips, and she frowned. "And I don't like you thinking every suggestion I make means I don't admire what you're trying to do with Joey. Or that I don't understand what you're up against. Because I do – on both counts."

He paused while she stared at him, her eyes sending mixed signals of temper and desire.

"And I'm looking forward to spending a lot more time with you."

He watched as she stiffened her shoulders. He gave her props for the fact that her voice didn't waiver, since he was still feeling a bit unsteady himself. At the same time, he wished she would relax the armor she'd put around herself to ward off even the slightest hint of criticism. If she would just open up a little bit to listen to some options, he could help her get Joey into some after-school programs that would keep him off the streets and out of trouble.

Maria was having none of it, though.

"While I certainly appreciate you taking Joey into work with you this week, any sort of personal relationship between the two of us is absolutely out of the question. It's obvious we have completely different ideas about what's best for a teenaged boy, and I don't want to spend the little free time I have arguing."

Ritchie admired a woman who stuck to her guns. Even when she was wrong.

"There are more enjoyable things we can do than argue." He leaned in closer, enjoyed the way her eyes went kind of jittery and nervous. "Are you daring me to kiss you again?"

"No, I –"

"Because I think that's a great idea," he said, taking her back into his arms before she had a chance to protest.

This time he was prepared for the heat. He did not intend to lose control again, but he wanted more of her. Wanted to figure out why this feisty, loyal, and utterly fascinating woman with a stubborn streak a mile wide was affecting him like no woman ever had before. He knew the need he had for her wouldn't burn out until he had her in his bed. And if he had anything to say about it, that would be very soon.

Chapter Four

"It's about time you got here!" Vivienne was pacing back and forth in front of a large sculpture, her brightly colored, oversized caftan flapping with each step, in stark relief to the black silk leggings that hugged her slim legs.

"I'm early," Maria pointed out, not that Vivienne would care. Maria worked part-time for the temperamental artist at her studio/gallery in the Design District.

"What difference does that make? I need you right now to take down that painting!"

"The one right here in front?"

"Yes, yes. I don't want that garbage in my show. I can't imagine what I was thinking."

Two days ago, she'd declared it her masterpiece, but Maria wisely didn't mention that as she and Vivienne lifted the painting off the wall and carried it into the back room.

"What do we hang in its place?" Maria asked, thinking of the expanse of empty wall space that would greet attendees as they entered the gallery.

"Nothing," Vivienne said sharply. "Let them wonder about it."

Vivienne was a sculptor, first and foremost, and, in her words, "dabbled" in canvas and oil. Her age was somewhere between fifty and seventy-five; no one could pin it any closer. Her reticence about her background was part of her mystique.

THE MILLIONAIRE'S
Convenient ARRANGEMENT

At the moment, her sculptures were a hot item, and not only in Miami. And because she so rarely painted, collectors put a high value on those works. Maria thought that the piece of "garbage" they were now hauling into the back room would have sold for enough money to pay Maria's rent for a year. Maybe even buy the whole building.

Meanwhile, as people arrived and the gallery filled with voices, Maria imagined what it would be like to have her own showing one day. She also made sure the little cards with the discreet prices of the sculptures and paintings were present, the trays of canapés were refilled, and the mojitos flowing.

When Ritchie walked in looking distinguished and moneyed, with Joey lagging behind him, Vivienne moved in for the kill.

"You like?" she asked, with that faintly Eastern European accent she sometimes affected. Vivienne had lived absolutely everywhere and, as far as Maria could tell, had no discernable accent at all.

Maria walked up to them, balancing an empty tray and a collection of long-stemmed glasses.

"He's not a patron of the arts, Vivienne. This is Ritchie Perez," she said, introducing him grudgingly. "He's the lawyer I told you about who's been helping me out with Joey this week."

"Ah," Vivienne said, causing Maria to instantly regret some other confidences about Ritchie she'd shared with her part-time employer earlier that same day. It was just that he'd made her so darned mad during their dinner. And so aroused afterward. She sighed.

"Ritchie, this is Vivienne, the owner of the gal–"

"There's no need for that introduction," Ritchie said smoothly and turned to Vivienne, accepting the hand she offered and lifting it to his lips. "Your face is as instantly recognizable as your work."

Maria rolled her eyes as she watched Vivienne's reaction to Mr. Charming.

"I've admired, in particular, your studies of the vanishing Florida Everglades," Ritchie continued.

"And you dare suggest this gentleman is not a patron of the arts?" Vivienne asked, raising one delicate eyebrow as she cast a sideways glance at Maria.

"Come," Vivienne said, before Maria could respond, taking Ritchie's arm. "I insist on giving you a personal tour of my gallery. I think you might particularly like to see..."

Maria stood there for a moment as their voices faded away, hoping she wouldn't have to put up with a lecture later from Vivienne about what a lovely young man he was. She took the tray back into the kitchen and, predictably, found Joey there, sitting at a small table making dinner of the food he'd managed to cajole out of the caterer.

And felt instant remorse. Ritchie might have been a little annoying on their date, with all his unsolicited advice about what she should be doing differently with Joey, but he had really gone over the top helping her out this week. She'd have managed somehow without his help, of course, but knowing that Joey was at Ritchie's office while she was at work all day had really relieved her mind.

She smiled at the caterer, reloaded her tray, and took it back out into the gallery to place strategically near several sculptures Vivienne was hoping to sell.

So okay, she owed him. Still, it didn't give him a right to judge her or anyone else who was struggling to raise a child on their own. As if it was her fault Joey kept getting in trouble. She'd moved them out of that neighborhood, hadn't she? Made sure he was in a good school. Nagged him about homework. She was doing the best she could. But what had really grated was that he seemed to think Joey was at a disadvantage just because Maria was a single "mom."

Well, she was pretty sure she knew a great deal more than he did about single-parent families, sitting up there every day in his fancy office. Ritchie had insisted on picking Joey up in the morning. She'd driven past the building later just so she'd know where her brother was, not because she was interested in seeing where Ritchie worked. And had been glad she'd overridden Joey's protests and made him wear his dress pants and a shirt with a collar. She watched from her car while people in expensive suits carrying briefcases walked into the building and wondered if they were other lawyers in Ritchie's office.

Their date hadn't gone very well. Except for those kisses she tried not to think about. After he took Joey to the office on Monday for the final day of suspension, she'd probably never see him again.

Except, of course, for Wednesday nights at St. Theresa's.

THE MILLIONAIRE'S
Convenient ARRANGEMENT

• • •

Ritchie sat at his desk Monday afternoon and studied the small sculpture of a rare species of frog, indigenous to the Everglades, which now commanded attention on his credenza. An original Vivienne. There was something compelling about it that he couldn't quite put his finger on. *For fifteen thousand dollars, it had better be compelling,* Ritchie thought. He still couldn't quite get used to the fact that he could spend that kind of money on a piece of art without even thinking twice about it.

But the fifteen thousand dollars he'd spent Friday night was a good investment in more ways than one. He knew enough about art to know the sculpture itself would appreciate. More importantly, he'd secured a commitment from the artist to create a piece specifically for the charity auction benefiting a scholarship program for kids from Miami's roughest neighborhoods, an event Ritchie's firm helped sponsor.

"So how much did she charge you for that?" He looked up and saw Joey standing in the doorway to his office.

"Enough," he said.

"Man, I don't know why people spend so much money on that stuff."

"Don't you have anything else to do?" Ritchie asked pointedly.

Joey shrugged. "If that lady down the hall sees me standing around, she's gonna make me go out and pick up a bunch of fancy coffee drinks again. Man, there's a coffee machine right in the kitchen!"

"Sorry if we don't have more challenging work for you to do," Ritchie said drily.

Joey sank into the visitor's chair across from Ritchie's desk and shrugged again.

"It's not like you really need a kid like me in this place." He kicked the corner of the desk idly, and Ritchie tried to ignore it.

Joey fidgeted in his chair.

"You think I don't know the only reason you let me hang around is 'cause you want to bang my sister?" He looked around the fancy office and smirked. "Rich guy like you? She'd be smart to do you becau–"

Ritchie was around the desk in seconds, before Joey could even get the rest of the words out. The kid probably thought lawyers were soft guys who sat behind a desk all day pushing papers around. Joey stuck out his chin with what Ritchie recognized as false bravado, even as Ritchie

THE MILLIONAIRE'S
Convenient ARRANGEMENT

leaned down and looked him right in the eye.

"She doesn't even like you," Joey said, squirming. "She thinks you're bossy."

Ritchie's face was close to Joey's. "When you're in this office, I'm your boss. And that's the last time you're going to make a stupid, disrespectful comment like that about your sister."

"You wouldn't dare touch me," Joey said, but his voice sounded small and scared.

"Am I touching you, Joey?"

"You don't scare me," Joey said, but his face went pale, and Ritchie could read what was going on in his mind. The kid grew up in the kind of neighborhood Ritchie knew all too well. He expected Ritchie to smack him around. He needed to learn that being strong didn't mean beating up someone smaller.

Ritchie spoke slowly, calmly.

"You are going to sit there in that chair and not move, and you are going to keep your mouth closed until I tell you otherwise. You got that?"

Joey nodded.

"All right," Ritchie said then went back behind his desk, turned back to his computer, took a phone call from a client, and reviewed a file for an upcoming hearing. He glanced over at Joey periodically. The kid squirmed a little in the chair, but kept his mouth shut.

Around three o'clock, Joey inched his phone partway out of his pocket and sighed miserably. Ritchie stifled a smile. Three o'clock was when Sam's younger sister Olivia – his wife's sister, actually – showed up after school to work at the office. Joey had followed her around yesterday with the kind of starry-eyed devotion a thirteen-year-old boy would predictably have for a cool and confident sixteen-year-old girl.

Ritchie caught his eye. "Get out of here."

Joey swallowed visibly. "You mean...go home?"

He was probably imagining how he would explain to Maria getting thrown out of Ritchie's office when he'd already been suspended from school.

"No, I don't mean go home. I mean get out of my office, and go to the file room. See if you can't find something useful to do for the rest of the day." Richie tried not to smile. "Olivia might need help making copies."

"Yes, sir!" Joey said and then bolted out of the chair.

Joey wasn't a bad kid, Ritchie thought, just a kid who needed some boundaries. And a positive male influence that he wasn't getting by hanging out in his old neighborhood or sitting around an apartment alone while Maria held down two jobs.

Ritchie was planning to spend more time with both of them.

Chapter Five

She was going to the game, but that didn't mean she had to enjoy it. When Ritchie cruised up in an expensive SUV, she thought *typical.* One luxury car wasn't enough, she supposed, remembering the sleek sports car with leather seats as soft as butter he'd used to take her to dinner. She felt herself blush as she recalled the little fantasy she'd had about making out with him on those soft seats.

"So how many cars do you have?" she asked as she climbed in the passenger side.

Ritchie grinned. "This is the one I use most of the time. The other one is just to impress girls."

"Right." She turned and looked out the window so he wouldn't see her smile.

Joey climbed into the back, looking young and really excited, and she felt a twinge of guilt. She should have been taking him to Marlins games herself, but it just wasn't something she ever thought of. And she really couldn't afford it anyway, not as long as she was saving every penny so they could move to a bigger place. But Joey had been so excited when Ritchie called and invited them that she just couldn't say no. Even if it meant she had to sit through another lecture about the challenges facing single mothers and the importance of having a male influence for a kid Joey's age.

So she'd said yes, mostly because he was right that it was good for

THE MILLIONAIRE'S
Convenient ARRANGEMENT

Joey to spend some time with a man he could look up to. Someone like Ritchie who, she conceded, was successful, honest, generous and, from all indications, close to his family. The only thing she didn't like about him was his assumption that keeping Joey out of trouble was more than she could handle on her own. It was as if he thought single mothers were the root cause of juvenile delinquency. It was an insult to the way her own mother had struggled, and the courage she'd showed when she'd found herself pregnant and unmarried at eighteen. When he talked about Joey needing a male influence and more structure, all she heard was *Maria, you just aren't good enough.*

But it was just a baseball game. At least, with Joey along, she wouldn't be tempted to embarrass herself again by kissing a man who was so completely unsuitable for her.

Despite her intentions otherwise, Maria found herself really enjoying the game. It was certainly a different experience watching from the butlered suite, helping themselves to the spread of food Ritchie had ordered. He'd explained that his firm bought the suite mostly to entertain other lawyers who referred cases to them, but neither of his partners were using it tonight so they had it all to themselves. She wondered if it would be terribly gauche to wrap up some of the leftover hotdogs and hamburgers and salad and donate it to the soup kitchen – they probably just threw it all away.

Ritchie apparently noticed her glancing at all the unused food, because he leaned over and said, "I ordered extra because I didn't know what you guys would like. Besides, we donate whatever's left to St. Theresa's."

Okay, Ritchie was a really nice guy. Maria tried to remind herself of all the reasons why starting any kind of relationship with him was a bad idea.

• • •

Ritchie was surprised what a good time he was having hanging out with Joey. His own nieces and nephews were too young to appreciate the finer points of baseball, but Joey absorbed statistics and sports strategy like a sponge.

"You play baseball at all, Joey?"

"Nah," he said, while he chomped his way through his third hot dog.

"I don't really play sports. I like video games mostly. But this is cool."

"I played a little baseball in college," Ritchie said. When he was Joey's age, baseball had been the focus of his life. It had probably been responsible for keeping him out of trouble too, while he dreamed of a future in the big leagues. By college, those dreams had shifted into more realistic goals. But he still remembered the feeling of being out there on the field, the sun at his back, crowds in the stands.

"Yeah? That's cool." Joey slurped his coke. "My brother used to play soccer. I liked going to the soccer field with him when I was really little."

Ritchie turned and looked at him. "I didn't know you have a brother. He doesn't live around here?"

"He got into some trouble," Joey said. He looked around, apparently making sure his sister hadn't come back from the restroom yet, and lowered his voice. "Maria doesn't like me to talk about it." He scraped the toe of his sneaker across the floor. "She thinks people will look down on us if they find out Tito's in prison."

"You have a brother in prison."

"Tito didn't do anything. It was all a big mistake. And some asshole prosecutor just wanted to make a name for himself. He didn't care."

"What was he convicted of?"

Joey shrugged. "Something about drugs. But Tito didn't sell drugs. Maria says some of the guys he hung out with did, but not Tito."

Ritchie was starting to get a bad feeling about this. "How long has he been in prison?"

Joey shrugged again. "I don't know." He bit his lip and looked like he was concentrating. "I was, like six or something. I don't remember a lot about it."

Seven years, Ritchie thought. Seven years ago, he would have been an assistant state attorney. Prosecuting drug-related crimes and gang violence. He'd handled hundreds of cases each year. It was impossible to remember every one. He hadn't been the only one prosecuting those cases, so there was still a good chance he wasn't the one who sent Maria's brother to prison. But the thought that he might have been made him feel suddenly cold inside.

"Tito won't let me visit him." Joey said. "Maria goes whenever she can.

"And I send him letters and stuff."

Joey glanced back over his shoulder. Maria was coming back toward them, a smile on her face.

"Listen," he said, leaning close to Ritchie, "don't say anything to Maria about me telling you, ok? She gets kind of weird about it sometimes."

"Sure," Ritchie said. "No problem."

Maria sat down beside him then jumped back out of her seat to cheer when the runner was tagged out on a triple play, ending the inning. Ritchie clapped automatically, but wasn't paying attention to the score any more. With one brother in prison, no wonder Maria was so sensitive about the parenting decisions she was making raising Joey. Anyone who spent any time at all with the two of them could see the bond of genuine love and affection they shared. She was putting everything she had into making a good life for Joey.

But the job she'd taken on was a hard one and, frankly, the odds were against her. Ritchie knew from experience that kids from tough neighborhoods in a single-parent home with siblings or other relatives who'd done time typically ended up in the system themselves before they were through high school. And from what Maria had told him, Joey'd already had a few minor run-ins with the police. Ritchie felt a rush of admiration and respect for Maria, in addition to the physical attraction that already made him want to spend more time with her. He could do a lot to help her with Joey if she'd just let down her guard a little and accept his help. Unfortunately, he might not get the chance.

If it turned out he was the "asshole prosecutor" Joey mentioned, he couldn't ask Maria out again without telling her. And he had a pretty good idea how that conversation would end.

• • •

Maria couldn't remember when she'd had such a carefree day. Although Ritchie had seemed a little quiet on the way home. Or maybe it was just that Joey wouldn't stop talking about the game, the ballpark, the seats, the food, everything.

Now, sitting beside him in the car, she felt a nervous flutter that hadn't been there in the crowed stadium. This wasn't a date, exactly, and

Joey's fast-paced patter pretty much drowned out the low music playing on the car's speakers. But there was something intimate about the way Ritchie's hand rested casually on the steering wheel as he drove, as she breathed in the scent of his cologne.

"Thanks so much," she said as he pulled up in front of her building, starting to open the car door.

"I'll walk you guys in," Ritchie said, turning off the ignition.

"That's all right, you don't need to."

"I want to," he said, stepping out and closing the door firmly.

There was no reason to feel so nervous, she thought as she unlocked the door to their apartment. It's not like he was going to make a move on her with Joey standing right there. And her apartment was nice, even if it was small. She'd just offer him a cup of coffee. No, soda. Coffee took time to brew. Then he'd be out of there.

She turned to ask him if he'd like something to drink as they walked in the door, then her throat went dry and her pulse quickened as she found herself standing way too close to him. Her mind just blanked as she imagined him pulling her into his arms, his lips covering hers firmly but gently, his body pressing her back against the door. *Get a grip, Maria,* she told herself and took a sharp step back. He wasn't going to kiss her right here in front of Joey, for heaven's sake. But now he was staring at her as if he knew exactly what had been going though her mind.

Joey was just standing in the middle of the room grinning at the two of them, oblivious to the electricity that was suddenly charging the air between her and Ritchie. "So are we gonna like watch a DVD or something? We've got some cool ones."

"Sorry," Ritchie said, "I can't stay that long. I thought we'd just relax a few minutes and talk."

"That's no fun." Joey looked so crestfallen that Maria had to suppress a laugh. "Haven't you had enough fun already for one day?" she asked.

Joey shrugged.

"Next time, kid," Ritchie said. "But if you don't want sit out here listening to boring adult talk, you don't have to. I don't mind if you go hang out in your room."

"Dude," Joey said, "this *is* my room."

Ritchie stepped back. "This is your room?"

"It's a really small apartment, I know," Maria began, feeling the sexual tension from just a few moments ago drain away, replaced by embarrassment. "As soon as I can afford..." Her voice trailed off.

He turned to Joey. "Where do you sleep?"

"Let me show you," Joey said. Marie watched while her little brother pulled out the couch and converted it into a bed.

"Cool, huh?"

Ritchie looked confused. "Where do you keep your stuff?"

"It's mostly in that closet," he said, gesturing. "Or that cool trunk we found, over there in the corner. I've got some stuff in boxes, too," he added, "until we get a bigger place."

"That's right," Maria said. "This is just *temporary*, until we can move again." She wanted to...she didn't know what she wanted to do. A man like Ritchie couldn't possibly understand the economic realities of her life. He had two luxury cars and a suite at the baseball stadium. She'd had to stretch to afford a one-bedroom apartment in a neighborhood that wasn't all that great, but was still way better than where they used to live. She'd have had the two of them living in her car rather than have Joey stay in his old school, live in his old neighborhood, spend his time with his old friends.

She hadn't been there for Tito and there was nothing she could do about that now. But another year in their old house and Joey could have ended up heading down that same path. And maybe she couldn't give him a nice house in the suburbs with a yard and a bike and a dog, but she thought she was doing pretty well considering all she had going for her was an unfinished art degree and the willingness to work hard.

Joey looked at them both impatiently. "If we did watch a movie, we could make popcorn."

Ritchie laughed, and she felt her tension ease a little.

"Are you actually hungry already? I think you ate seven hot dogs before I lost count."

Joey shrugged.

"Boys his age are always hungry," Maria said. "It's just a fact of life." Joey, she noticed, was already headed for the kitchen.

"I remember." Ritchie said. "Sorry sport, I have to get going. We'll do the movie thing another time."

"Yeah, thanks, Ritchie. I had a great time," Joey called back then disappeared, and moments later, Maria could hear him rooting around in the fridge. The kid's stomach was a bottomless pit.

"I know this place doesn't look like much," she began, as she followed Ritchie to the door.

He leaned in and gave her a quick kiss that was nothing like the lingering one she'd imagined earlier, but almost managed to melt her bones anyway.

"I'm not judging where you live, Maria."

Maybe not. But she knew he had to be thinking that a pullout couch was not an ideal situation for Joey. She and Ritchie lived in different worlds. She certainly couldn't bring a man home with her for the evening, not when she lived in a tiny apartment with her thirteen-year-old brother. And she wasn't about to spend late nights anywhere else and leave Joey on his own. Dating anyone at all just wasn't practical right now. And dating Ritchie was impossible.

"I'll call you," she heard him say as he walked down the hall toward the elevator. Maybe he would call her, she thought, but what would be the point?

Chapter Six

Ritchie leaned back in his chair. At 1:00, the verdict had come in on the product liability case he'd taken to trial when the insurance company for the manufacturer of a defective toy refused to settle. The two million dollar verdict would leave his client – a ten-year-old and his family – with plenty of money left over after the medical bills for reconstructive surgery. More importantly, the product was off the shelves.

Ritchie's partners were already down at their favorite pub waiting to buy him a late lunch and a celebratory beer before he took the rest of the day off and slept for about fifteen hours.

It had been almost a month since he'd seen Maria or Joey. They hadn't shown up at St. Theresa's the Wednesday after the baseball game, and the next two weeks he'd been immersed in a trial that had consumed every minute in his day. He'd called her once – okay, twice –left a message explaining that he was underwater in a case for a few weeks, but asked her to give him a call back and just let him know how she and Joey were doing. She hadn't called.

He tried to convince himself it was just as well. He'd looked up the file on Tito Martinez. He honestly didn't remember much about the case. It had been about a year before he left the State Attorney's office to open this practice with Jonathon and Sam. There'd been a lot of aggressive gang activity at that time. And a series of drug and weapons busts where the police had recovered guns that were used in a drive-by shooting that had gotten a lot of notoriety when a nine-year-old girl was killed. Ritchie had been at the forefront of an initiative in the State Attorney's office to crack down on gang activity, particularly drug-related.

He'd prosecuted Tito Martinez along with a whole group of gang members who'd been rounded up in a drug operation. Five kilos of cocaine and a kilo of crystal meth had been confiscated and kept off the streets of Miami. The police had also seized unregistered firearms. He tried to picture Maria's brother specifically, but he drew a blank. There'd been so many of them back then, and Ritchie had been proud of his reputation as a prosecutor who didn't cut deals with drug dealers or gang members. He took most of those cases to trial instead of pleading them down, and had a solid track record for getting the maximum sentence imposed.

Joey had claimed his brother had just been at the wrong place at the wrong time. Ritchie doubted that was the case. You didn't just stumble into a gang house when a major drug and weapons deal was about to go down. Not and walk out alive.

That the kid had just turned 18 had been a tough break for him. But in Ritchie's experience, those kids were hardened long before 18, and he'd tried younger ones as adults and gotten convictions. Miami juries had been fed up with punks who tarnished their city's reputation, increasing the crime rate and driving down property values, screwing up urban renewal efforts and turning parts of the city into places the tourists were warned not to visit.

His jaw tensed as he thought about Joey. Shoplifting, vandalism, fighting at school. Maria had confided that much before she shut down at dinner. The kid was on a path that led right to where his brother was sitting. It wouldn't take much to straighten him out – that had been evident at the office when Ritchie had made it clear that mouthing off disrespectfully about his sister was out of line and wouldn't be tolerated.

He was basically a good kid, but he had lousy friends and too much time on his hands. He ought to be playing a sport, burning off some of that excess energy. A kid could learn a lot from being part of a team. Joey's excited interest at the baseball game made Ritchie think the kid would enjoy getting out there in the field with a bat and ball. No offense to the job Maria was doing, but the kid needed more people in his life he could look up to – someone other than a brother who was a gang member serving time on drug and weapons charges. Kids that age were crying out for a role model. If an appropriate one wasn't available, they'd latch on to an inappropriate one.

The social services system wasn't set up to help kids like Joey and single parents like Maria who were just trying to make ends meet. Most of the so-called "early intervention" programs didn't kick in until it was already too late.

Not his problem, Ritchie thought as he headed out the door to have a celebratory drink with his partners. When his cell phone rang, he was pleasantly surprised at the name that popped up in the display. When he heard what she had to say, he decided the celebration would have to wait.

• • •

A sick fear was clawing at Maria, squeezing her lungs until she could barely take a breath. She hadn't been in a courtroom since the day of Tito's sentencing. No one had told her. She'd been off on a summer-long art program in Italy, paid for by the scholarship she'd won for the body of work she'd done in her high school AP art class. For Maria, it had been the opportunity of a lifetime. She'd had no clue that while she was studying the great works of art, strolling through museums, taking her sketch pad to charming little trattorias and the Trevi Fountain... her brother Tito had been sitting in a jail cell in Miami waiting to find out what sentence the judge would impose.

There was nothing you could do, her mother had told her when she returned from Italy to find out her brother had been arrested, and the trial she hadn't even known about was already over. *How could I let you come home, spoil something you worked so hard for, when there was nothing you could do?* She'd sent him postcards, Maria had thought bitterly. Bright shiny postcards from Rome and Florence and Venice. Dashed off with a cheerful note about all the wonders she was seeing. While what Tito was seeing was his future disappearing right before his eyes.

She hadn't been paying attention, not really, not for a long time. She'd been angry their last few years of high school when Tito withdrew, when he shut her out of his life. He'd hurt her, hurt the bond they'd had their whole lives, and she hadn't had a clue what to do about it.

She'd sat in a courtroom like this one. Sat and watched and listened when the Judge gave Tito the maximum sentence. Sat there frozen in disbelief and stunned horror as they led him away.

Helpless, helpless, helpless was how she'd felt that day and how she felt now, sitting in another courtroom, with a pale and terrified Joey at her side. It wasn't the same. Joey was thirteen. They weren't going to send him to prison, for heaven's sake. This was juvenile court. They'd said they found drugs in his locker. Joey swore he didn't do it, that he didn't know how they got there.

Tito had sworn he didn't know about the drugs, the guns, too, when he was arrested.

They wouldn't lock him up. But she was so afraid they might take him away from her. Think she was unfit to raise him, that he was out of control. Put him in some kind of juvenile detention center where he'd be exposed to the very sort of kids she'd been trying to keep him away from by moving out of the old neighborhood, starting a new life.

She sat in the back of the courtroom with Joey, waiting for their case to be called. She hadn't wanted to call Ritchie. Didn't want to go crawling back to him for help when she hadn't returned his calls, when she'd decided not to see him anymore. Hadn't wanted to call him and admit that maybe, just a little, he was right; maybe she couldn't handle Joey on her own, maybe she was kidding herself. But at the last minute, she'd called because Joey was more important than her pride. She didn't know if Ritchie knew anything about criminal law or juvenile law, or if he could even help, but she knew he went to court. His last message to her had been about some trial he was tied up in. When she called him, thank God, he'd picked up the phone and said he would come.

She looked back every time the courtroom doors opened, and she felt like the vise clamping her lungs loosened just a little when Ritchie walked through the door. She'd never seen him in a suit before – looking like a lawyer – and something niggled in the back of her mind but was swept aside in the wave of relief that washed over her.

He motioned for them to step out into the hallway, holding the heavy courtroom door open for them. They walked down to a bench in the corner, and Ritchie sat directly facing Joey and looked him in the eyes.

"You tell me exactly what happened. That's the only way I can help you."

Joey's lower lip trembled, and Maria just wanted to pull him close and hug him and make all his troubles go away. But he wasn't a little boy anymore.

"I didn't do it!" Joey said, his eyes filling up and his voice cracking. "They found some joints and some other stuff in my locker, but they don't belong to me. I didn't put it there. Somebody else did."

"Somebody else put drugs in your locker at school."

"I swear, Ritchie."

He nodded. "I believe you."

Maria saw something change on Joey's face then, and she realized he hadn't expected anyone to believe him. She hadn't believed him herself.

"Seems to me," Ritchie said, "the only reason somebody would put drugs in your locker and tip off the school is because they wanted you to get in trouble. Serious trouble. Somebody has that kind of grudge against you, I figure you know who it is."

Joey looked down at his shoes. "I'm no rat."

"That's not going to work with me, kid." Ritchie's voice was calm, but the look in his eyes conveyed the kind of quiet strength that demanded respect and made you feel like he could see right through any evasion. Maria figured anybody would have a hard time lying to him, especially an already terrified thirteen-year-old boy.

She leaned forward, but Ritchie stopped her in her tracks with a look, said "I've got this," then turned back to Joey.

"Somebody sets you up like this and you think you're supposed to just take it and not say who it was? If you don't know what bullshit that is, then you're not as smart as I thought you were."

Ritchie just looked at him, steady, and waited, while Joey stared back, looking like a deer caught in the headlights.

Maria thought Ritchie would lose his temper, raise his voice, or threaten Joey with the consequences if he didn't cooperate. But Ritchie didn't do any of those things. He just held Joey in that unwavering gaze while the seconds ticked by.

"Bobby Scranton and Jim Marcus," Joey blurted.

Ritchie nodded. "Now tell me why."

"Those were the guys I got into a fight with at school last month.

THE MILLIONAIRE'S
Convenient ARRANGEMENT

When I got suspended?"

"Go on," Ritchie said.

"We all got suspended, and Bobby's dad was really pissed off. Bobby said he and Jim were going to get me back for it."

"All right." Ritchie checked his watch. "We better get back in there."

Maria put her hand on his arm before they went back through the door. "Can you...Is it going to be okay?"

The look he gave her was equal parts compassion and exasperation.

"Just leave it to me, and don't worry." He paused. "But if anything like this ever happens again, don't wait until it's almost time for the hearing to call me."

He motioned for Maria and Joey to take a seat, put a hand on her shoulder briefly, then walked up toward the front of the courtroom where the lawyers were congregated, shaking hands and greeting people. It looked like he knew just about everybody, including the clerk who was sitting in the front beyond the little gate and past the lawyers' tables. It was puzzling. Marie wouldn't have thought Ritchie's work as a personal injury attorney would have brought him to the same place dealing with the same people who handled criminal matters involving juveniles.

She glanced over as two young women in suits, both with their arms laden with file folders, paused on their way up the aisle.

"Isn't that Ritchie Perez?" one woman asked the other.

"Who?"

"Oh yeah, it's him. He left the State Attorney's office what, six years ago? So that was before you got here."

"Thought so," the other woman said, "cause I'd have remembered a guy who looks like that. Yum."

The other woman laughed and waived at Ritchie when she caught his eye as he turned back from the clerk's desk.

"All rise!" the bailiff ordered, and Maria stood up, her eyes transfixed on Ritchie as he walked back toward the table where the attorneys sat. She'd seen him before. And it wasn't on a billboard or a late night TV commercial. Seven years ago, she'd seen him walk back across a courtroom facing exactly the same way. Looking exactly the same – polished, in his element, invincible.

When the Judge sat down at the bench and told everyone to be seated, Joey had to tug on her arm to get her attention. She sank slowly into her seat, but everything that happened next was a blur to her until Joey's case was called, and Ritchie motioned them forward.

It was over incredibly fast, and she couldn't even follow what was going on. Apparently, Ritchie had already worked something out with the Assistant State Attorney, and the Judge appeared to be going along with the recommendations. She tried to focus. The prosecutor was talking now.

" ... and after consultation with Mr. Perez, we're recommending that this matter be continued and, if the young man can stay out of trouble for the next six months, my office will drop any charges."

The Judge frowned at Joey and then addressed his comments to the prosecutor.

"This young man is thirteen years old, and in the past three months there have been incidents of shoplifting, vandalism, underage drinking, truancy, and now we have possession of a controlled substance and drug paraphernalia. It seems that at the very least, we need to have social services take a look at the home environment, and ordinarily I'd be inclined to order that he be placed in a juvenile detention facility pending further recommendations."

Maria couldn't breathe.

Ritchie stepped forward. "Your Honor, there are extenuating circumstances here that I've already discussed with the State Attorney's office, and my client is cooperating with the authorities in identifying the students who actually brought the drugs into the school." He paused a moment. "And I'm willing to make it my personal responsibility to make sure Joey Martinez stays completely out of trouble."

The Judge tapped his pen on the bench while Maria waited. Finally, he looked down at Joey sternly. "Young man, if I agree to this deal your attorney is proposing, I don't expect to see you back in this courtroom again."

"Yes, sir," Joey said. "I mean, no, sir, I won't be back here. Sir."

The judge looked at the file on his computer screen. "Parents deceased. Who is the legal guardian?"

Maria stepped forward and Ritchie said, "Your Honor, his sister, Maria Martinez."

She tried to look older, more responsible, someone who was capable of keeping a teenaged boy out of trouble.

"Ms. Martinez," the Judge said. "Do you consent to the conditions proposed by your brother's attorney and recommended by the State Attorney's office?"

"Yes, sir." She didn't care what the conditions were, didn't understand what exactly was going on, but if it kept Joey with her and out of the juvenile justice system, then whatever it was, she'd do it.

"Very, well." The Judge turned back to Ritchie. "Mr. Perez, against my better judgment, I'm going to continue this case. If Joey Martinez stays out of trouble – and I mean completely out of trouble – for six months, the case will be dismissed without any record of a juvenile charge for drug possession. But Mr. Perez, this young man is being released on your recommendation and under your supervision, and I am holding you personally accountable if he ends up in my courtroom again, is that clear?"

"Perfectly, Your Honor," Ritchie said.

"Fine," the Judge said, nodding to the clerk and handing her some papers from the file. "Next case on the docket."

Maria let out the breath she had been holding and turned with Joey to walk back out of the courtroom behind the man the Judge had put in charge of making sure Joey stayed out of trouble.

The same man who was responsible for putting Tito in prison seven years ago.

THE MILLIONAIRE'S
Convenient ARRANGEMENT

Chapter Seven

As they walked out of the courthouse together, Maria's mind was reeling. The Judge had made it pretty clear that without Ritchie's intervention, Joey would have been on his way to a juvenile detention center.

He'd talked to a judge about Tito, too. But in that case, his words had been more along the lines of lock him up and throw away the key. Tito had no college degree, no job experience, and a felony criminal record. When he finally got out of prison, who would hire him? His future had been destroyed. Destroyed by the man who couldn't see – or hadn't bothered to try to see – that Tito was different from the gang members he'd associated with.

She'd hated Ritchie Perez for seven years without even knowing his name. Hated him because he wouldn't give Tito a chance. And she'd be indebted to him forever because he did get Joey that chance. They were outside on the courthouse steps now, and Joey was staring up at him as if was a god. What was she supposed to say?

"I – I want to thank you for coming here today, Ritchie," she said. "I don't know how we'll ever repay you." She knew her words sounded stiff and formal, and she saw his eyes narrow.

"You don't need to 'repay' anything, Maria," he said.

God, her hands were shaking. She had to get out of here. Get Joey out of here. Go someplace where she could think.

THE MILLIONAIRE'S
Convenient ARRANGEMENT

"So," she faltered, "I guess we'll be going home now. Thank you, again. I'll—"

"Not so fast, Maria," Ritchie said, putting a hand on her arm. "We're going to go someplace right now and discuss this."

Oh, God, did he know he was the one who put her brother away? Did he realize that *she* now knew? Tito must have been just one of so many nameless, faceless defendants he'd processed through the system, she realized. That was probably how he looked at it. He wouldn't even remember Tito's name.

She shook his hand off and turned to face him.

"There's nothing to discuss." Her words sounded sharper than she'd intended.

Ritchie raised his eyebrows, giving her a sardonic look that made him look like a dark angel.

"Oh, so it's drop everything, Ritchie and come save us, after a month of not bothering to return my phone calls. Then it's thanks and goodbye, on the courthouse steps, before we even have a chance to discuss what happens next with Joey."

"No, I mean, I'm sorry, I didn't call you, but…"

He interrupted her. "Look, this isn't about you not calling me. I shouldn't even have said that. You don't want to see me again socially, that's fine. But you called me today to help Joey, and that's what I intend to do. And the first thing we need to discuss is Joey's living situation."

She felt her mouth drop open. "Our living situation is none of your business."

"The Judge just made it my business. When he put me in charge of overseeing Joey's conduct and made me personally responsible for keeping him out of trouble. For the next six months until this case is dismissed, it makes the most sense for Joey to live with me."

"I'm moving in with you?" Joey looked awestruck. "Cool. Do I get my own room?"

Maria turned to Joey. "You are not moving in with Ritchie. *I'm* your legal guardian, in case you've forgotten." She turned to look at Ritchie. "This is absolutely ridiculous."

"I'm offering to help you out, Maria. Look, I might as well be blunt. You saw how close the Judge was to bringing in Social Services. What do you think some caseworker would put in their report about a kid who's already been in trouble sleeping on the couch in a one-bedroom apartment while the only adult works two jobs and is hardly ever home?"

Marie felt herself bristling. "I do the best I can."

His voice softened. "I know you do, and I admire you for it. But you might have to face the fact that right now your best just isn't enough to give Joey the support he needs."

"Well, that's your opinion." Where did he get his nerve? Life was easy enough when you were a rich lawyer with your own business. He obviously had no concept of how regular people lived.

"Want to take any bets on what the opinion of the court would be?" Ritchie asked.

When she was silent, he continued. "Because I think we both know the answer to that."

"Joey's in school most of the time I'm at work at the restaurant."

"That's another thing we need to discuss," Ritchie said. "Putting aside for the moment the fact that Joey got drugs planted in his locker, that school has a low rating because the teachers spend more time with discipline issues and drug problems than they do teaching. It's not the best environment for your brother."

"I sold my house and *moved* to get Joey into that school because it's better than where he was."

"Sometimes better still isn't good enough," Ritchie said, and turned toward Joey again. "You're changing schools."

"No way," Joey said, but the way he said it made Maria think he wasn't posing any real objection.

Well, she was. "You can't just take over our lives like this. I won't have it," Maria said.

He turned that level gaze on her then. "Watch me."

Chapter Eight

Over lunch, Maria tried to marshal her arguments. Ritchie could all but see the wheels turning in her head. He was convinced Joey was a good kid – if he had to steamroll over Maria to do what was in the kid's best interests then he would. The fact that he was attracted to her as a woman was no reason to stand aside when a boy's future was on the line.

Too bad she had to fight him on every issue. It would be so much easier if she would just let go of her pride enough to see that everything he had suggested was in Joey's best interests. She was obviously too close to the situation to comprehend how much the kid was struggling, and how easily he could end up in serious trouble if some pretty drastic changes weren't made right now.

But no, she took every attempt to help as an insult, and dug her heels in. And even though he felt her tenacity was misplaced, he admired her for it. The more her temper flared, the more he wanted to channel all that energy into something that would give them both a lot more pleasure. He had to be crazy to try to pursue a relationship with her now that he'd realized he put her other brother behind bars. If she hadn't called him for help – if Joey hadn't gotten into trouble – he probably would never have seen her again. She hadn't returned his phone calls, and that would be that.

But fate had stepped in, and Ritchie wasn't one to ignore fate. If she knew already that he was the attorney who had prosecuted her brother, that explained her sudden resistance to every suggestion he made. If she didn't know, he'd have to tell her. And soon. Because, thanks to the Judge, he was going to be seeing a lot more of her.

They were sitting at an outside café on the waterfront. Joey seemed to have rebounded quickly and managed to eat two burgers and a massive quantity of cheese fries. As soon as he finished, Maria had given him some money to go down the street and get ice cream so she could talk things over with Ritchie.

The second he was gone, she started, apparently realizing she needed to shift tactics and take a softer approach. Ritchie wondered how long it would take until that temper of hers took over again.

"Listen, I don't want you to think I don't appreciate what you did for Joey – for both of us – this afternoon. But I can tell how much this has shaken Joey up. He's not going to be a problem from here on." She took a measured breath and continued.

"So, as much as I appreciate your offer to have Joey move in with you for six months, it's really not necessary. We couldn't disrupt your life that way."

She smiled at him, and he knew it must have cost her. Humble was not her style.

"It doesn't work that way, Maria," he said, and watched the smile fade from her pretty face.

"I don't know what you mean," she said.

"I mean, when you ask me to drop everything and run over to the courthouse and get Joey out of trouble, I'm happy to do that. And I was happy to take on responsibility for watching over him because that was what it took to keep the Judge from removing him and conducting a home study and dumping that kid into a system that's going to hurt him more than it would ever help him. But when I make a commitment to help, I'm all in. Don't expect me to put a temporary fix on this legal problem then step back and just wait for you to call me when the next crisis happens."

He leaned forward. "Because the way things are headed, there will be a next crisis. And it won't be as easy to make a deal with the prosecutor and the court next time."

"I think you're overstating it. This was a wake-up call for Joey. He'll stay out of trouble from now on," she said.

"Why not make it easier for him to do that? I like you, Maria. And I like Joey. He's a good kid, and I want to help. But I don't have time to run back and forth between your apartment and his school checking up on him."

"I'm not asking you to do that."

"That apartment isn't big enough, and you know it. That's why the best solution is for him to move into my house, where he has his own room. I can make sure he's home when he's supposed to be, he's in the right school, and he's doing the right kind of activities. You know he's interested in sports. I can get him in some great programs after school and on weekends. No more hanging out with his friends from the old neighborhood, and no more sitting around an empty apartment thinking up ways to get in trouble while you're at work."

"So you'll help him but only if it's your way." Her jaw was set stubbornly, and she narrowed her eyes, still holding onto her temper but clearly by a thin thread.

"That's right. If you want me to help him, you have to give me a chance to do it my way."

"And if I say no?"

"Then you might as well make a reservation for him to move into a cell with your brother Tito."

Her face paled. "You knew," she said, her voice a whisper. "You spent time with us, with Joey, you took me out on a date, you knew I was attracted to you. You kissed me," she said, and a bit of the color came back into her face. "You must have realized that if I knew who you were, I'd hate you."

"I didn't know. Not until the baseball game when Joey mentioned his brother. His brother who was serving time in prison."

She sat there, just staring at him.

"Obviously, there was a good chance I'd prosecuted him. The timing made sense. So I looked up the file."

"You don't remember it."

"I prosecuted a lot of people. Gangbangers and drug addicts and pushers. So no, I can't put a name and a face to them all."

"Tito was different," she said, and he cut off the sharp retort he'd intended when he saw the sudden tears spring into her eyes. "You destroyed his life, and you don't even remember his face."

He imagined her brother hadn't needed any help in destroying his own life, but he didn't say so.

"Joey is what matters now. I'm offering to get him out of trouble and back on track. You want to walk away from that because you think I'm responsible for where your brother Tito ended up, go ahead. But Joey's the one who'll suffer for it."

He could see the struggle on her face. "I get that I'm the last person you want to accept help from right now. Joey needs a more stable environment, structure, a new school, activities, all the things I can provide. But he also needs you."

She looked up, surprise and a hint of resignation on her face. She knew she'd run out of options.

"Of course he needs me. We could come up with a schedule, have him spend some time at your house and some time at home with me each week."

Ritchie shook his head. "That's not going to cut it."

"Then I don't know what you're suggesting."

"I'm suggesting that for the next six months, the most convenient arrangement is for both of you to move out of your apartment and move in with me."

• • •

"Are you out of your mind?" She spoke so loudly that other people in the café turned to look at them. She took a deep breath and lowered her voice. "You must be out of your mind."

"Think about it," Ritchie said, "and you'll see it makes perfect sense."

"It doesn't make any sense at all. Why are you doing this? It's not enough that you've taken one brother away from me, now you want to take over Joey's life and control mine?"

"Look, I understand how you feel about your brother Tito, but—"

"You don't understand anything."

"I understand that Joey needs help, and he looks up to me."

"He won't once I tell him who you are, what you did."

"Maybe not." He leaned forward. "Maria, did you ever think that part of Joey's problem is that he sees his brother as a victim, not someone who made some really bad choices?"

"Well, since you don't even remember Tito's case, I don't know how you can say that."

"I didn't make a habit of prosecuting innocent people. I went back and looked at the file, Maria, and there was plenty of evidence against your brother. But from what Joey told me it was all some big mistake. Tito was just at the wrong place at the wrong time, and the only reason he's in prison is because some overly zealous prosecutor wanted to make a name for himself. Me."

"Tito was just a kid! He deserved a second chance. You could have recommended probation, made a plea bargain. He didn't have to go to prison for ten years. You didn't care about anything but how many convictions you could get."

"First of all, Tito was not a kid. He was eighteen, and that's an adult. Your brother was dealing drugs, and he was right in the middle of it when the police raid came up with not just drugs but illegal guns being sold. People don't just stumble into a major deal like that. Just because you don't want to believe it doesn't mean it wasn't true.

"What's your excuse for Joey shoplifting? Going back and vandalizing the store? Skipping school? Fighting in the hallways? Coming home drunk at thirteen?"

"Shoplifting was the first and only time. He was just going along with his friends, and he knows it was wrong. He didn't start that fight at school. He– "

"Do you even *hear* yourself? If he's drinking at thirteen, what's he going to be doing at fifteen? What's your excuse going to be when it really is his drugs they find in his locker at school?"

"That's not going to happen."

"That's right. Because for the next six months, Joey's going to be living in my house under my rules. And I'm hoping you'll be there with him, and we can turn this around together."

As Joey walked back to the table, traces of chocolate ice cream still on his chin, Maria grasped a futile hope that he'd put up an argument about moving into Ritchie's house just to be obstinate, but no such luck. Wouldn't you know, the one time she needed him to be churlish, moody, and disagreeable was the one time he couldn't be more cooperative. She could have wiped that eager smile off his face with a few well-chosen words about Ritchie's role in Tito's conviction, but she didn't have the heart. Ritchie thought he had the answer to everything? Fine, let him figure out a way to tell Joey, and she'd be there to pick up the pieces and take her brother back home where he belonged.

But it had better be soon. The last thing she wanted was Joey finding this out from somebody else. Not that the wealthy lawyers and socialites Ritchie hung out with were likely to make a connection between Joey and one more in a long string of forgotten defendants from Ritchie's days as a prosecutor.

At any rate, Maria figured Joey had had enough to handle already today. And she was feeling guiltier by the minute that she hadn't entirely believed him when he'd told her the drugs in the locker at school weren't his. She had to admit, having Ritchie stand up for him in court had made an impression.

"So when do I move in?" Joey asked. He looked over at Maria belatedly. "It's okay, isn't it? I mean, it's not like I want to move out of your place, but the Judge said so, right?"

"Right," Ritchie said smoothly.

"So," Ritchie continued, "I was just telling your sister she's welcome to move in too. I've got plenty of room, so it's no big deal."

"Awesome," Joey said, looking over at Maria. "You're gonna do it, right?"

"I don't know," Maria said.

"Come on, Sis, it makes sense, you know? I mean, we're supposed to stick together, right?"

"I'll think about it."

"What's there to think about?" Joey said, pushing.

"I said I'll think about it," Maria said more sharply than she intended, and Joey shrugged his shoulders.

"All right," she relented and saw his eyes brighten. "I'll try it for one week. Just to help you get settled. But I'm not giving up my apartment," she said, turning to look at Ritchie. "Not that I could anyway, 'cause I signed a lease for a year, and it's only been a few months."

"Then it's settled," Ritchie said, nodding.

She hated the smug look on his face. Sure, she needed to be there for Joey, but she hadn't bought into the idea that Joey had to live at Ritchie's house full-time. It still seemed to her that rotating him back and forth between Ritchie's house and her apartment would be a workable solution. It would also give both her and Joey a little distance from the guy who seemed intent on deciding what *he* thought was best for her brother and just ignoring her objections. Joey was *her* brother, and it was *her* decision what was best for him.

"I'll give it a week," she said to Ritchie, "and then we'll see."

Chapter Nine

"This is where you live?" She'd figured out by now that he was seriously wealthy, but still, she hadn't expected to be moving into a...mansion was the only way she could describe it.

"I used to have a condo, but I have fundraisers here sometimes, and it just made more sense for entertaining."

"I bet," Maria said, as she walked through the marble entranceway and gazed though the open floor plan to the wide terrace that spanned the back of the house, looking out over the water. Ritchie's house was huge. But she doubted if the size was going to do anything to reduce the awkwardness she felt staying here with him.

"Come on," Ritchie said, "I'll show you your rooms."

Ritchie headed up the stairs carrying one of Joey's boxes, and Joey hurried along behind him. They stopped at Joey's room first. It was at the rear of the second floor, with a wide bay window that faced the water. The full-size bed had a headboard of dark mahogany and matched the chest of drawers and the desk that angled out from one corner to take advantage of the view. There was a window seat in the bay window, Maria noticed, with a thick cushion. Photos of sailboats were framed and mounted on the wall.

"Wow," Joey said, dropping his duffel bag on the floor.

"We can get some posters, fix it up for you," Ritchie said.

"Dude. This is so cool," Joey said.

THE MILLIONAIRE'S
Convenient ARRANGEMENT

"Your bathroom is through there," Ritchie said, gesturing toward a door, as Joey's eyes bugged out.

"I get my own bathroom? No more girl stuff all over the counter?"

The corner of Ritchie's mouth twitched. "You get your own bathroom."

"Cool."

Joey flopped onto the bed and laid on his back, his eyes widening again, when he noticed the flat screen TV that was flush to the wall opposite the bed.

"Don't get too comfortable," Ritchie said.

"Huh?"

"You've got more boxes to bring up from the car."

"Right," Joey said, leaping up and tearing out into the hallway.

"Don't run in the house!" Maria called after him, but his feet were already flying down the stairs. "I'm sorry," she said, turning to Ritchie. "I think he's just a bit overwhelmed." *And so am I,* she thought. After six months of living here, how was he ever going to adjust to her small apartment again? She hoped she was doing the right thing, even as she admitted to herself that Ritchie really hadn't given her any other option.

She followed him down the hallway to her room and tried not to look as star-struck as Joey had.

She wouldn't say this room was exactly feminine, but the colors were softer. The walls were a muted peach color, and both the window treatments and the thick cover and fat pillows on the bed were pure white. The bed itself looked like an antique, with a painted wood headboard and intricate carvings along the top. It was a bed for romantic dreams, and she suddenly felt keenly aware of Ritchie, standing in the hallway behind her. An image came unbidden of Ritchie lowering her onto that bed, slowly undressing her, his eyes dark with passion. Rolling with him over and under the thick covers, sinking into the softness of the bed, pressed against the hardness of his body…She pushed the image resolutely from her mind and turned back quickly, only to find herself against his chest. She saw the awareness flicker in his eyes and felt the pull in her own center, and she stepped back abruptly.

"I'll go get your bags," he said.

Maria walked across the room and stared out at her own view of clear blue sky and water as calm as glass, taking several deep breaths to steady her nerves.

This was not going to work. She couldn't be in the same room with him without conflicting feelings of physical attraction and immediate guilt because of what he had done to her family. To Tito. Tempered by what he was doing to help Joey. But his way, always his way.

If she ended up in bed with him, she didn't know how she'd ever forgive herself.

And she was afraid that if she stayed here that was exactly what was going to happen.

• • •

As days and then weeks went by, Maria was surprised how rarely she actually saw Ritchie. Depending on her schedule at the restaurant and the gallery, often entire days would go by with no communication other than a few text messages coordinating where Joey was and what time he'd be home. She still felt guilty that she wasn't able to spend nearly as much time with Joey as she'd like, but she had to admit it was doubtful he even noticed. Joey was now playing not one but two sports, and he participated in extracurricular activities at school. She hoped he was making friends.

If he had any spare time when Maria wasn't home, Ritchie made sure he was either at Ritchie's office or at his partner Sam's house, where sixteen-year-old Olivia was tutoring him.

Sam and Camilla had invited them over for dinner, and Maria was nervous as they approached an even more grandiose home than Ritchie's. What could she possibly have in common with these people? Ritchie was wealthy, she knew that, but something about him seemed down to earth, and he'd told her about the poor working class neighborhood he'd grown up in, right here in Miami. When she'd said she'd rather not go, Ritchie had pointed out that since Joey was spending a couple afternoons a week at their house with Olivia for tutoring, Sam's family just naturally wanted to get to know Maria.

Besides, he said, it was no big deal.

No big deal, she repeated to herself even as her stomach churned when a cool, sophisticated blonde opened the door to greet them. Before she could say a word, Joey pushed past her.

"Hey Camilla. This is my sister, Maria. Is Olivia here?"

Camilla moved aside. "She's on the terrace with JD."

"Cool." Joey took off through the wide doors, and Camilla extended her hand to Maria. Her grip was cool and firm, her eyes appraising.

"Hello Maria, I'm Camilla. Obviously," she said, laughing. "Thank you for sharing Joey with us."

"Thank you for putting up with him," Maria said, managing a smile.

"Sam's out back manning the grill," Camilla said to Ritchie, and he headed through the house, abandoning Maria almost as fast as Joey had.

Maria heard a soft cry from upstairs, and Camilla turned, heading toward the wide staircase and motioning Maria to come along.

"There she goes – come with me, and we can chat while I get Sophia up. Honestly," she said, looking back over her shoulder at Maria as they went up the stairs, "that baby is determined that I never get a moment's rest. She's up at the crack of dawn, and she almost never goes down for a nap. So when she conked out right after lunch today, I just let her sleep."

Camilla laughed. "I had about a hundred and one things I should have gotten done, but I have to confess, I spent about two hours just sitting on the terrace reading a book."

Maria wondered why Camilla didn't have a nanny, but thought it would be rude to ask.

"You're probably wondering why I don't just hire some outside help," Camilla said, making Maria wonder if she could actually read her mind.

Maria flushed. "No, I –"

"It's okay," Camilla said, and pushed open the door to a bedroom designed for a baby princess. Maria was vaguely aware of frilly pink curtains, of a dreamy mural on the wall, of a soft thick carpet, and child-sized furniture with dozens of plush stuffed animals, but her attention was riveted to the cherub who had pulled herself upright, holding onto the crib rail and cooing delightedly at Camilla.

"Gaa...daaa..." The little rosebud lips, rosy cheeks, soft curls falling over her forehead. She looked like a Botticelli angel.

"That's the most beautiful baby I've ever seen. No wonder you don't have a nanny; you must want to spend every second with her," Maria said.

Camilla grinned. "Oh, I knew I would like you. But I didn't know I would like you this much."

"Thank you, but...how did you know you'd like me?"

"Well," Camilla said, adjusting Sophia in her arms, "the way Joey talks about you, of course, but really, I mean, I've never seen Ritchie so smitten, so you had to be someone really special."

Maria stopped short. "Ritchie? Smitten? No, I think you misunderstand. Ritchie and I aren't...involved. Not at all. He's helping me with Joey, and it made sense to move in, but it's nothing..."

Maria felt the color rise in her face. "I'm not sleeping with him."

"Hmm," Camilla said. "Maybe you should be."

"It's not like that."

"If you say so," Camilla said, but she smiled in a way that told Maria she wasn't buying it.

Maria needed to change the subject, fast. But she was saved when Sophia reached out and grabbed onto a fistful of her hair, yanking so hard that it almost brought tears to her eyes.

"Sophia, no," Camilla said, extricating the tiny fingers. "I'm so sorry."

"Can I hold her?"

"Fair warning," Camilla said as she handed Sophia over. "She grabs noses too."

"I'll watch out," Maria laughed.

Downstairs, they stopped just inside and looked out through the French doors onto the terrace, where Joey was helping Camilla's son JD build an elaborate Lego project.

"I really can't thank you enough for letting Joey spend time here. After just a few weeks of Olivia helping him, I already see an improvement in his grades."

"I'm the one that should be thanking you," Camilla said. "When he's not doing homework with Olivia, JD follows him around like a puppy. He has so much patience with him. Most thirteen-year-old boys wouldn't."

It was no small blessing, Maria realized suddenly, to have people look at Joey and see a good kid, see someone they'd want their six-year-old to hang out with, to look up to. This was a whole new beginning, and these people were part of it. She felt sudden tears spring into her eyes. She'd gotten used to people looking at Joey and just seeing trouble. To be honest, she'd started to see him that way herself.

By the time they were sitting around the large table on the patio eating burgers fresh off the grill, Maria wondered why she'd been so nervous about coming here. She'd expected an uncomfortable evening, but Sam's family acted like there was nothing in the least unusual about Maria and Joey suddenly taking up residence in Ritchie's house, and she felt herself relaxing and enjoying both the food and the company. Although her home had been humbler by far – and her backyard certainly hadn't boasted a spectacular water view –it reminded her of the cookouts they'd had when her stepfather was still alive, back when everything had seemed so simple and perfect. Back when she and Tito were the same age Joey was now.

Joey had already put away two fat, juicy hamburgers and a mountain of potato salad before Olivia talked him into sampling a tofu burger, which he reluctantly proclaimed was "not bad." Although Maria was pretty sure he would eat dirt and proclaim it "not bad" if Olivia suggested it.

After dinner, Joey ran around the back yard with JD, roughhousing and probably showing off a bit for Olivia, who seemed suitably impressed when he kicked off his shoes and did a back flip off the edge of the pool. In his shorts and t-shirt. JD followed him, doing a cannonball, and Camilla looked over at Maria and rolled her eyes.

"Welcome to the insane asylum," she said, opening an outside cupboard to remove several oversized striped beach towels. "Swim suits optional."

Later, Olivia got out her acoustic guitar, and Maria leaned back on a chaise, listening to the soft strains of the guitar blending with Olivia's sweet and surprisingly soulful voice. Joey and JD were wrapped in the towels, momentarily worn out, and Camilla was sharing a wide lounge chair with her husband, baby Sophia snuggled close on her lap. Maria glanced over at Ritchie, the long length of him sprawled out on another chaise near hers.

To an outsider, they would look like two couples – two *families* – sharing an evening together. For a moment, she felt almost overwhelmed with longing, the urge to reach across the short space separating her chair from Ritchie's and slip her hand into his almost too powerful to ignore. What would it be like to lean on Ritchie's strength, to have the kind of trust and commitment Camilla and Sam obviously shared? To face life's challenges with someone else at her side, to not be so alone?

Just then Ritchie turned his head, looked at her, and smiled a slow smile. She looked away, every nerve ending in her body tingling. She had to get a grip. This was not her life. She and Joey didn't belong here. It was a temporary arrangement. One that she'd been forced into with no other choice, by a man who she had no business feeling attracted to. Not after what he had done to Tito.

But the warm glow of the evening still followed her later when Sam's family said goodbye and Camilla walked them to the door.

"We'll have lunch," Camilla said. "Soon."

"I'd like that," Maria said and meant it.

Maria had hoped having Joey in the backseat would ease the tension she felt riding back in the car beside Ritchie, but within sixty seconds, Joey was fast asleep. She reached over to turn on the radio just as Ritchie reached over to adjust the temperature in the car, and their hands brushed, sending an electric shock up her arm. She jerked back.

"Sorry."

"No problem," Ritchie said, and she wondered if he'd felt it too.

Maria turned her head, staring out the window and watching the lights stream by. And tried not to remember what it had been like to be held in Ritchie's arms the night they'd gone on their one date. Tried not to think about how it had felt to have his mouth on hers.

Chapter Ten

Ritchie pulled his sports car into the driveway and drummed his fingers on the steering wheel for a few moments. This was ridiculous. He was sitting in his own driveway, hesitating before walking into his own house.

The truth was, Maria was driving him crazy. Ever since they spent the evening at Sam and Camilla's house – an evening Ritchie thought had gone perfectly well – Maria had been avoiding him like the plague. Not that she'd gone out of her way to be in the same room with him before that, but things had definitely gotten worse. If he walked into a room, within moments, she made an excuse to be somewhere else. And he was getting pretty fed up with it.

He didn't expect gratitude, and he knew she hadn't gotten over the fact that he was the one who had prosecuted her brother. But dammit, the point was Joey now, and this arrangement wasn't going to work if she couldn't manage to be in the same room with him for more than five minutes.

They had to confront this, and there was no time like the present. Especially since he'd just dropped Joey off at a sleepover with one of his new friends from his baseball team.

Typically, Maria cooked dinner for the three of them if Ritchie got home that early, and the kid served as a buffer. Not tonight. Ritchie had already texted Maria that he'd be picking up some takeout on the way home. He grabbed the containers of food and went into the house, just in time to hear Maria's door close upstairs. He set them on the bar and walked up the steps to knock on her door. She opened it a few inches and peered out at him.

"Yes?"

"Are you coming down to eat?"

"Oh. I thought since Joey wasn't here..."

"I texted you."

"I thought you just meant I wouldn't need to cook anything." She opened the door a little wider, and he saw that she was wearing what looked like long cotton pajama pants with a drawstring around the waist, slung low on her hips, and a stretchy little cap-sleeve t-shirt that had some art museum logo on it. There was nothing indecent about the outfit, but he thought it was somehow sexier than a flimsy negligee would have been. He felt himself go hard and, as a result, his voice came out harsher than he intended.

"For heaven's sake, Maria, you're not my housekeeper. You're my guest. I picked up dinner for both of us." He tried not to sound annoyed, but did she have to make everything difficult?

"Coming?"

She shrugged one shoulder in a move that was typically Joey.

"Sure."

Maria followed him down the stairs, then got out plates while Ritchie started opening the takeout containers.

She looked surprised when she looked into the containers to find a meal of fragrant roasted chicken, beans, rice, plantains, crisp salad, and soft bread. There were little containers of guava barbeque sauce guaranteed to make your mouth water and thick slices of cheesecake for dessert.

"Not what you expected?" Ritchie tossed his jacket over the back of one of the stools in the kitchen and rolled up his sleeves.

"I guess I was expecting something...I don't know, fancier?"

"Sorry to disappoint."

"No, this is...perfect."

"Let's load up our plates and take it out on the patio." Maybe if they ate out back where the lights were dimmer, he could get his mind off the way her breasts filled out the simple little shirt she was wearing, stop thinking about what was under the thin cotton pajama bottoms slung low on her hips.

Maria hesitated by the French doors leading out back. "Don't you want to go...change or something?"

"And let the food get cold?"

"I feel a little underdressed."

"You're fine. Come on."

They took their plates out to the terrace and set them on the table. Maria was perched on the edge of her seat, looking like she was ready to take flight at any moment.

"Could you relax?"

"It's just a little weird. Without Joey here."

Ritchie nodded, then got up, walked into the house, and selected a bottle of wine from the under-the-counter cooler, opened it and grabbed two glasses. Maybe after some dinner and some wine, Maria would lighten up a bit.

By the time he walked back out, she had pulled her chair closer and was sitting at the table, her posture stiff. He grinned and sat down across from her and poured them both some wine.

"I'm not really much of a wine drinker." She picked up the glass and took a small sip, then raised her eyes to him in surprise. "This is really good."

"I'm glad you like it."

"You didn't have to do this," she said, gesturing to the plates of food.

"It's just dinner, Maria."

She took another drink of wine and started in on her meal. She looked younger, more vulnerable, sitting there in the simple cotton shirt and pajama pants. Her face seemed innocent without a trace of make-up, and when a light breeze moved over her, he smelled the faint scent of exotic flowers. No wonder she seemed stressed around him. He really had steamrolled her into moving in here, had completely taken over every decision about her brother's life. And, as he reminded himself, he was the enemy.

"I know it's just dinner," she said. "But when you do thoughtful things like this, it just makes it harder."

"Harder to what?"

She raised her eyes. "Harder to keep hating you."

"You don't have to hate me, Maria."

"Yeah, I do," she said, and her eyes looked sad. "I really do."

"Well, here's an idea. How about a truce."

"A truce?"

"Yeah, a truce." He took a bite of chicken and rice and washed it down with some wine, then picked up the bottle and refilled both their glasses.

"Let's declare a truce for as long as you and Joey are living here. Then when you move back to your apartment, you can pick up right where you left off, hating me."

"You're making fun of me," she said, her eyes flashing with sudden passion.

"I'm not. I'm just being practical. I think we both agree that, for the time being, living here is in Joey's best interests."

He knew it cost her to agree with anything he said, but she nodded. "His grades are up, he's playing sports, no problems at school, and he's making friends – the right kind this time. What do you want, for me to admit you were right all along?"

"Maria, that kid's got a solid foundation, and that's all you. It was the situation you were in. I don't think there's anything more you could have done. I just have more...resources. That's all."

"There you go again, sounding all reasonable."

"I'm a very reasonable man."

"Hmmm. Reasonable is not the first word that comes to mind. Assertive, confident, maybe just a bit arrogant..." Her voice trailed off, and she took a deep breath and exhaled slowly. "Look, it's not that I don't appreciate everything you've done for Joey. I *know* we'll never be able to repay you."

"Dammit, Maria." He slammed his palms down on the table and stood up, pushing back his chair. She looked startled, and maybe a little frightened. Marvelous. Just marvelous.

He walked over to one of the wide chaises, sat down, kicked off his shoes, and leaned back, then spoke in a level tone without looking at her.

"It's not about repaying me. And you know what? It's not about Tito or about you carrying around years of resentment and anger about something you can't change and I can't change." He closed his eyes for a few seconds, then opened them and turned to look at her. "It's about Joey."

She didn't say anything. He watched as she got up from her chair, and he thought she was going to go back into the house, and retreat to her room again. Instead, she poured the last of the bottle of wine into their glasses then carried them over and stood next to the chaise. He figured it was her move.

"Mind if I sit down?"

"Be my guest." He shifted over and patted the seat next to him. She handed him his glass of wine and then set hers down on the terrace before taking a seat beside him on the chaise. She leaned against the backrest, not looking at him, staring instead up at the stars that had begun to appear in the evening sky.

They sat there awhile, stretched out side by side, not talking, until their wine glasses were empty. He thought about going into the house to get another bottle, but then decided not to interrupt what almost seemed like companionable silence. Finally, she spoke, her voice soft and her words seeming to be carefully chosen.

"Everything changed when Tito went to prison. For my mom to lose her husband so young was bad enough. But she pulled herself together. Joey was so little. He needed her to be strong for him, and she was. But Tito and me...something like that should have brought us closer. When you have a twin, that person is like the other half of you. But he wouldn't talk to me. It was like he turned into someone I didn't even know."

She signed. "I don't know why I'm telling you this. I guess it's the wine talking. I just wanted you to understand."

Maria and Tito were twins? Ritchie hadn't realized that. Somehow it made it worse.

"I want you to tell me," Ritchie said. "I do want to understand."

The air was so still, the night so quiet. Maria didn't speak for so long he thought she might have fallen asleep. He watched the rise and fall of her chest as she breathed, and he felt an unexpected surge of tenderness. She turned her head toward him then, and her eyes were clear and intense.

"I didn't know what to do with the grief, the sadness, so I lost myself in my art. Tito just lost himself."

He knew it was pointless to tell her not to blame herself. To tell her that her brother had made choices that led him to where he was today. But she couldn't help blaming herself any more than she could stop blaming him. And he had no business lying here beside her wanting to offer comfort she didn't want from him, wanting to pull her into his arms and make love to her, watch her eyes cloud over with pleasure and all the sadness slip away.

She sat up suddenly, setting her empty glass back down on the stone terrace. She turned to face him.

"I said I can't stop hating you, Ritchie, but that's not the worst of it."

He just watched her, waited.

She laughed, and it was a hollow sound with no joy. "Hating you I could deal with. It's *wanting* you that keeps me awake at night."

It was like the world stopped spinning on its axis. One of those moments when everything stands still. Like the moment when the jury files back in at the end of a long trial and everyone in the courtroom holds their collective breath, waiting for the verdict.

"Tell me what you want, Maria."

"Why don't I just show you," she said, and just like that, she was on top of him, all hot and fast hands, lips fastening onto his, their legs tangling, her body pressing tightly against his. He felt his pulse shoot into overdrive, and he was instantly hard. Her hands were in his hair, her lips locked on his, and before he had a moment to think, his own hands pushed up the flimsy cotton t-shirt, slid up her ribs, and moved none too gently over her breasts, skin to skin. His mind ordered him to slow down, but his body wasn't getting the message. His strokes became more demanding as her nipples instantly responded to his touch, hardening under each rough caress.

She called out his name, arching above him as her hands moved to his shoulders for support. He pulled her tighter, then let his mouth take over, felt a taut nipple against his tongue, and heard her gasp. His hands moved down her body, siding over her hips, and his mind flashed for a second to their first and only date. He remembered the restraint he'd exercised against the temptation to move his hands up under the short skirt she'd worn.

With no hesitation now – and no restraint – he pulled the drawstring on her pants loose and slipped the waistband down over her hips then let his hands wander over her perfectly rounded bottom. She wasn't wearing anything – not even a thong – under those pj pants, and it almost undid him.

She was fumbling with his belt, murmuring, "Now, Ritchie, now," and her words seemed a little slurred. *I guess it's the wine talking,* she'd said earlier, and the recollection was like a cold splash of water on his face. Would she be all over him if she hadn't had more than half a bottle of wine? He tried to remember how many times her glass had been refilled.

He caught her wrists, pulled her hands away from his belt, and she looked at him, confusion showing on her face.

"Don't you want me?"

"Oh, God, Maria, more than you know."

"Then what's the matter?"

His head was starting to clear. Her shirt was still pushed up, and he could see already reddened marks where his face – not shaved since seven a.m. – had scraped against her delicate skin. He gently lowered her shirt and pulled the loose pants back over her hips.

"What's the matter," he told her, "is that we've had too much wine."

"I'm not drunk!"

"Of course not," he said, swinging his legs over the side of the chaise and scooping her up into his arms.

"What are you doing, Ritchie?"

"I'm putting you to bed."

"Mmmm. Yes, take me to bed."

"Not take you to bed – *put* you to bed, darling." She leaned against him, and he carried her into the house, shutting the terrace door behind them. God, she weighed almost nothing. He carried her up the stairs and down the hall and laid her down on the soft comforter on her bed. She smiled and reached out her arms to him.

"I'll be right back," he said, and she smiled again.

Ritchie walked over to the closet, pulled a light blanket down from the shelf, unfolded it, and walked back to the bed. Her eyes were closed, her breathing deep and regular. He put the blanket over her and shut off the light, watching her for a moment before he walked out of the room, closing the door behind him.

THE MILLIONAIRE'S
Convenient ARRANGEMENT

Either way, she'd hate him in the morning, but what the hell, she hated him already.

It may have taken few glasses of wine to open up a part of her she'd closed off to him, but now her behavior over the past weeks made a lot more sense. Ritchie had wanted her in his bed since the first night he saw her at the soup kitchen. How ironic that when he finally had her exactly where he'd wanted her, he was the one who had to call a halt. Maria wanted him, probably as much as he wanted her. She just wouldn't admit it unless a little too much wine loosened her self-control. The response he'd felt when his hands were on her body didn't lie.

He would never take advantage of her when she was intoxicated, but he had no qualms about using that information to his advantage when she had a clear head. Things were about to get a lot more interesting.

But for now, his best chance of getting any sleep tonight was to go swim a few dozen laps in the pool until he wore himself out. Then he'd try to put that delectable body a few doors down the hallway from his room completely out of his mind.

Chapter Eleven

Someone just shoot me. Maria groaned and rolled over, tangling herself further in the blanket. Her head was pounding and she felt mildly queasy. She'd had too much wine to drink, that much she remembered. She had a sudden vision of herself rolling on top of Ritchie on the chaise by the pool. Grabbing him. Kissing him.

Oh God. Had she...No. *That* she would have remembered. But how had she ended up here, in bed? Wait, they'd been rolling around on the chaise, and then the next thing she remembered, Ritchie had picked her up and said...Wow. She must have passed out. If she hadn't, she would have made even more of a fool of herself, whereas Ritchie had been the perfect gentleman and just tucked her into bed. She felt her cheeks flush at the memory, partly from embarrassment but – if she was honest with herself – just as much from the memory of what his hands had felt like on her skin, the way her body had felt pressed against his.

Maria took a long shower and took her time getting dressed, putting off the moment when she'd have to face him. Hoping maybe he'd gone into the office. It was Saturday, and she wasn't scheduled at the restaurant. She was working at the gallery later this afternoon, and Joey wouldn't be back until much later.

She could smell the coffee as soon as she started down the stairs. She took a deep breath and walked into the kitchen. And there he was, learning against the kitchen counter, a mug of coffee in one hand and an unreadable look on his face.

"How do you feel?"

How about really, really embarrassed. She looked for any hint of condescension, but the question seemed sincere.

"I'm okay," she said cautiously.

"Hungry?"

"Do you cook?"

"I'm a man of many talents," he said.

After last night, she had to agree.

"You want an omelet?"

Her stomach wasn't quite ready for that. "Just some toast. And coffee," she added, walking over to the counter to pour herself some. "But go ahead and make whatever you want."

"I've been up awhile. I ate."

"Ok."

Richie cut two thick slices from a loaf of Italian bread and dropped them in the toaster while she stood there, sipping her coffee.

The small talk had been bad enough, but the silence was making her nuts. Should she apologize for practically jumping him last night? Well, it's not like he put up any resistance. In fact, if she hadn't had so much wine, he wouldn't have put her to bed – he'd have gone to bed with her. Or maybe made love with her right there by the pool. Her body tingled at the thought. Of course, if she hadn't had so much wine, she never would have rolled on top of him and kissed him and...

She jumped when the toast popped, and he looked over at her and grinned.

"Something on your mind?" He had just enough of a smug look on his face to make all thoughts of an apology for her behavior fly right out the window.

"You're just lucky I passed out last night, or we might have done something we'd both be regretting this morning." She plucked a piece of toast out of the toaster and took a bite. It settled her stomach a bit, but not her nerves.

He grinned at her.

THE MILLIONAIRE'S
Convenient ARRANGEMENT

"Why? Would I have been that disappointed?"

Just who did he think he was, standing there, in his low slung jeans and his faded University of Florida Law School t-shirt and his bare feet and that *smirk* on his face, looking way more sexy than any man had any right to look.

"Of course not," she said indignantly. "I just mean I realize I was the one that started something last night, and I just want you to know that if I hadn't been drinking, I never would have kissed you or…or…"

"Or climbed on top of me out by the pool?" He set his coffee on the marble island and walked around it.

She took a deep breath and exhaled slowly, trying to ignore the grin on his face. She abandoned her toast and took a step backward as he moved closer.

"Absolutely not. I simply wasn't in full possession of my faculties last night," she said primly.

He was just a little too close now, and she could feel her back pressing against the counter. Her heart started to beat a little faster.

"Do you know what you're doing now? Fully in possession of your faculties?"

"Yes, of course."

"Good."

He took the coffee mug out of her hands and set it on the counter.

"Wh– what are you doing?"

"If it's not obvious, then I'm not doing a very good job of it." He reached out and hooked two fingers into the waistband of her shorts, pulling her gently forward until she was pressed up against him.

"It's my turn to make the first move. You okay with that?"

Before she could form an answer, his mouth covered hers, and a fire shot through her straight to her core. She put her hands against his chest, gripping his shirt, then wrapping her arms around those hard muscles. She kissed him back, thrilling wildly when he lifted her up, leaned her against the counter as she wrapped her legs around his waist and arched backward. She'd thought it was just the alcohol last night that had made her feel so dizzy, but she wasn't drunk now. His strong hands were under her shirt, unhooking her bra and pushing it out of the way, and then his mouth was on her bare breast, his lips moving closer to the taut peak while the pad of his thumb brushed over her other breast.

She felt his warm breath on her nipple as he leaned his head back to look at her face, his chin resting on the underside of her breast, and a quick thrill ran through her.

"Do you want me to stop? Tell me now, Maria."

"No. I don't want you to stop."

Then his thumb was moving in rhythmic circles over one nipple and his mouth closed over the other one and she couldn't even think anymore. She grabbed his head, gripping his hair with both hands and moaned as she strained toward him, clamping her legs tighter around his waist. He was doing things to her she'd only imagined before, and it felt incredible. Why had she been so afraid to get this close to someone? God, if she died right now, she'd die happy.

But why did it have to be Ritchie who made her feel this way?

He lifted his head, and his mouth trailed up over the top of her breast, to her collarbone, and made her shiver.

"Take me to bed, Ritchie. Take me to bed now. And I don't mean tuck me in for the night."

"Are you sure?"

In response, she fastened her lips on his and kissed him like she'd never kissed anyone before. When she slid her hand down between them, pressing her palm against the hard length of him straining against his jeans, he pulled back.

"Whoa. Let's try to at least make it to the bed."

Then she found herself boosted up higher, her legs coming loose from around his waist as he put her over his shoulder and strode out of the kitchen and toward the wide staircase. The feel of his hand at the top of her thighs, holding her in place, was intoxicating, and being pressed against his shoulder created a delicious pressure that was almost unbearable.

When he tossed her unceremoniously onto his bed, she bounced on the mattress and laughed out loud at the incongruity of it all.

"Something funny, Miss Martinez?"

She was about to make a clever retort when he peeled off his shirt and, suddenly, her mouth went dry.

"I'm just a little nervous," she whispered.

"Hmm. That's probably because you're wearing too many clothes. I can help you with that," he said, leaning over and pulling her shirt over her head. Then he slid her bra straps off her shoulders so it fell forward.

"Now where were we when we paused downstairs?" he asked. "Ah, yes, now I remember."

His eyes had a wicked glint as he leaned forward, putting one knee on the bed, and lowered his face to graze her breasts. His chin was soft, and she realized that of course he had shaved this morning. The smooth touch was every bit as erotic as the rough beard had felt the night before. She felt her nipples tighten, and she arched toward him, letting the feeling ripple through her entire body. *Just let it happen. Don't overthink it. No*, said another voice in her head, *you have to tell him.*

He stepped back and unfastened his jeans then reached over and pulled a foil packet out of the drawer in the bedside table. He slipped onto the bed beside her, wearing only his boxers, and she thought, *wow*, and then *this is really it.*

He leaned over her, on his side, his leg brushing up against hers.

"You're so quiet all of a sudden."

"I have to tell you something."

"Uh oh." He sat up. "Is this one of those moments where you tell me you are secretly married to a Columbian drug lord? Who carves out the heart of any man who looks at you?"

"I think I saw that movie." She laughed nervously.

"What is it, Maria?"

"It's just...I've never done this before." She couldn't look at him, but when she looked down, all she could see was the evidence of how ready and willing he was to do what they were about to do, and she wondered why she hadn't just kept her mouth shut. It was just so *embarrassing*.

He frowned. "If you mean you don't usually have casual sex, Maria, I get that. This attraction between us has been coming on for a long time." He put his fingers under her chin, forced her to look at him. "I've wanted you since the first night I met you at St. Theresa's."

"I used to think about you." Her voice was a whisper. "About this. At night. Back before I knew..."

His voice hardened. "Tito's not in bed with us. *This* isn't about him, it isn't about Joey. It's just you and me right now."

He paused and spoke more gently. "If you think I'm going to think less of you because we ended up in bed together, then you don't really know me at all."

"No, it's not that..." The longer she waited, the harder it was to get the words out.

"I've never had sex before!" she said, almost shouting. "Oh crap."

"You've never had sex before," he repeated, looking at her like he was in shock. Oh great. Now he thought she was some kind of a freak. A twenty-six year old virgin.

"It's not like I planned it that way, it just...the time was never right, that's all." She knew she sounded defensive. She sounded like an idiot. "I shouldn't have told you. I should have just fumbled my way through it."

He looked like he was trying not to laugh, and she felt sick.

"Trust me," he said, "I would have figured it out before long."

His gaze dropped down to her breasts, and she felt her nipples tighten of their own will. Suddenly she felt too naked, too vulnerable. She grabbed a pillow from the other side of the bed and held it in front of her.

"Don't do that." He pulled the pillow away and she sighed, hating that the breath came out on a half sob. Dammit. The last thing she wanted to do was look like a fool.

"We're not going to do this, Maria."

"Because I told you I'm a virgin."

"Because now that I know that, things are more complicated. We've got issues between us, Maria. I know I said Tito has nothing to do with it, but are you sure you want the first guy you have sex with to be the same guy who put your brother in prison for ten years? It would be different if this were just a casual thing between two people who are just having a good time. You raised the stakes, Maria. I'm sorry."

"You can't do this. You can't humiliate me like this." Her eyes filled up with tears, and she blinked them back, furious with herself. "You can't carry me up here to your bed and then just walk away because I was...honest with you."

"No. I can't."

"So what does that mean? Now I'm confused."

"I still want to touch you. We're just not going to have sex."

"Not going to...okay."

He leaned back over her again and started tracing circles with his fingertips around her nipples. And she started finding it hard to talk.

"So, how far did you go in high school in the back seat of your boyfriend's car?"

"I was a good...Catholic girl," she managed to get out.

"Um hmm. You're a good Catholic girl now," he said then his mouth took over one of her nipples as he slid her shorts down over her hips. He cupped her with his hand, stroking her gently through the thin fabric of her panties, pushing her knee to one side to give his hand better access. He slipped one finger under her panties and started stroking in a slow circle, and she gasped.

"Not this far," she said. It was too much. She couldn't get her bearings. His mouth on her breast, one hand skillfully manipulating her other nipple, and his other hand stroking her in those maddeningly slow circles. Every time she got close to the edge, he seemed to sense it and kept her trembling there.

"You're so beautiful, Maria. Let go for me."

Waves of pleasure broke over her without warning, and he kept on stroking her, holding her, while her whole body clenched, and she heard herself cry out his name. It seemed like it went on forever, and then he was kissing her while she felt the aftershocks of the most intense orgasm she'd ever imagined. She wondered if it felt like this just making out with him, what would it be like to actually have sex?

As she laid there afterward, leaning her head on his shoulder while he trailed a lazy hand down her breasts and her belly, giving her fresh shivers and tremors, she made a conscious decision to just be in the moment and not think about anything else. She wasn't going to spoil this. Ritchie was pressed against her thigh, and the thought of the hard length of him made her tremble again.

"Can I touch you?"

"Yeah," he said, nuzzling her neck.

"Show me how."

When he didn't respond, she slid her hand tentatively under the waistband of his boxers and closed it around him, gaining confidence as she moved her grip up and down slowly, watching his reaction.

"God, Maria."

"Am I doing it wrong?" She knew she wasn't.

Emboldened, she moved lower on the bed, sliding his boxers down, and trailed kisses down the length of him and back up again while she continued to move her hand faster. When he came, it was her name he shouted, and she felt a primal thrill of knowledge as old as time.

Then he was stroking her again, before she had a chance to get nervous. Her heart was racing as he took her higher and higher, his eyes locked on hers when she went over again. Finally, they laid side by side, and she waited for her breathing to come back to normal. When he reached over and held her hand, she almost came apart at the incredible sweetness of it.

"I never did anything like this in the backseat of anybody's car," she confessed.

"So tell me your story. I want to know." When she turned her head to the side, he said, "Come on, you can't possibly be embarrassed to tell me anything now."

"Well, like I said, I was a good Catholic girl. And when my stepfather died, I just got focused so much on art that I really didn't have that much interest in dating."

"Wait, your stepfather? I'm confused."

"Joey's my half-brother. Mom married my stepfather when Tito and I were ten. And he was the best thing that ever happened to us."

"What about your father?"

"I don't have a father. Not in any sense of the word."

"I'm sorry – I wasn't trying to make you sad."

"It's okay. Anyway, I had some boyfriends in high school and college, but I never wanted to let anyone get that close. I was afraid."

"Afraid?"

"Afraid I'd make the same mistakes by mother did. She got pregnant in high school. To a guy who dumped her as soon as he found out. Her parents never forgave her. It wasn't easy when Tito and I were little. Single mother with a high school education and suddenly she has twin babies to raise, with no support."

Ritchie squeezed her hand.

"So there was no way I wanted to end up like that."

"That's a hard life. Being a single mom with two kids before she was even out of her teens. Especially if she didn't have family she could depend on."

"I'm not saying our life was horrible or anything. My mom loved us. And I probably learned a lot from those lean years. Like not to take things for granted. But she worked really hard. She had to hold down two jobs, and finding day care that she could afford was always a problem. I always swore I was never going to end up like that."

He looked at her thoughtfully, casually brushing a stray lock of hair from her forehead and tucking it behind her ear, his hand pausing to brush the side of her jaw and send fresh tremors rushing through her. "But here you are."

"What?"

"Working two jobs. Taking care of Joey. And worrying about reliable care when he's not in school."

She laughed. "Yeah. I never thought about it that way." She shook her head. "Best laid plans and all that."

All of a sudden, she felt a little too exposed. Not just physically, but like she was letting Ritchie see too much inside her head. And her heart. She shivered.

"Cold?" he asked.

"A little," she lied, and in moments he had the soft comforter pulled up from under them and tucked around her.

"Anyway," she said when he turned on his side again to face her. "I guess if you're asking why I'm still a virgin at twenty-six, that's why. At first, I was never going to have sex until I got married, and I didn't want to get married until I finished school, got my degree, established myself as an artist. Then when my mom died and things fell apart, and I had Joey to take care of, well, I just didn't have time think about dating."

"And you've never been tempted until now?"

He had a smug look on his face again. "Well, I was tempted once. When I was in Paris. I got into a prestigious art program in Philadelphia, and the summer before my freshman year, I won a scholarship to study abroad. Jean Paul. That was his name. An art student, like me. French."

"Of course."

"He had very liberal views about politics and art and, well, a lot of things. He quoted poetry and told me we were destined to be together."

"I'm sure. You resisted, I take it?"

"Only after I caught him with another student. Apparently, Jean Paul was also very liberal with his affections."

"Jean Paul was an ass."

"Yeah, that too. Anyway, after I almost fell for all his talk about how 'special' I was, I realized how close I had come to risking everything. I wasn't even on birth control pills, and I would have trusted a guy like that to protect me?"

"You were going to trust me."

She felt her cheeks flush. "I got caught up in the moment, but I still saw you get a condom out of the drawer. Beside, my issues with you have nothing to do with trust."

"Issues? There's more than one?"

She gave him a light shove back onto his back and rolled over onto him, propped her elbows on his chest. "Well, aside from the obvious one that I really don't want to talk about right now, yeah."

The look he gave her made her blood pound in her veins. "So, what other issues do you have with me?"

"Well, you're a little too sure of yourself sometimes."

He nodded. "And?"

"Bossy. You can be kind of bossy."

"You don't like being told what to do."

"I definitely don't like being told what to do."

"Well, that's a pity."

"Why, you thinking about bossing me around?"

"I'd like to boss you around right now…in bed."

Since they were pressed so closely together, she was sure he felt her tremble.

"Well," she said, running her tongue across her lips in a way she was pretty sure had the desired effect, if the sudden pressure against her thigh was any indication. "I guess I could make an exception…in bed."

His voice was brisk, but the expression in his eyes was playful. "Slide your body up higher and grab onto the posts on the headboard."

She slid up his chest and reached up tentatively for the posts.

THE MILLIONAIRE'S
Convenient ARRANGEMENT

"Like this?"

"Higher. I want your breast so close to my lips that you can feel my breath on your nipple."

"Ohmigod."

"Now, whatever you do, don't let go of the posts."

"You mean whatever you do." She paused. "What are you going to do?"

"Plenty."

And he did. For someone who'd just had her first orgasm with another person, Maria figured she'd had quite an education all in one day. And they hadn't even had sex yet.

• • •

"I don't get it," she said, much later, as she lay stretched out beside Ritchie on his bed, her limbs languid. She hadn't realized it was possible to feel so exhausted and feel like her body was shimmering with energy all at the same time.

"What?" Ritchie rolled onto his side and propped himself on one elbow. He traced her jaw line with the tips of his fingers, then down her neck, barely grazing her collarbone, before he moved on to her shoulder. She felt her nipples tighten.

"What?" he repeated, continuing to trace light patterns down her arm. "What don't you get?"

"How can you do all this stuff with me and you don't want to have sex with me? I mean, what difference would it make?"

He didn't answer at first.

"Ritchie?"

He sighed and sat up, and she bit back a protest when he stopped stroking her and rested his hand on the bed.

"One, I *do* want to have sex with you. Which should be obvious. And two, it does make a difference. If I'm ever going to move from that guy you made out with to that guy you slept with, first you're going to have to come to terms with the fact that I prosecuted Tito, but it was his own actions that caused him to end up where he is today."

Maria sat up too, crossing her arms over her breasts as the euphoria of a few moments ago disappeared and was replaced by a cold, empty feeling in her chest. It looked like nothing had changed after all.

"Maybe you're the one that has to come to terms with the fact that just maybe you made one mistake in your prosecutorial career. Just maybe you were so intent on racking up convictions that you forgot what justice means."

"He's not the innocent you think he was, Maria. Look, I know your brother had a rough time, but so did you. The same things happened to you, but you didn't end up in a gang house selling drugs and guns." He hesitated.

"Listen, maybe I did take too strong a stand back then on no plea bargains for gang members and drug dealers. Maybe I didn't look close enough for the rare case where cutting a deal wouldn't just result in one more gang member back out there faster– selling drugs and committing other crimes as soon as his feet hit the street. Maybe I'd do things differently now. But that doesn't change the fact that your brother was right in the middle of a whole lot of really bad stuff. The person ultimately responsible for Tito being in prison is Tito."

Unbelievable. Even when he admitted he'd do things differently now, Ritchie still – in the next breath –was justifying the way he'd brushed off any thought of a plea deal and put Tito in prison for ten years.

Sure, Tito never should have gotten anywhere near the gangs that had moved into the old neighborhood. But he'd only been on the fringes, and it was bad luck and bad timing that had put him in the wrong place at the wrong time when the police stormed that house and arrested everyone there. How different all their lives would be now if only Tito could have had a second chance. And Ritchie was the one person who could have given it to him.

Maria scrambled for her shirt and pulled it on over her head, then found her shorts and wriggled back into them.

"You think you know everything, but you don't. I can't believe I spent all morning in bed with you, doing . . . this."

His smile was sardonic. "So, aren't you glad we didn't take it any further? Aren't you glad you didn't have sex with me, Maria?"

She picked up a pillow and hurled it at him. As she stalked out of the room and back down the hallway, she thought she heard him curse.

Fine. She hoped he felt as lousy now as she did. She *was* glad she hadn't slept with him. And he was going to have to change his tune about the past if he expected her to get naked with him again anytime soon. Or anytime period.

Chapter Twelve

"I like this man the minute I met him." Vivienne looked up from the chaos of wood, steel, and Plexiglas from which, Maria knew, an amazing work of art was about to be born.

"Did you listen to anything I said?"

"Hmmm. Everything." Vivienne turned back to her project. "I like a man who takes charge in bed."

"Well, Ritchie thinks he can take charge of my life. Everything is black and white with him. No blurred lines. Tito is a criminal, throw away the key. That's what Ritchie thinks."

"And for you, everything is all black and white as well."

"That's not true."

"Tito was railroaded, he was innocent, he was in the wrong place at the wrong time."

"Yes? Well? That's true."

Vivienne turned and looked at her.

"Have you ever asked him?"

"What?"

"In all these years, have you ever asked Tito what happened that night?"

"Of course not. Make my own brother think I question his innocence? Why would I do that?"

"Maybe you should ask yourself why you *don't* do that."

"What do you mean?"

"Maybe you are afraid of what Tito might tell you. Sweetie, maybe you don't want to know."

"There's nothing to tell."

"Fine. Come have a cup of tea with me. I am tired of this piece for now."

"I'm restless."

"Then come. Take your tea and go paint for awhile."

"I thought you wanted me to start organizing your schedule for –"

"That can wait." Vivienne studied her shrewdly. "You have a different look about you today. An energy. You need to use it. Put it into your art."

"It's called frustration."

Vivienne shrugged. "Use it."

• • •

By the time Maria looked at her watch, she was shocked to see that six hours had gone by. She pushed aside the blackout curtains – Vivienne claimed there were times as an artist when she didn't want to know if it was night or day – and saw that it was dark outside. She'd been experimenting with a new medium, adding texture to her paintings, and for the first time in months, she felt like she'd made real progress in creating something on the canvas that resembled what she saw in her mind.

"It's very good."

She startled at the quiet voice behind her, and turned to face Vivienne, who was studying her latest effort still propped on an easel.

"Perhaps, before long, we will have a small showing."

Maria felt the sharp jolt of excitement shoot through her. But it was too soon.

"It's not ready for anyone else to see yet."

"Nonsense. Art is meant to be seen."

Right. Half the time, Vivienne put new pieces away ten minutes before a showing, judging them not worthy. But Maria knew better than to point that out.

Maybe she should think about a showing. But as she drove back to Ritchie's, she realized how much time it would take her to complete enough pieces to make that possible. Between her job at the restaurant, the work she did for Vivienne, and the time she wanted – needed – to spend with Joey, it just wasn't possible. Her feelings about Richie were getting more and more complicated, and that made it more important than ever that she maintain her independence.

Sure, Ritchie was paying for all the extras for Joey now, not to mention the food they were eating. But as attracted as she was to Ritchie on a physical level, and as much as she appreciated everything he was doing for Joey, there simply wasn't any future for her in a relationship with the man who was responsible for Tito being sentenced to ten long years in prison.

In April, Joey would have fulfilled the judge's requirement that he stay out of trouble for six months, and Ritchie's responsibility for Joey would end. Although she was sure Ritchie would want to continue to have some role in Joey's life, Maria and Joey would be back in her apartment. The last thing she wanted to do was depend on Ritchie to pay for Joey to stay in the sports programs and have the kind of opportunities that kept him away from the old neighborhood.

He was doing well in school, staying of trouble, bringing home good grades. Maria could never afford to pay the tuition for the private school where he was thriving, but maybe they had a scholarship program. Or would allow her to set up a payment plan. She might even be able to pick up a part-time job in the school office in exchange for reduced tuition.

Once Joey was through high school and in college, there would be plenty of time to pursue her own dreams. But for now, it was all about Joey. It had to be.

Chapter Thirteen

"Hold still, would you?" Ritchie breathed out a sigh in frustration. He didn't remember Halloween being this complicated when he was a kid. Zombie gory flesh? What happened to drawing a scar on your face with a magic marker and spattering some red paint on an old shirt? Oh well, it had been his idea to transform Joey from a plain old pirate to a zombie pirate, so he might as well suck it up.

"Come on, Ritchie, we're gonna be late."

"Not if you hold still." Ritchie used the putty-like substance to mold a realistic looking scar down the side of Joey's face and onto his neck, then used a sponge to dab on some nasty looking liquid from a bottle labeled "fake zombie skin" (as opposed to what, *real* zombie skin?), and finally, painted over it all with zombie blood.

He moved on to adjust the knife through the head, adding convincing amounts of fake zombie skin and zombie blood at the points of entry.

"Hang in there, almost done," Ritchie said, picking up the scissors and cutting slits in the billowing shirt of the pirate costume Maria had bought for Joey, then ripping the shirt into long tatters, adding generous squirts from the zombie blood spray bottle.

Joey's eyes widened as he look down at the ruined shirt. "Holy shit, Maria's gonna have a fit when she see this." His voice was giddy with excitement. "You just like, totally destroyed it."

THE MILLIONAIRE'S
Convenient ARRANGEMENT

"You were planning to wear the puffy shirt on another occasion?" Ritchie asked.

"Like, no way, but...oh, man," he said, as Ritchie finally turned him to face the mirror. "This is awesome."

"Here. Put the hat on and nobody can see the top of the band over the knife."

"Freakin' awesome."

The Captain Jack Sparrow costume Maria had picked up for Joey to wear to Sam and Camilla's pirate-themed Halloween party had been pretty amazing, right down to the beaded dreads, the sword, the wide sash, the tail coat, the puffy white shirt, and real boots. But Joey had balked, claiming that at thirteen, he was way too old to wear a costume on Halloween, especially one that looked like it came right out of an old Disney movie.

Maria was at work and was meeting them at the party later, and Ritchie had convinced Joey that if they just zombied it up a bit, it would be cool. Plus, he said, he'd heard directly from Sam that Olivia and some of her friends were dressing up, and did Joey want Olivia to think he wasn't a good sport?

Ritchie stifled a laugh when they got to Sam's house and Joey got his first look at Olivia and a couple of her friends decked out as pirates' wenches. And saw him swell with pride when Olivia said, "Hey Joey, cool costume." Joey shrugged one shoulder nonchalantly, but even behind the gory zombie skin, you couldn't miss the huge smile on his face.

Sam's only concession to the occasion was a pirate hat and a patch over one eye. Unless you counted baby Sophia perched on his arm wearing...what exactly was she wearing? It looked to Ritchie like an explosion of bright colored rags with feathers sewn through it, some of them a bit worse for wear.

"What?" Sam said, as Ritchie studied her through squinted eyes. "You don't like my parrot?"

They both started to laugh, and the baby joined in, bouncing and squealing and making them both laugh all the harder until Joey ran into the room, wiping a bloody smear from his mouth with his sleeve.

"Ritchie! It worked! It was so cool. Oh, man, Olivia and her friends *freaked out.*"

THE MILLIONAIRE'S
Convenient ARRANGEMENT

Ritchie nodded soberly. "Good job. Make sure you save some for your sister."

"Oh, yeah," Joey said and raced back out of the room with JD tearing after him, protesting loudly that he should have been a zombie pirate too because it was so cool.

"What was that all about," Sam asked as Sophia continued to bounce in his arms.

"Blood capsules," Ritchie explained.

"Blood capsules."

"Yeah. You bite down on them then you open your mouth, and let it..."

"I get the picture." Sam shook his head. "Why didn't they think of that when we were kids? So, Joey's zombie pirate? That your work?"

"Yep."

"Nice. She's going to kill you, you know?"

Ritchie grinned. "Hard to complain when the kid's so damn happy. I'll take my chances."

"Good," Sam said, "because look who just came through the door."

Ritchie turned around and almost dropped his beer. Maria hadn't mentioned picking up a costume for herself. He watched her as she walked across the entranceway. Olivia and her friends looked pretty and fun in the pirate wench costumes. Maria looked...incredible. She was wearing tall black boots with skinny heels, a short skirt, sheer black tights that hugged her gorgeous legs, and some sort of lace up top that made her waist look incredibly small and her breasts...he didn't even want to think about how it made her breasts look. All he wanted to do was pull her into a room where they could have some privacy, and he could slowly undo those laces until her ripe, full breasts filled his hands. He imagined her keeping those sexy boots on while she wrapped her legs around his waist and...he shook his head slightly to clear his thoughts.

"Excuse me," he said to Sam and then strode over to Maria, taking hold of her arm none too gently and pulling her outside onto the terrace.

"Where did you get that costume?"

"What? I rented it from that party place. What's the matter? Don't you like it?" She ran her hands down the short skirt, seeming to smooth it self-consciously.

"That's the problem," he heard himself growl. "I like it way too much."

Her eyes sparkled.

"And that's a problem?"

Ritchie moved in closer and toyed with the laces on her corset-like top. He tugged one of the strings lightly and saw her eyes widen

"Ritchie!"

"Don't worry," he said. "You're safe enough for now. But we'll be back at home later." It was strange how much his house had started to feel like home now that Maria and Joey were in it.

"I'm not doing that anymore."

"Um hmmm."

"Besides, with Joey as a chaperone I'm sure you'll be on your best behavior," Maria said with a wicked glint in her eyes and a smirk on those pouty red lips. Why had he never noticed her lips before?

He leaned in closer. The contradiction of the fresh, lemony scent of her hair and the wantonly sexy outfit was intoxicating. "Don't count on it," he said. Would anyone even notice if the dashing pirate he was portraying swept this saucy wench into his arms and thoroughly kissed her? Because he was really tempted to do exactly that.

"There you are!" Joey shouted, and they stepped apart, startled back into reality. Maria's cheeks were flushed, but Joey didn't seem to notice.

He ran toward them. "Maria, I just…" Suddenly, Joey faltered and a strange look came over his face. He stopped, clutched his stomach, and made a gurgling noise.

"Joey, what is it? What's the matter?" Marie started toward him, then gasped as a trickle of blood leaked out of his mouth and ran down his chin as Joey fell to his knees.

Marie dropped down and grabbed him by the shoulders. And Joey came up laughing.

"Gotcha!"

She rose and turned, her eyes narrowing as she looked at Ritchie, who was trying without success to keep the grin off his face.

Joey raced back into the house, bloody chin and all, hooting with laughter and proclaiming, *I just got my sister so good* to anyone who cared to listen. Which left Ritchie on his own to face the fiery temper of a pirate wench with murder in her eye.

"I suppose you think that was funny," she said, standing in front of him with her hands on her hips.

Ritchie wanted to point out that she was even sexier when she was mad, but he thought better of it.

Instead, he tried to take a reasonable approach.

"Come on, Maria," he said, extending his hands outward in front of him. "It was just a little bit of harmless fun."

"Harmless fun? He probably scared five years off my life," she said, but he could already see the faint trace of humor lurking behind her otherwise angry expression.

Ritchie gave up and started laughing.

"Oh, go ahead, have a good laugh. Enjoy yourself."

"Maybe we should forget about sports and enroll the kid in some acting classes."

Then he saw a hint of a smile on her lips. "He is pretty good, isn't he?"

"Oh yeah," Ritchie said.

"But don't think I've forgotten who bought him that stuff."

• • •

When Ritchie asked Maria to check the pool house to see if there was another case of cold beer in that fridge, Maria knew he was up to something. Especially since the Halloween-themed fireworks were just starting, and it looked like there was plenty of beer already iced down on the patio.

"This is the pool house?" Maria looked around as Ritchie shut the door. It was like a little apartment. "I thought it was just a place to change clothes. Someone could actually live here."

"Um hmm," Ritchie said, as he pulled her farther inside, then reached around her and locked the door.

"What are you doing?" She stepped around him, then turned and backed a few steps into the room.

He walked toward her, a wicked glint in his eye.

"You're quite the saucy little wench in that outfit," he said, moving closer. "Since I'm dressed as a pirate, I think I'm in the mood for a bit of pillaging."

"Pillaging? What does that even mean?" She backed up a little further.

"It means helping myself to whatever I want. And right now, I want to unlace that corset and put my mouth on your bare nipples."

"Ritchie! Quit joking around. Everybody's right outside."

She felt a wild thrill run through her as he moved even closer, reached up with his hand, and toyed with the end of one of the laces.

"Stop it, Richie, be serious."

"Oh, I'm perfectly serious, Maria."

He began methodically unlacing her corset, his eyes gleaming as he pushed the loosened top down over her shoulders, baring her breasts to the glow of moonlight and the reflection of the fireworks through the narrow slats of the shuttered window.

"Wait, Richie, we can't do this here." She felt a sense of panic rising. Then he closed his mouth over her nipple just as she heard a burst of laughter and applause at the fireworks outside the door to the pool house. The sound of the party going on so close nearby while Ritchie swirled his tongue around one nipple and pinched the other lightly between his thumb and fingers put an almost unbearable edge on her pleasure. She let her head fall back as she pressed her hips tighter against him and felt the hard length of him. This was crazy. They should stop now before it got completely out of control.

Then somehow his hand was under her skirt, pushing her panties out of the way, a firm palm caressing her bottom. His mouth was trailing across the top of her breast, to her collarbone and up the side of her neck, while his other hand still taunted her nipple, and she couldn't think anymore. Didn't want to think any more.

"Maybe next time you dress up, we'll play angry pirate and naughty wench," he said softly, his warm breath against the side of her neck sending shivers racing through her whole body. "You can sass me and stamp your feet in those pretty boots, and I'll put you across my knee."

"You'll...what?" Before she could get the words out fully, she felt his hand slide around between them, and he was stroking her faster and faster. Her knees gave out and she clamped her arms around his neck for support, kissing his wicked mouth like she was drowning. Her climax this time was startling and intense, with sharp claws that blurred the lines between pleasure and pain. It left her breathless and dizzy.

When she regained her senses, she was slumped across him on the now untidy daybed, and the sounds of laughter and fireworks were still going on outside. She'd probably never be able to think of fireworks the same way again.

"I don't know how you do this to me," she said, pushing herself up. In an easy move, he reversed their positions and had her under him.

"You look beautiful. All flushed and rumpled and so sexy I just want to touch you all over again." He shook his head. "You're like a drug. You make me crazy."

"Let me up," she said, pushing against his chest. "We can't keep doing this."

"You're right," he said, as he rolled over and released her. She looked back at him as she headed to the small bathroom to put herself back together, trying to look like a woman who *hadn't* spent the last twenty minutes making out in the pool house.

"You better come to grips with the past, Maria," he said. "Because it's only a matter of time."

Chapter Fourteen

"What the hell are you doing?" He raised his voice loud enough that a guard looked their way.

"Don't swear at me."

"Are you kidding?"

"I'm sorry I even told you."

Tito leaned back in his chair. "You're shacking up with the guy who prosecuted me."

"It isn't like that, Tito."

"Well, why don't you tell me what it is like, then, *little* sister?"

"By four minutes," she said, and he shrugged.

"Little sister," he said again, and she had to smile.

"I'm not sleeping with him," she said, but felt guilty as she said it. Sure, technically, she wasn't sleeping with him, but...

"Maybe not yet. But you're falling for him. I can tell."

Tito always had been able to read her mind, finish her sentences. It was pretty much the only thing that hadn't changed. Heaven knows she didn't want to be falling for Ritchie.

He shook his head. "What I don't get is how you got mixed up with that guy in the first place."

"I told you. I met him at Saint Theresa's. He volunteers there."

"What's some fancy lawyer doing passing out food to homeless people?"

"He's...different than you'd think. Joey got in trouble, and I needed help. By the time I found out he was the same guy who prosecuted you, he was already doing so much for Joey. Tito, he was a tough prosecutor but he has a good heart."

Tito laughed. "Yeah, right. My lawyer told me he wouldn't even discuss a plea deal. Wouldn't even discuss it. You be careful. He's playing the big hero now, but he's one cold bastard, and he'll turn on you just like that."

"He's changed. He even told me he'd do things differently now."

"People don't change."

She looked at him. "I hope that's not true."

"This guy's just telling you what you want to hear. I don't like you and Joey living in his house. I don't like you owing him anything."

"You act like I had a choice."

"Didn't you?"

"They would have taken Joey away from me," she said quietly. "Put him in a juvenile detention center. Maybe foster care. I couldn't let that happen."

"Damn. It's my fault. Maria —"

"He just got into the wrong crowd, Tito."

"And Assistant State Attorney Ritchie Perez is the guy to pull him out of that crowd, I suppose."

"Yes, he is." She leaned forward. "Besides, like I told you, Ritchie isn't with the State Attorney's office anymore. He has a private law firm, with his two partners, doing injury cases, and class action lawsuits. He doesn't prosecute people now – he helps people who've been hurt.

"Tito, Joey's playing sports now. He's in a really good school, a private school, away from all those bad influences – "

"How exactly are you paying for all that, Maria?"

"Ritchie's paying for it."

"Why?" He leaned closer. "Because that's what I don't get. He sure as hell isn't doing it to apologize for putting me in here." He drummed his fingers on the tabletop. "So, what's in it for Perez?"

"Well, he wants to help Joey."

"Nobody does anything for free, Maria. If there's one thing I've learned in here, it's that." He narrowed his eyes speculatively. "So don't tell me this guy doesn't expect something from you."

THE MILLIONAIRE'S
Convenient ARRANGEMENT

"The money doesn't mean anything to him, Tito."

"Guys like that think they can buy whatever they want."

She stiffened. "I'm not for sale."

"It would be a hell of a lot of trouble for the guy to go to, anyway, just to get laid." Tito jerked his shoulder. "I don't like it."

"Look, I didn't come here to fight with you, Tito. I wanted to talk you about something."

He just looked at her, and she continued.

"Joey's been saying maybe I could bring him to see you, maybe over the Thanksgiving holiday –" She watched his face close down.

"You know how I feel about that."

"Yeah, when he was little, I agreed with you, but Joey's thirteen now. He wants to know his brother."

"The answer's no, Maria. I don't want him coming here."

"He wants to know his brother."

"Drop it, Maria."

"Ok. Ok. Another six months and we'll all be a family again. He'll have plenty of time to get to know you then." It was what had kept her going.

"Look, Maria. We have to talk about that."

"Oh no. Tito, please tell me you aren't in trouble." Tito's original ten-year sentence had been shortened as much as it could be under Florida law. Although parole wasn't an option, he'd earned reduced time for good behavior – "gain time" they called it – and would end up only serving eight and a half years. Unless something went wrong.

"I'm still getting out in May."

"Then what's the problem."

He averted his eyes. "I just – I think what I need is a fresh start."

"It will be a fresh start for all of us. You can go to school part time, have a career. It's not too late. I'll be there for you."

"I don't want you to be there for me. And I don't want Joey hanging around his ex-con brother."

"No, Tito –"

"Look, especially now. You and Joey are living with this rich lawyer –you think he wants anything to do with some loser he sent up eight years ago?"

"You are not a loser. Tito, you're twenty-six years old. Stop talking like you're life is over. It was one mistake."

"Are you for real? Grow up, Maria. Nobody's going to hire me. You really think I'm going to fill out some community college application and go back to school?"

"I know you took some classes when you first got in here, earned some credits."

"Yeah, and they shut that program down. Nobody is going to give an ex-con a second chance."

"I'll help you get back on your feet. Maybe I can get you job with Vivienne at the gallery."

"I don't want her charity. I don't want your help, Maria."

"Tito – "

"Don't you get it? Every time I look at you, I remember how I threw my life away."

She felt her eyes fill up and blinked back the burning sensation.

"Aw, shit. Don't cry. Look. Maria. I just want to go someplace new. This guy I know in here has an uncle in Texas. Has an auto body shop. The guy owes me a favor, said his uncle could hook me up with a job."

"Don't, Tito."

"The best thing for you and Joey is if I just head out that way when I get out. I've messed up your life enough already. I wasn't even there for you when Mom died."

"It doesn't matter, Tito. None of that matters. I just want you back home again. It'll all work out. Just give it a chance."

'Yeah, well, I gotta go. Thanks for coming by, Sis."

He stood up, then hesitated, still looking at her. "Look, forget what I said about Perez. If Joey hanging around this guy keeps him from ending up in a place like this, then I'm all for it. And as long as Perez is treating you right, you do what you want. I got no business telling you how to live your life."

He crossed two fingers in a sign of solidarity they used to do as kids that she'd almost forgotten, then headed back toward the corridors that would take him to his cell.

She stared after him a moment and tried to see her brother the way he used to be. Was she just kidding herself that they could erase eight years, start over, and put the past behind them?

As she left the correctional facility, the familiar sense of institutionalized hopelessness bore down on her. After all the years, and all the visits, you would think she'd be used to it. But Maria felt the same ache in her chest, the shortness of breath that never let up until she had driven through the gate and turned onto the highway.

Reluctantly, she admitted to herself that Tito was right about not bringing Joey here. This was no way for him to see the brother who by now was mostly a distant memory. One that she kept alive with the stories she told him about her and Tito growing up together, the photos they had of a much younger Joey perched on Tito's shoulders, laughing. Memories she shared of the too short period before her stepfather died, when all of them had been a family.

But that was the past and this was now.

It had honestly never occurred to her that, when Tito finally got out, he would want to go anywhere but home. She was starting to realize that she hadn't just lost her brother for eight and a half years – she might have lost him forever.

And there was one man who was responsible for that. The man she was currently living with, had started to care about, and had almost had sex with. It was like she'd been two people lately – Tito's sister, who lived every day with the pain Richie Perez had caused her family…and Joey's sister, who couldn't help but admire the way Richie had stepped up and turned her little brother's life around.

The two sides of Maria would collide when Tito was released in May, and the answer wasn't for Tito to leave prison and just quietly disappear. It might not be possible for both Tito and Ritchie to be part of her life. If that turned out to be the case, she knew where her loyalties lay. She'd let Tito down once before, when she'd been so wrapped up in her grief over the loss of their stepdad that she'd closed her eyes to anything but her art. She hadn't seen the path her twin brother was heading down until it was too late. She wouldn't let him down again.

• • •

When she walked in the door, her thoughts were still on Tito. Which is probably why finding Joey and Ritchie in the family room shouting and laughing over the latest edition of Grand Theft Auto hit her in exactly the wrong way.

"Aren't you supposed to be doing homework?"

"All done," Joey said, eyes still glued to the screen as a character dragged an old woman out of a car, jumped in, ran over three pedestrians and crashed through a fire hydrant.

"So did you eat yet?"

Ritchie grunted and jerked his head toward an open pizza box with a few slices remaining. His hands were gripping a controller, his eyes glued to the screen.

The car T-boned a taxi then swerved to the right, careening around a corner where a man with a briefcase leapt out of the way just in time.

"Dude, your wanted level is off the charts. You better get outta there!" Joey reached over, grabbed a slice of pizza, and crammed a huge corner of it into his mouth.

Maria watched Ritchie's car take off while cop cars with wailing sirens joined the pursuit from all corners of the gaming world. She shook her head and walked back out to the kitchen, leaving the shrieks of pure male adrenalin behind.

"Dude! That's so freakin' awesome!" Joey shouted, as Maria opened the fridge and considered her options, deciding on a container of Greek yogurt and a bottle of Mexican beer. She wandered out onto the terrace and sat at the round table, sipping her beer and watching a storm gather on the horizon. Distant lightning lit up the sky and reflected off the dark water, creating an eerie glow.

She was so lost in her thoughts that she didn't notice when the shouts died down and the light dimmed, until Ritchie sat down across the table from her, setting his own beer down on the glass surface with a quiet thunk.

"That's your idea of dinner?"

"Said the man who ate half a large pizza for dinner."

"Actually, we put away two large pizzas. The kid has an appetite."

"Sounds like he has an appetite for violence, and you don't mind feeding that either."

"Whoa, where'd that come from?"

"Grand Theft Auto? Seriously?"

"GTA's a classic. What's gotten under your skin?"

"I don't know, maybe driving to a prison to spend some time with my brother, who is exactly where I *never, ever* want Joey to end up, and I come here and find the two of you in the middle of a video game crime spree." She looked over at him, and he was laughing. *Laughing.*

"It's a game, Maria. A *game*. Besides, this it GTA IV, the one with the morality choices. And Joey knows the difference between a game and real life."

"How do you not get why this upsets me?" Then, to her horror, she broke into tears.

He was at her side in seconds, pulling her out of the chair and just holding her.

She pushed her hands against her chest. "Let me go."

"Huh uh. Why don't you start by telling me what's really got you so upset. Because I don't think it's Joey playing a video game."

"He doesn't want to live with me. He doesn't want to be anywhere near me."

"You know that's not true. Joey's crazy about you."

"No, not Joey. Tito."

He tilted her chin up, brushed his knuckles against her cheek, and waited.

"He'll be out in May. That's six months from now. He used to be excited about getting out of prison, getting his life back together. But now he seems to have just given up."

Ritchie nodded.

"I thought everything would be okay as soon as he was released. We could finally put our lives back together. Be a family again. But Tito doesn't want that." She heard the bitterness in her own voice and tried to choke it back, took a few deep breaths.

"Tito doesn't want to put his old life back together. He wants to get as far away from Joey and me as possible. He thinks he's some kind of a bad influence. That having an ex-con as a brother is just going to hold Joey back."

"He has a point."

"I can't believe you'd say that." Annoyance turned to cold fury. This man ruined Tito's life, and he wasn't the least bit sorry. She twisted out of his embrace.

"Don't talk about him like he's some common criminal."

"He's an ex-con, Maria. And you should give him credit for not wanting to drag you and Joey down with him."

"I can't believe you are for real."

"Much as you might want to, Maria, you can't change the past. You can't make the last eight years disappear."

"I lost my brother eight years ago. I'll be damned if I lose him again."

She gathered up her empty yogurt cup and her half-empty bottle of beer, and marched back into the house, leaving Ritchie alone to stare out over the water.

Chapter Fifteen

"Are we there yet?"

Ritchie grinned back at Joey and slowed the car, parking on the street in front of his parents' modest home. It wasn't the house he'd grown up in. A few years ago, he and his sisters had finally convinced their parents to move into a nicer section of town. But it didn't matter what house it was – walking through the front door still meant going home. And the neighborhood was a lot like the one he'd grown up in. Before drugs and gangs had driven away the small businesses that once flourished, driven away the working class families who'd taken pride in their neighborhood.

He glanced over at Maria, sitting stiffly beside him. She'd resisted when he first invited them for Thanksgiving dinner with his family, but since her brother had made it clear he didn't want her showing up at the prison with Joey in tow, she'd given in. He'd played the 'Joey card' and he wasn't ashamed to admit it. Besides, it would be good for the kid to soak up some of the loud, crazy comfort his large family dished out on holidays along with the turkey and the sweet potato casserole and way too many pies. But the truth was, he'd wanted *her* to see where he came from.

The front door burst open and assorted nieces and nephews spilled out onto the porch.

He was out of the car and around the other side before Maria had gotten out, and helped her out with the plate of cookies she'd baked.

Cutout cookies, shaped like turkeys, and decorated with colorful icing and sprinkles. A family tradition she'd carried on for Joey and that he'd insisted she bring along today.

"I should have baked a pie," Maria said, looking down at the homemade cookies that Joey had helped decorate.

"Don't be ridiculous," Ritchie said. "They're going to love these."

"I shouldn't have come." She'd gone from being stiff to looking like a bird that wanted to take flight.

"Well, I'm glad you did," he said, and whatever Maria was going to say in response was cut off as his mother hurried down the porch steps, wiping her hands on her apron.

"So these are the two you've been keeping from us," she said. "Hello Joey, welcome." She put her hands on his shoulders, bent down slightly, and kissed him on both cheeks.

"Go on in the house now with my grandbabies," she said, laughing as the younger kids grabbed onto his arm and pulled him along, Ritchie's five-year-old nephew tugging on Joey's pants leg, asking him if he knew how to play Mario Kart.

"You must be Maria," his mother beamed. "Ritchie! Take that plate of food for her so I can say hello."

"It's just some cookies, Mrs. Perez—"

"Please, call me Giana," she said, giving Maria a hug and kissing her on the cheeks as soon as Ritchie took the plate out of Maria's hands. "Or Mama G."

Mama G? It looked like Maria had already passed some kind of unspoken test. His sister Rosalie had been practically engaged to her husband, Eduardo before their mom had invited him to do the same.

She turned to Ritchie, giving him a playful slap to the side of his head before pulling him into her arms and hugging him.

"Why you wait so long to bring Maria and her brother to meet your family?" She turned back to Maria without waiting for an answer.

"Never mind. You come with me, we get to know each other," Ritchie's mom said. Maria looked back over her shoulder with a slightly panicked look as his mom swept her up the steps and into the house as effectively as the assorted nieces and nephews had taken control of Joey.

From the gleam in his mother's eye, she was already making plans

THE MILLIONAIRE'S
Convenient ARRANGEMENT

about Maria. Ritchie chuckled to himself. He hadn't exactly explained the nature of his relationship with Maria to his mother. Who was he kidding? He didn't exactly understand the nature of his relationship with Maria himself.

But he sure liked the way she looked sitting at his family's table, he thought later as he watched her laugh at a joke his uncle told.

"What's going on with those partners of yours, Ritchie?" his dad asked, as he passed one of the bowls of stuffing around the table for the fourth or fifth time. Half the group was still eating turkey and fixings, while the other half had moved on to dessert. They had already made a serious dent in the pies, and two-thirds of Maria's cookies were gone.

His father had just turned 60 and was still working as a foreman on a construction crew. If you did that kind of manual labor your whole life, Ritchie figured, you didn't need visits to the gym to make up for that fourth helping of turkey and stuffing. His dad's skin was weathered from the years of outdoor work in the Florida sun, but Ritchie imagined he still climbed the scaffolds as confidently as he'd done more than two decades ago when Ritchie used to tag along at construction sites. Back then, all Ritchie had wanted was to put on a hardhat and follow in his father's footsteps, but the old man had pushed him down another path altogether.

"Sam and Camilla are doing the whole family thing," Ritchie said.

"Camilla's sister Olivia made a tofu turkey," Joey said. "They invited Maria and me, but we came here instead," his expression making it clear that he was *much* happier with the menu Ritchie's mom put on the table. Joey flushed a little and gave a shy smiled when Ritchie's mom reached over and tousled his hair and said she was glad.

Watching the exchange, Ritchie wondered why it hadn't occurred to him before to bring Joey over to his parents' house. Spending a little time weeding Mama G's garden and sitting at the kitchen table drinking cold lemonade and sampling the hot sweet bread and rolls she had baked every Wednesday and Saturday for as long as he could remember might be exactly what the kid needed. It sure was a great memory from his own childhood, and had kept him grounded in the simple things in life.

"So where's Jonnie?" his mom asked, and Ritchie grinned. He'd never get used to her nickname for his partner Jonathon, and he doubted anyone but his mom would have dared to refer to the fifth generation

Bostonian with his fancy pedigree as "Jonnie." Not that Jonathon was uptight or anything – he just carried that air of formality that was part of his breeding, from the family estate he'd grown up in to the toney private schools he'd attended. But there was no such thing as formality in Mama G's house.

"Did he go back to Boston for the holiday?" his mom persisted. It was probably the only excuse she would accept for his nonappearance at the Perez family holiday table.

"He's got a hot date," Ritchie said, and grinned as he got the exact reaction he was looking for. "Going to some fancy restaurant for dinner."

"A hot date!" His mom shook her head then brandished her fork in the air. "Thanksgiving is not the time for a hot date. Thanksgiving is the time for family. Next time you tell Jonnie to bring this 'hot date' here so we can meet her."

"Okay, Mama," Ritchie said. "But you know Jonathon. Chances are by next week the romance will be over."

"That boy needs to settle down and find a good woman. A man needs a good woman," she said, and looked over at Maria with a gleam in her eye. "A woman who knows how important family is."

Here it comes, Ritchie thought.

"Look at Maria, here," his mom continued. "It's a good woman who takes care of her little brother like you do." She turned back to Ritchie. "And beautiful too. A woman like Maria is a treasure, and the right man would be a fool to let her get away."

"And don't forget she bakes really good cookies," Ritchie's brother-in-law chimed in from the other end of the table. "That's important."

"So, Mama, you want me to fix Maria up with Jonathon?" Ritchie asked innocently, then grinned when Maria almost choked on a bite of pie.

"You think I can't reach across the table and smack you?" his mom said.

"Mama," Ritchie said, laughing and feigning to the side to avoid an imaginary blow.

"You always did have a smart mouth," she said, but laugh lines around her eyes belied the stern expression she was trying to put on.

"Behave yourself," she said. "And pass me that plate of cookies Maria made."

• • •

Fix her up with Jonathon? Sure, Maria knew Ritchie was just teasing his mom for being so obvious about her opinion that Maria was a good match for *Ritchie*, but it made her wonder just exactly what his mother – his whole family, for that matter – thought her relationship with Ritchie was. Did they think it was strange that she and Joey were living in his house with him? Or did they just assume that she and Ritchie were sleeping together?

When she'd asked Ritchie about it, he'd given her a look and said, *"Stop worrying about it, I don't discuss my sex life with my mother."* So she still didn't know exactly what he *had* told his family.

Anyway, whatever Ritchie had said about them, his family had certainly been welcoming. Ritchie's nieces and nephews seemed thrilled to have an older boy with Joey's gamer skills in the house, and Joey was soaking up all the attention. And Mama G was fussing over him like the grandmother he'd never had.

It made her happy, but it also made her yearn for a family of her own. She imagined how different their lives would have been if her stepfather hadn't died. If her mother hadn't gotten cancer. If Tito hadn't started spending time with all the wrong people.

She looked over at Joey, laughing as he shoveled a fork full of apple pie into his mouth with one hand while surreptitiously slipping a piece of turkey under the table in his other hand to the stocky bulldog lying quietly by his feet. If sitting here, surrounded by someone else's family, was a little bittersweet for her, well, it was worth it to see Joey so unreservedly happy.

When Ritchie's sister Rosalie asked her if she was doing any Black Friday shopping, she saw Joey sneaking glances at her. His face broke into a grin when she said, "I might be going by a certain electronics store to do a little early Christmas shopping." She hoped Ritchie's appreciation for loud video games extended to having the latest edition of Rock Band hooked into the Xbox in his family room. What she'd do when they moved back into her small apartment she wasn't sure, but at least for the next few months Joey could rock out to his heart's content.

"Are you and Joey spending Christmas here in Miami, Maria?"

Rosalie asked as she deftly moved the saltshaker out of the reach of the toddler perched on her lap just before his chubby fist closed around it.

"Yes, do you have any family here?" Mama G asked.

None that she'd be spending the holiday with, other than Joey. All of a sudden, it seemed like everyone was looking at her, waiting for her to answer. She straightened her shoulders. There was nothing wrong with a small, quiet Christmas. Just her and Joey, like always.

"No, I – "

Ritchie broke in before she could answer. "Maria, Joey, and I are heading over to the house in Bimini for the holidays," Ritchie said.

Ritchie had a house in Bimini? She knew she was staring at him with an expression of complete shock on her face. Because going to Bimini for Christmas was news to her.

"Cool!" Joey said. "Where's Bimini?"

"It's in the Bahamas," Maria said.

"Cool! I've never been out of the country. I can't wait to tell the guys at school."

"Ritchie, I don't know. Joey doesn't even have a passport."

"Come on, Sis, you're not leaving me at home!"

"No, of course not. I just don't think – "

"Relax," Ritchie said, cutting her off again. "Since he's under sixteen, he doesn't need a passport for Bimini. You have one, right?"

"Yes." She hadn't been out of the country since her trip to Italy to study art in what now seemed like another lifetime ago, but her passport was still valid.

The bigger issue was why would Ritchie announce plans for the holidays that he hadn't even *discussed* with her? Mama G was beaming her approval, as if this confirmed her suspicions that there was more to their relationship than Ritchie just taking her little brother under his wing.

Ritchie leaned over and whispered in her ear, "I'll explain later." But she wished he'd thought about explaining *before* blurting his plans out in front of everyone. Now, Joey was all excited and it would look strange to his whole family if they *didn't* go, but Maria wasn't at all sure that spending Christmas with Ritchie in some tropical paradise was a good idea.

She managed to get through the rest of the dinner, the football game on TV, and all the hugs and farewells with a smile on her face. But as soon as they were in the car she turned to him.

"So explain to me why you told everyone we're going to Bimini for Christmas, and this is the first I've heard about it."

"I'm sorry. They were asking about your family and your plans, and I knew the second you said it was just you and Joey for the holidays, my mom would have insisted you join in the whole Perez family Christmas. My family can be a little overwhelming. And actually, the idea just occurred to me while we were at the table."

He glanced over with an apologetic smile. "If I'd thought of it earlier, I'd have mentioned it."

What kind of person decided on the spur of the moment to take off for the Bahamas in a few weeks? A person who owned his own business and had enough wealth and power to do whatever he wanted, she supposed.

"I just don't like people just assuming they can make plans for me." She had this lump in her throat that was making it hard to swallow. Was there anything in her life that she had control over anymore?

"Come on, Maria," Joey piped up from the back seat. "It sounds cool."

"I know it sounds cool." And if she refused to go, she'd be the bad guy with Joey.

"Look," Ritchie said, as he merged into traffic. "If you don't want to go, it's no big deal. But if you do, you'd be doing me a favor. We have some rental property there."

"We?"

"Jonathon, Sam, and I. It's an investment. We rent it out most of the year, but we left it open for two weeks over Christmas this year. Jon and I were planning on going down there, taking care of some repairs from the last tropical storm that went through there, and having some downtime. Getting in some sport fishing."

"Oh, so Jonathon's going too?" Now it was beginning to make sense. He was leaving town for the holidays anyway and was feeling guilty about just leaving her and Joey here. Or maybe he was worried what kind of trouble Joey might get into while he was off school and Maria was pulling double shifts at the restaurant. Anyway, with Jonathon there, it would be more business."

"No, Jonathon has a trial coming up and can't take the time. It would have been the first vacation I've had in a long time. I was planning to just cancel it and deal with the repairs long distance." He looked over at Maria. "But then when everyone was talking about Christmas plans, I thought, why not just take you and Joey down there and make it a fun trip? How long has it been since *you* had a vacation?"

Had she *ever* had a vacation? Not since she studied that summer in Italy, when her future seemed full of nothing but good things.

Joey piped up from the back seat. "We took that trip to Disney, remember Maria?"

It had been Joey's 10th birthday, and it had taken her almost a year to save up enough money for the three-day park hopper passes, even with her Florida resident's discount. She'd chosen one of the economy family hotels on the property. She could have gotten a cheaper place to stay a few miles out, but figured the convenience of the free shuttle busses from the hotel to the parks, plus the huge kid-friendly pool and food court and refillable drink mugs was worth the price. But it made her heart ache now to think that a three-day trip to Orlando almost four years ago was the only vacation Joey had ever known.

"All right, let's do it," she said and heard Joey's whoop of delight. She just hoped she didn't regret it. If managing her conflicted feelings about Ritchie was difficult now in the day-to-day routine they'd established, she could only imagine how much harder it would be at a vacation paradise in the Bahamas.

"I have to talk to my boss at the restaurant. And Vivienne." She looked back at Joey. "So don't get too excited yet." Futile words, she knew. Joey was already way past excited at the prospect of a real vacation, and a Christmas spent somewhere he'd never been before. With Ritchie, whom he already regarded with something close to hero worship.

"I'm glad you decided to go," Ritchie said, reaching over and touching her hand, sending a charge of energy shooting through her that had her already second-guessing her decision.

But really, what other choice did she have?

Chapter Sixteen

Ritchie climbed up the narrow circular staircase to the artist's workroom above Vivienne's gallery. The view out the floor to ceiling windows was amazing. But the view inside the studio took his breath away. An immense sculpture dominated the center of the room. Twisted metal wires partially covered with plaster and intersecting through Plexiglas were visible in the clearly unfinished work, but already it seemed like a living, breathing thing. To his left, a large canvas stretched across ten feet of wall space, and Vivienne was using her hands to create wild swirls of paint in sweeping arcs. Finger painting on steroids, he thought, and took a startled step back when she then balled a paint rag into her hand and slammed it repeatedly into the canvas.

But what really captivated his attention was a group of paintings casually arrayed on the other side of the room, against the wall. He never would have recognized them as Vivienne's – she was apparently taking part of her work in an entirely different direction, and it was fresh and exciting, with something he would think of as almost naiveté running through it, *if* he didn't know that Vivienne was the artist.

He stepped over for a closer look. There were street scenes he recognized from Florence, countrysides with flowers that seemed to weep in the falling rain, a view of Biscayne Bay showcasing a sleek sailboat. He leaned closer and grinned. If he could talk Vivienne into including that one in the donation she was making to his charity auction, he'd bet Jonathon would ensure the betting went into high numbers, and likely end up taking it home himself at the end of the evening.

He heard Vivienne step up behind him and turned.

"I had no idea you were taking your work in this direction. Is there any chance you'd consider donating one of these for the auction in addition to the sculpture we discussed? The sailboat in particular..."

Vivienne smiled. "You'd have to discuss that with the artist."

"I don't understand."

She laughed. "This isn't my work, darling. We had them out yesterday to review. I'm trying to convince Maria she has enough for a small showing. But the girl is stubborn."

"These are...*Maria's?*"

"You are surprised? Didn't she tell you I give her studio space as part of her compensation for helping me in the gallery?"

"Yes, but...I had no idea she was this good."

"Neither does she." Her eyes narrowed. "I would almost be jealous of such raw talent but, after all, I am Vivienne."

"And incomparable," he said, and was rewarded with the smile that had been photographed almost as often as her art.

He turned back and studied a scene from South Beach that completely captured the mood of the area. He could almost feel the heat of the sun on his shoulders as he stared into the painting. He felt an odd sort of anger bubbling up in him.

"I can't believe she's wasting her time waiting tables in a restaurant when she can create something like this. What is she thinking?"

"I imagine she's thinking she has to pay the bills. That she has a younger brother to raise and educate. And that art is a fickle lover at best."

"She could sell a single one of these for more money that she makes waiting tables for a year."

"Perhaps."

"You don't think the quality is there?"

"Her work needs to be shown. Not just these pieces. All of it."

"There's more?"

She gestured through a doorway for a smaller studio, and he walked in. The pieces here were bolder, less refined. They seemed to draw their power from raw emotion. He stared at a half-finished canvas on an easel that took his breath away. And was instantly transported back to an afternoon he'd once spent in Florence.

"She needs to show them," Vivienne repeated. "Simply having the talent, creating the work, is not enough."

"Well, what's stopping her?"

Vivienne shrugged, pulled off her paint splattered gloves, and deposited them in a basket already littered with gloves and rags, just outside the door.

"Insecurity. About her talent and about her future. And time. She doesn't have enough of it."

"How can you allow her to let this talent go to waste?"

Vivienne laughed. "Allow her? Believe me, I have offered to support her – a loan – if she would quit her job and devote real time to pursuing this, her life." She gestured expansively. "Our Maria, she is not one for having her hand out."

Vivienne paused, her eyes narrowing. "What she needs is a patron of the arts to take an interest in her work."

"She's living with me, I'm paying the bills. I'll tell her to quit the damn job and pursue this."

"I can imagine how well that would go over," Vivienne said dryly.

"You're right. She'd never accept it." He paced across the room, considering. There had to be away to help Maria move forward with her art without her balking because she thought it was some kind of charity. The woman could be so damn prickly sometimes. But an idea was forming in the back of his mind. What good was it to have connections, if you couldn't use them?

"There might just be a way to get around all that."

Vivienne smiled. "I thought there might. Now, let's go into my office, and we can discuss the sculpture I'm donating to your charity auction."

"Would you consider doing one of those events where you create a piece of art during the party and at the end of the evening we auction it off?" He'd gotten the idea when he saw her working on the large abstract canvas. It reminded him of a performance he'd once seen in New York by a master Japanese artist. A man, once a contemporary of Andy Warhol, who continued painting – and performing– into his 80's.

She gave him a cold stare. "No, I will not." She paused. "And the fact that I use a large canvas and punch it with my hands does not mean I imitate Ushio Shinohara."

Ouch. How did she know what he'd been thinking? But then, Vivienne had a reputation for her uncanny ability to read people. It was in part what gave her the ability to create art that felt so personal to so many people. It was the reason she was the perfect artist to showcase at his fundraiser.

"I wasn't suggesting –"

"Well, see that you don't."

"Vivienne, you compare to no one. A sculpture by the one and only Vivienne will ensure the event is a success, and that it will raise the funds to make a real difference."

"Hmm," she said, giving him a narrow glance. But she slipped her arm through his and they walked together to a small office on the other side of the studio. He walked out of the gallery twenty minutes later and pulled out his phone. And wondered if it was any accident that Maria's paintings had happened to be fully in view on the very day Vivienne agreed to meet with him at her studio.

• • •

"Holy shit!" Joey yelled as Ritchie pushed the throttle forward and the boat took off, planing over the water. Ritchie just looked back over his shoulder and grinned. Maria didn't even give Joey an admonishing look herself, because she knew exactly how he felt.

When Ritchie asked her if she'd rather take the speedboat or the yacht she'd thought he was joking. So not the case. The three partners had a yacht – *a yacht* - with an actual crew. But they used it for longer trips, he explained, like down to Key West. Bimini was a short 45 miles from Miami, and a fast boat could make the run in under two hours. The 35 foot Baja Outlaw they were now flying over the water on was like no other speedboat Maria had ever seen. When she'd told Ritchie it looked like something drug runners would use, he'd just laughed and told her criminals weren't the only ones who liked power and speed.

Ritchie told her he and Jonathon had planned to sail over. At that point, she gave up being shocked that there was apparently yet another boat in their fleet. The sailboat, Ritchie explained, was Jonathon's, and, being familiar with Ritchie's skills as a sailor – or lack thereof – there was no way he'd be lending him his sailboat.

But don't worry, he'd assured her. He was more than capable at the helm of the Baja. As they sliced across the water, Joey's shouts of pure joy disappearing into the wind and spray, Maria tugged her life jacket closer and said a little prayer just in case.

It seemed like no time at all until they had arrived. Maria and Joey waited on the boat while Ritchie stopped in the marina in Alice Town and took care of customs. Now that the boat wasn't moving, Joey entertained himself exploring the surprisingly roomy cuddy cabin in the boat and asked excitedly if he could sleep there one night while they were in Bimini.

"You'll have to ask Ritchie about that," she told him. Personally, Maria thought the windowless cabin was a bit claustrophobic, but she had to admit it was luxurious. She left Joey playing with his 3DS in the bed and went back up to the fresh air just as Ritchie stepped onboard.

In no time at all, they were pulling up to a private dock in front of a cottage-style house that way exceeded her expectations of what a beach rental would be.

"How many bedrooms are there?" she asked as they stepped up from the dock onto a wide brick patio that led to a brick walkway. Wooden chaises with brightly colored pillows were on one side, facing the water, and a wide hammock graced the other side of the walkway. Maria pictured herself curled up in the hammock with a book, swaying gently in the ocean breeze, and sighed.

They continued up the steps onto the wide wraparound porch, then stepped in through the French doors.

"Four bedrooms," Ritchie said. "It sleeps 10 comfortably. We get a lot of extended family rentals or two families vacationing together."

"What does it cost to rent this place?"

"About $1,800 a night. But we do weekly rentals at a reduced rate. Housekeeping's included. If they want a private chef, that's extra of course."

"Of course."

"Ritchie, it's lovely to see you again. Welcome back to Alice Town."

THE MILLIONAIRE'S
Convenient ARRANGEMENT

A tall, tanned, and gorgeous blonde wearing cut-off shorts and a tank top under a chef's apron came into the room from a doorway Maria assumed must lead to the kitchen.

"Jillian, hello. Meet Maria and Joey Martinez." He gestured toward the blonde, "Jillian Rowe, personal chef extraordinaire."

"It's nice to meet you," Jillian said, clasping hands with Maria and then turning to Joey to smile. "Please let me know if you have any special dietary restrictions or preferences. It's my job to make your dining effortless and memorable."

"Thank you," Maria said. Would this gorgeous woman be staying here at the house with them? How well did she know Ritchie? Stop it, she told herself. You're being jealous of a private chef? Jillian wasn't here to seduce Ritchie – she was just here to do her job.

Maybe it was Maria's experience with the temperamental executive chef at the restaurant where she waited tables in South Beach that made her find this woman more than a little intimidating. Of course, the long legs, clear blue eyes, perfect face, and blond ponytail weren't helping either.

"Cool," Joey said. "Can you make pizza?"

"Absolutely," Jillian answered. "Why don't the two of you make a list of foods you like and foods I should avoid? I'll leave my iPad on the island in the kitchen and pick it up later." She turned to Ritchie and smiled. "I already know what you like."

I already know what you like. Right. Maria forced herself to smile graciously. "I'm sure whatever you're used to preparing for Ritchie will be fine for me."

"I'm gonna make a list," Joey said. "Thanks Jillian! A private chef. Your job must be so cool," he said, following her. "Did you ever cook for, like, rock stars or any famous people?"

Their voices trailed off as they disappeared into the kitchen.

"Ritchie," Maria said quietly, "do we really need a private chef? I'd be happy to cook for the three of us."

"You," he said, moving closer to her, "are on vacation. You deserve the chance to just relax and enjoy yourself. So, no cooking. Ok?"

"Ok," she said dubiously.

"Don't worry," he laughed. "I've always been in good hands with

Jillian."

That's what she was afraid of.

• • •

Ritchie spent the morning dragging Joey around on a tube behind the boat, while Maria reclined on one of the outside chaises reading a book, listening to music, and enjoying the view. Wearing a bikini that made him wish he were stretched out beside her, enjoying a view that wasn't the glistening water. But it was hard to resent the time out in the boat when the kid was so damn over-the-top excited to be bouncing along on the round, flat tube. Ritchie cut the boat to the side in a sharp turn and sent Joey flying over the wake, shrieking happily and hanging on tight as the tube went airborne. Nothing scared that kid. Ritchie was already looking forward to taking the two of them snorkeling. Just thinking about what a kick Joey would get out of swimming through the hull of an old wrecked ship made him grin.

After one more spin around the Bay, Ritchie cut the motor and hauled the tube back in with Joey protesting that it was way too soon to quit.

"Aren't you hungry, kid?" Ritchie gave Joey a hand onto the swim platform at the rear of the boat. "I heard Jillian saying something about baking her special chocolate chunk cookie bars. Of course, if you're not hungry…"

"I guess I could eat," Joey said, grinning up at him.

"Thought so. Besides, you've gotta save some energy for when we go snorkeling this afternoon."

Joey wrinkled his nose. "That doesn't sound as much fun as tubing."

Ritchie chuckled. "That's what they all say, until the barracudas show up."

"No shit! Barracudas? Are you serious?"

"If you're lucky, we might see some tiger sharks too. They like to hang around the hulls of old sunken ships."

Joey was looking at him, his eyes wide and round, and his jaw slightly slack.

"You better not be putting one over on me, Ritchie."

Ritchie grinned and rubbed his hand over the kid's wet hair. "Just wait and see."

THE MILLIONAIRE'S
Convenient ARRANGEMENT

Apparently, the afternoon of snorkeling had taken on a new appeal for Joey. Ritchie walked up the short walkway toward Maria. She looked like a vision in her striped bikini – he hoped she kept that on this afternoon – huge sunglasses and a wide brimmed straw hat. Why hadn't he noticed before how her legs seemed to go on for miles? His fingers itched to undo the bow of fabric that held the front of her bathing suit top together. He imagined doing just that, and her slowly sliding her sunglasses down to look at him with those dark, expressive eyes while the bikini top fell away, and his hands cupped those beautiful breasts. Then he would lean down and...

The image shattered as quick feet pounded behind him and Joey pushed past, running up to Maria to chatter excitedly and drip cold salt water on her smooth skin. She sat up with a startled yelp, the sunglasses falling off sideways, but the bikini staying well in place. Oh, yeah, that's right. They had an adolescent boy with them. Not to mention a private chef, Ritchie reminded himself, as Jillian came out across the wide porch carrying a tray with conch salad, fruit, sweet rolls, and a pitcher of iced tea.

Stop acting like a hormone-crazed teenager, Ritchie told himself. After all, he was the one who drew the line in the sand about not sleeping together. Right now, he was trying to remember exactly why he thought that was so important. Oh yeah. Because taking the virginity of a woman who still blamed him for prosecuting her brother and ruining his life was not a great idea. It didn't matter that said brother was a punk, up to his neck in the illegal activities of a drug-dealing, gun-selling street gang, and Ritchie had just been doing his job.

"If there's nothing else," Jillian said, "I'm heading off to the market to get some provisions for dinner."

Ritchie looked up. "Why don't you see if you can pick up some fresh grouper? Or maybe tuna steaks. I'm in the mood to fire up the grill tonight."

"Sure," Jillian said. "Anything special you'd like to go with it?"

"How about your potato salad."

"All right. I'll get some vegetables you can toss on the grill, too. And maybe whip up something for dessert."

"Don't put yourself out," Ritchie said. "We'll still have the chocolate cookie bars."

"Not if I can help it," Joey said, already eying the plate of thick, chocolatey bars.

"Okay, okay," Ritchie said. "Make us something for dessert, but don't wait around. We may be out on the boat pretty late."

"Just make sure you get out of the water before the sharks start to feed," Jillian said, winking at him as she whisked off her apron and headed back toward the kitchen.

"Sharks feeding?" Maria hissed. "Is there something we should be worried about?" She glanced over nervously at Joey who, if anything, seemed even more excited about snorkeling.

"It's been weeks since anyone was eaten," Ritchie said.

Maria narrowed her eyes. "Go ahead and make fun of me. But I'm having serious doubts about this. It's too dangerous."

"Oh come on, Maria," Joey said, bypassing a second helping of the conch salad to shovel another cookie bar into his mouth. "Ritchie's just fooling around. It's totally safe, right Ritchie?"

"Well, I wouldn't say *totally* safe . . ."

He actually didn't mind her being cautious. And that little worried crease between her eyes *was* pretty cute. "People who are just a little bit nervous stay alert. They're less likely to make stupid mistakes."

"I'll keep that in mind," Maria said.

"Don't worry," Ritchie said. "I've been doing this since I was a kid. Just stay close to me, and I'll protect you."

Exploring the glistening underwater environment with Maria staying close to him was something Ritchie was looking forward to.

Chapter Seventeen

Right. It's a good thing to be nervous. Maria sat on the swim platform at the rear of the boat and watched as Joey pulled on fins and lowered into the water, adjusting his mask and snorkel just as Ritchie had instructed.

Despite the heat of the day, the water felt cool. Here goes nothing, she thought as she followed them in. Fascination replaced nerves as she watched a school of fish swim by, and then they went deeper to see colorful sea anemone clinging to the rocks, tentacles waving gently in the current like bright flowers swaying to a summer breeze. When she felt herself getting short of breath, she swam back up to the surface, cleared her snorkel with a quick puff of air, then took a few steadying breaths.

She felt Ritchie beside her, moving through the water, his leg brushing her thigh. In the quiet of the undersea world there was a sense of unreality, and as their bodies touched a spark ran through her. Floating, weightless, the urge to press her body closer to Ritchie almost irresistible. He pointed ahead to the shipwreck, and signaled Joey to swim in that direction, then took Maria's hand and guided her down into the crystal waters. A majestic stingray glided across the sandy bottom beneath them, and schools of yellow fish swam in and out of the sides of a sunken ship that functioned as reef. She felt a quick panic when Joey disappeared through one of the gaping holes in the side of the ship. Ritchie gave her hand a squeeze then followed Joey, and Maria went back to the surface where she could float on her stomach and take short, shallow dives to watch the colorful world below her.

She hadn't been sure it was a good idea to come along on this trip, but she had to admit she hadn't felt this relaxed and free from stress in a very long time. She raised her hand in the water, turning it from side to side, as a school of striped fish, their sides as round and flat as dinner plates swam leisurely past her, then suddenly picked up speed and flitted off in another direction. A long silver fish moved smoothly through the water, razor sharp teeth bared in its underbitten jaw, eyes small and round. Barracuda. It turned slowly, cruising like a silent stealth missile, its small smooth scales glinting in the sun-drenched water, then shot forward in a surprising burst of speed, snapping its prey cleanly in half. Maria swam back to the surface to get a few breaths of air through her suddenly dry throat, while keeping a careful eye on the whereabouts of the barracuda below. Ritchie had told her they typically didn't bother snorkelers or divers. Still. Seeing one up close was like coming face to face with a prehistoric predator.

She pulled herself onto the swim platform, took off her snorkeling gear, and spread one of the thick towels on the sun pad to stretch out in the warm air. With her sunglasses and hat shielding her eyes, the heat and the gentle rocking of the boat soon lulled her to sleep. She was back underwater again, watching a school of brightly colored fish swim in changing geometric patterns. Suddenly, they scattered, and she looked around to see what had frightened them. Something was swimming toward her from the depths beyond the shipwreck. At first, it looked like the barracuda she'd seen earlier, but much larger – at least six feet long. And headed straight for her. She knew she should get out of the water, but her legs wouldn't move and instead, she found herself sinking farther away from the sunlight and into the shadowy depths below. Just when the giant predator's jaws were almost upon her, she realized it wasn't a barracuda at all, it was a diver, in full scuba gear. She struggled to see who was behind the mask as the diver's hand clamped on her ankle and pulled her downward. Her snorkel gear was gone, her hair floating freely around her face. Oddly, she didn't seem to need to breathe. But she knew she had to get to the surface. She knew there wasn't much time.

"Maria." Ritchie's voice.

"It's you," she said. "I was so afraid."

"You don't have to be afraid ever again," he said. She heard his voice clearly inside her head, saw only the bubbles rising up through the water.

A cloud must have passed over the sun, because the day got darker. Or maybe it was evening by now. When sharks come out to feed.

"We have to go back to the surface. To the boat," Maria said,

"You know I can't do that." His voice had changed, but it was still familiar. She reached out and pulled off his mask.

"You shouldn't have done that," Tito said. He put his mask back on and pushed her away.

"Tito! No!"

He continued to look up at her as he sank farther and farther away, down into the depths.

"Don't go! Don't go!" She called to him, but now every time she opened her mouth it filled with salt water, and she could only make a gurgling sound. She tried to swim after him, but without her fins she couldn't get her body to move downward and she kept floating higher and higher, closer and closer to the surface, where finally a glimmer of sun broke through the clouds. She felt hands gripping her shoulders, lifting her up.

She opened her eyes and was looking into Ritchie's face. He had both hands on her shoulders, and she was half sitting on the deck of the boat. For a moment, she felt completely disoriented, then the dream faded into the background.

"Maria, wake up."

"Whoa, Sis, are you ok?" Joey was leaning against the side of the boat, giving her a look that was half concern and half embarrassment.

"I'm fine." She sat the rest of the way up. "I was just dreaming, that's all. I must have fallen asleep."

"Man, that must have been some dream," Joey said. "You were yelling so loud. We heard you as soon as we got near the boat. Shit."

"Watch your language," she said automatically. Then her eyes narrowed. "What exactly was I yelling?"

Joey shrugged. "I don't know. So, what was it, some kinda' nightmare?"

"I don't remember that well." She looked at Ritchie. "Except the part where a giant barracuda was swimming toward me, and then it turned out to be you in scuba diving gear."

"Not a very flattering image you have of me." Ritchie leaned in closer. "If I ever do take you diving, I promise not to turn into a barracuda."

"Hey," Joey said, "Do you really know how to scuba dive?"

"Sure."

"Can we do it? Will you show me how?"

"Not this trip," Ritchie said.

"Aw, come on."

"People who take a few quick lessons on vacation are idiots," Ritchie said, sternly. "It takes a lot of training to dive safely."

Joey looked down, scraping his toe along the deck of the boat, clearly disappointed.

"But I'll tell you what, Sport," Ritchie said. "When we get back to Miami, I'll sign you up for a certification class. Pass that and I'll take you for some open water practice myself. That way you'll be ready to go next time we come to Bimini."

Joey looked up, eyes shining. "Really?"

"You bet." Ritchie reached over and ruffled Joey's hair, and Maria looked away. Why was Ritchie making promises like this, getting Joey's hopes up? How was she ever going to provide these kinds of experiences for Joey once their lives got back to normal?

"You want to go stow the gear?"

"You bet!" Joey said, gathering up the assortment of fins, snorkels, and goggles, and lugging them below deck.

She felt Ritchie's finger lightly under her chin, forcing her to look up at him.

"What's the matter?"

"You shouldn't promise him things like that."

"I like spending time with Joey."

"But what's he going to do when the six months is over and you aren't part of our lives anymore? Have you thought about that?"

There was a long pause.

"I don't make promises I don't intend to keep. And I have every intention of staying part of Joey's life for the long term."

She started to turn her head but the look in his eyes stopped her.

"And I'd like it — very much - if that means I'm going to be part of your life, too."

That was the problem. She did like having Ritchie in her life. She was starting to like it way too much.

...

Maria woke up the next morning to the sound of laughter coming from downstairs.

There'd been too little laughter in Joey's life. And, she realized guiltily, she hadn't even thought about it until now. She'd been too busy keeping food on the table and rent paid, and keeping up with a kid who outgrew his jeans and sneakers faster than she could buy new ones. About the only thing the two of them had done together as a family in the past few years was go to Mass on Sundays and volunteer at St. Theresa's Wednesday nights. Thanks to Ritchie, she could take a step back and just enjoy Joey being a kid. And maybe Joey was starting to see her as someone who wasn't just put on this earth to nag him.

Maria pulled on her robe, gathered up her shower supplies, and walked down the hall through Ritchie's bedroom into the master bath he'd told her was one of the selling points on the vacation rental ads. He wasn't kidding.

The whirlpool tub tempted her for a moment, as she imagined herself luxuriating in a swirl of bubbles while the hot jets sent streams of water to massage her entire body. No. Because that just led to thoughts of Ritchie taking off his clothes and slipping into the oversize tub with her.

She adjusted the five showerheads, tilting her head into the gentle stream from the large rainforest head as the steam rose around her. She poured some shower gel onto one of the soft washcloths that had been sitting in a basket on the marble counter and began rubbing it over her body.

When she'd stepped in, the shower had still been slightly damp from Ritchie's use earlier, and she imagined his lean, muscled body with the rivulets of steamy water cascading over it. A shiver ran through her despite the heat of the shower. Ritchie's body wash was sitting on a shelf built into the tile. She opened the cap and lifted it to her nose. The scent that was so uniquely Ritchie filled her lungs, making her ache with a vague sort of longing. She tilted the bottle and leaned her head back, squeezing a small amount onto her collarbone, letting it run down her body between her breasts as the streams of water washed it away. She squeezed a little more into her hand and more boldly rubbed it across the top of her breasts so that the clean, masculine scent washed over her. Maria closed her eyes and imagined Ritchie standing right behind her, imagined that it was his hands and not her own caressing her body. The scent of him surrounded her, and she picked up the soft washcloth and brushed it over her breasts, then slid it down her body slowly until she was moving it gently between her legs.

She had to stop this. She was just making herself want him more. Maria opened her eyes and snapped the lid shut on the body wash, returning it to the shelf. Then she put a generous amount of her own shower gel on her body and tried to wash away the lingering scent.

But even after she toweled off and got dressed, she could still smell the underlying scent of his body wash clinging to her skin.

As she rounded the corner and headed toward the kitchen she heard Joey laughing again. Ritchie joined in, and a light feminine laugh blended with his. Jillian. She was leaning forward with her hand on his shoulder as they both looked at something Joey was showing them on Ritchie's iPad.

Ritchie looked up as she stepped into the kitchen and their eyes met and held. His were so intense and she felt the air heating between them, and blushed. It was ridiculous. There was no way he could know what she'd been doing in the shower. He couldn't look right through her and read her thoughts.

She broke eye contact and poured herself a cup of coffee.

"Can I fix you an omelet?" Jillian turned her perfect face toward Maria.

At least if she was cooking, she wouldn't be standing so close to Ritchie. Maria knew she shouldn't be jealous. It was none of her business what sort of relationship Ritchie might have had with the picture-perfect personal chef in the past.

"Thank, you," Maria said. "That would be great."

"Any special requests?" Jillian asked, as she moved toward the array of chopped vegetables, fresh herbs, and cheeses spread across the cutting board in neat little piles.

Stay away from Ritchie, Maria wanted to say, *that's my special request.* Instead, she said all of it looked great, so whatever Jillian added to the omelet would be fine.

When Jillian slid it onto her plate a few minutes later, garnished with a generous helping of fresh tropical fruit, Maria had to admit that it was probably the best omelet she'd ever eaten.

"This is delicious."

"Thank you." Jillian smiled and ruffled Joey's hair. "You want seconds, Joey?"

"Sure. Can I help you?"

"Come on over." Maria watched in amazement as Joey the junk food addict sorted through the selection of chopped mushrooms, peppers, and other fresh vegetables and piled them onto a plate for Jillian to slide into his omelet as soon as she flipped the eggs – and by flipped the eggs, she meant casually and literally tossing them into the air. If Maria did that, the omelet would either land on the floor or be stuck to the ceiling.

"Hey," Joey said, "can you teach me how to do that?"

"Sure," Jillian said. "Go talk Ritchie into a second omelet and you can be the chef."

"Cool."

"But first," Jillian said, as she added some cheddar cheese and folded the omelet over, "you have to eat this one before it gets cold."

Joey, of course, didn't even think about giving Jillian an argument. He just hopped back on his stool at the bar and waited for Jillian to slip his second helping of fluffy omelet perfection onto his plate and fill his glass from a frosty carafe of almond milk.

"I try to limit the amount of dairy. Organic almond milk has more protein and less allergens," Jillian explained.

Joey just nodded, like it made perfect sense to him, and took a big gulp of his drink. Maybe Maria could get Jillian to start making observations about how doing your homework without complaining was good for the soul, and sneaking out of the house at night was seriously uncool.

Maria finished eating and poured another cup of coffee to sip outside on the terrace. She felt like she could never tire of the amazing view. The water seemed impossibly blue, the sky impossibly clear. Reality would be waiting for them when they got back to Miami, but for now, she just wanted to let go of all the worries and strains of her everyday life and just be.

Ritchie wandered out with his own cup of coffee and sat down on the end of the chaise she was reclining on. He reached over and casually ran his hand over the top of her foot, and she felt tingles run the length of her body. In the background, she could hear Joey's excited voice as he attempted the feat of omelet flipping.

Ritchie left his hand resting casually on her ankle, and she tried not to squirm. Did he have any idea the heat he was generating from that simple touch?

"So, what are your plans for the day?" he asked, shifting in his seat to face her, his hand moving slightly higher on her leg. Every coherent thought drained out of her brain.

"Um. . ." What *had* she been planning to do with her day? Focus. "I might go into town awhile. Check out the shops."

He nodded and seemed completely unaware that his fingers were now absently tracing a pattern on the calf of her leg. She felt her muscles tense instinctively and forced herself to relax. Jillian probably wouldn't become this flustered from such a casual touch. Jillian *never* seemed flustered around Ritchie. To the contrary, she seemed relaxed, friendly, just a little too friendly, in Maria's opinion, crossing that fine line between employer and employee. But who was she to judge? She had no hold on Ritchie.

How could Ritchie *not* realize what his touch was doing to her? He looked at her then and reached up to remove the sunglasses shielding her eyes. All of a sudden he seemed very aware of his hand idly stroking her leg. He moved it to the back of her knee, and she caught her breath. Ritchie shifted on the side of the chaise and leaned his head closer to hers as his hand slid higher. He was now gently stroking the inside of her thigh, and she felt her nipples tingling under the thin cotton blouse. He was going to kiss her. She parted her lips slightly and started to lean forward, when she sensed a movement in the doorway.

"Ritchie, your omelet's ready," Jillian said, and Maria turned and saw the chef watching her, speculation in her eyes.

Joey burst through the doorway behind Jillian. "Ritchie, come on, I made it myself, I flipped it and everything! Jillian taught me how."

"I'll be right there, Sport," Ritchie said, standing up as Maria eased back against the pillow on the chaise and put her sunglasses back in place.

"Cool," Joey said and raced back toward the kitchen, Jillian following behind him.

Ritchie stopped in the doorway, and Maria could feel him looking at her, waiting for her to turn her head and look back at him. When she did, she was glad the sunglasses shielded her eyes, because she didn't want to reveal how affected she had been by the little interlude that really amounted to...nothing. Did it?

The look in Ritchie's eyes was both heated and determined. "Later," he said simply, holding her gaze for a long moment before turning and going into the house.

All Maria could think was that it was only a matter of time until those strong hands were on her again. And once Ritchie had her alone, she wouldn't have the will or the desire to stop.

Chapter Eighteen

It was only two days until Christmas, and Joey was more excited than Ritchie had ever seen him. The stubborn kid with a chip on his shoulder that he'd first met at St. Theresa's seemed to have disappeared altogether. Which proved his point. Joey was a good kid, thanks to all the sacrifices Maria had made raising him on her own. All the kid had needed to get him through a rough period was a strong male influence taking an interest in him, someone who'd both give him opportunities and also hold him accountable.

Ritchie had pulled a top of the line artificial tree out of storage and taken Maria and Joey shopping for crazy beach souvenirs and shells in place of traditional ornaments. Now, he was enjoying sitting back, having a cold beer, and watching them decorate. Jillian had left an impressive array of snacks for the occasion. For some reason, Maria seemed uncomfortable when Jillian was around, and had offered again to cook Christmas Eve dinner herself. But the last thing Ritchie wanted was for Maria – who worked too hard already – to spend the holiday in the kitchen. Maria probably just wasn't used to having someone wait on her.

"This is so good!" Joey shoved a handful of the popcorn Jillian had drizzled with caramel into his mouth. "You need to find out how to make this, Maria! I'll ask Jillian."

Maria made a face. "You don't like my popcorn?"

Joey laughed. "You just put a bag in the microwave. This is *real* popcorn. I saw her make it."

THE MILLIONAIRE'S
Convenient ARRANGEMENT

He turned to Ritchie. "She put the kernels in a big pot on the stove in some oil and then put a lid on it. When it started popping, it was like the whole pot was going to explode! And she melted butter and everything. Then when it was in the bowl, she dumped salt on it, and then she poured this stuff off a pan on the stove, and she let me stir it all up with my hands."

"I hope you washed them first," Maria said, glancing over at him while she hung a starfish on the tree.

"Jillian says it's really important to have clean hands when you're working with food preparation," Joey said solemnly, and Ritchie had to stifle a laugh.

"I'm sure," Maria said.

Ritchie reached for a deviled egg – another of Jillian's specialties – and grinned. She'd infused the egg mixture with some kind of seafood, and there was a bite to the flavor that could be hot sauce or could be vinegar. All Ritchie knew was that he liked it.

"You should try these, Maria."

"I'm baking cookies later," she said.

He nodded. "Good. Do you need any cookie recipes? I think Jillian... "

She turned around with her hands on her hips. "I have my own recipe, thank you very much."

"Ok." Ritchie lifted his hand palms up.

"In fact," she said, "maybe I'll just check the pantry now and see if I have to pick up any ingredients."

Maria walked briskly toward the kitchen, and Ritchie turned to Joey.

"What's up with your sister?"

Joey shrugged. "I don't know. She gets all goofy whenever I say anything about Jillian. And man, when you and Jillian were out on the porch laughing yesterday she looked" — he shot a quick glance toward the kitchen and lowered her voice — "really pissed."

"Really?"

"Yeah. Hey, you don't have anything going on with Jillian, do you?"

"With *Jillian*? No, of course not. Why?"

Joey lowered his voice again. "Because I think Maria's jealous."

"You don't say. Why would she be jealous of Jillian?"

THE MILLIONAIRE'S
Convenient ARRANGEMENT

Joey shrugged. "Well, duh, Maria *likes* you. And Jillian's pretty hot. Besides, girls are weird. You haven't figured that out yet, dude?"

Could that really be what was going on? Ritchie decided he might just put Joey's theory to the test. And have a little fun while he was doing it. As long as he made sure Maria figured out that, despite their complications, she was the only woman he was interested in.

• • •

"You have got to be kidding." There was no way she could balance on that. It was crazy.

"Come on, Maria, it'll be fun." Joey was practically bouncing up and down on the dock.

"Christmas Eve would be a really bad time to die," she said. "Think about it, Joey, you'd be crying while you open your presents in the morning."

"It's a great way to relax," Ritchie said.

"Dying?"

"Paddleboarding."

"I'm sure."

Ritchie was standing waist-deep in the water holding onto the paddleboard.

"Well," Ritchie said, turning slightly away. "It's not for everyone." He paused. "Jillian's out on one all the time. But maybe it's just not your thing, Maria."

Jillian's out on one all the time? So, was Ritchie standing around watching Jillian paddling back and forth in her bikini? Well, that was just great.

"I never said I wouldn't try it." If Jillian could get up on one of these things, then Maria was going to give it her best shot.

"So, can I go first?" Joey was shuffling from foot to foot on the dock, clearly impatient at all the conversation it was taking to get the activities underway. At Ritchie's nod, he was off the dock and into the water.

"Shouldn't he wear a life preserver?"

"*Ma-ri-a! No,*" Joey said indignantly.

"I have some inflatable PFD's in the boat," Ritchie said. "For today though, we're staying right by the shore, so don't worry."

THE MILLIONAIRE'S
Convenient ARRANGEMENT

Maria watched as Joey followed Ritchie's instructions, getting on the board on his knees first, then carefully standing up.

"Just find your balance," Ritchie said, reaching up to take the shorter paddle off the dock.

"It's like a surfboard!" Joey said, moving his left foot ahead of his right and crouching in surfer position...and promptly flipping off the board and into the water. He came up sputtering a few feet away.

"Let's try that again," Ritchie said, as Joey climbed back up. "This time, keep your feet even, about shoulder width."

"Ok," Joey said, clearly concentrating.

Ritchie handed him the paddle, but kept ahold of the board until he fastened the ankle strap, then slowly released it. Joey wobbled a bit but hung in there and started to paddle, seeming to gain his balance as he picked up a little speed.

Maria sat down on the dock, wrapped her arms around her knees, and just watched. Ritchie's muscles rippled, the sun glistening on his wet skin as he called instructions to Joey. His arms weren't bulky at all, but she could see how strong they were just in his casual movements. And the etched lines of his chest made her sigh.

It was more than how he looked, though. There was something undeniably sexy about a successful and confident man taking the time to make a kid Joey's age feel special. A strong man, opinionated and a bit stubborn to be sure, but with so much patience.

She hoped he'd reserved some of that patience for her. She'd tried surfing once back when she was in high school, and had been an abysmal failure at it. If she couldn't even manage to get up on a board when it caught a wave, she had no idea how she'd maintain her balance completely still in calm water.

It rankled to know that Jillian – who looked like a cover model and was a fabulous chef – apparently excelled at it. And she was being silly. There wasn't any reason to think he had a past with Jillian, and even if he did, it wasn't any of her business.

Anyway, Joey seemed to be getting the hang of it. By the time they came back to the dock about twenty minutes later she was thinking it might not be so bad after all. Until it took her all of ten seconds to fall off. After her fourth attempt, Ritchie came up with a new approach.

THE MILLIONAIRE'S
Convenient ARRANGEMENT

"It's nerves more than anything," he said. "You get up there and the only thing you can think about is that you're going to fall off. So you do."

"Here," he said, patting a spot slightly past the center toward the front of the board. "Just try sitting right here for little while. Until you get more comfortable with it."

She climbed onto the board and settled herself gingerly, sitting cross-legged.

"But how – " She gasped as Ritchie easily hopped onto the board himself, standing directly behind her.

"We're going to tip over!"

"Relax," he said, reaching down and touching her shoulder lightly. "I'm just going to paddle around a little until you stop thinking about it and start enjoying it."

"Dude," Joey said, "if you're just going to paddle around like that, I'm gonna go watch Jillian cook."

Maria watched him scramble back up onto the dock and head into the house.

"You don't have to do this, Ritchie. We can go back in."

"You'd rather be watching Jillian cook?"

Was he grinning at her? She gritted her teeth and decided just to focus on keeping her balance. After a few minutes she realized they weren't about to tip over and surprised herself by starting to relax.

It was actually pretty amazing to be this close to the water, sitting on a board. Schools of tiny fish darted about near the sandy bottom. The water sparkled in the morning sunshine, and the gentle laps that splashed over the board felt cool on her skin.

They glided over the water, Ritchie's smooth, experienced strokes seeming effortless. He turned, passing their dock, but, she realized with surprise, they were much farther out now. She could no longer see down to the bottom, although the water remained surprisingly clear.

"Shouldn't we go back in a little closer?"

"I wanted to give us some room to maneuver." She realized that the board had slowed, and they were just gently drifting, instead of moving with purpose. She glanced back behind her and saw that Ritchie had set the paddle down, crossways on the board.

"Shift onto your knees now, and then slowly stand up."

THE MILLIONAIRE'S
Convenient ARRANGEMENT

"We'll flip!"

She felt his hands on both of her upper arms, just below her shoulders. "Don't you trust me?"

"Okay, but I warned you…"

She leaned forward onto her knees, certain that she'd find herself flung into the cool water at any moment. But to her surprise, the board remained steady.

"That's it," Ritchie said. "Now, just stand up, one foot at a time."

He ran his hands down the sides of her arms to steady her, and she shivered.

"Keep your feet parallel, even with your hips," he said and moved his hands down to both sides of her hips. "There. That's it. Don't stand on the rails."

"The rails?"

"The edges of the board. Just keep your feet centered, and you'll be fine."

"You make it sound easy."

"It is easy."

She felt him let go of her as he reached down and picked up the paddle, then handed it to her.

"You try."

He moved closer, his chest pressing against her back as he reached around her to position her hands. She could smell the clean male scent of him, mingling with the sea air.

"No, don't look down, keep your eyes on the horizon. Relax, you're trying too hard."

She was afraid to relax. If she allowed herself to relax she might melt right into him. She never would have imagined that learning to paddleboard could feel so… intimate.

"Now pull back in a smooth stroke. Like this." His voice was like a caress, his breath warm on her neck as he bent his head close to hers. Their bodies pressed tighter together as he guided her, moving them smoothly through the water.

"You're a natural."

"More like you're a great teacher." She felt a warm glow, but it was just as quickly overshadowed by an image of Ritchie standing like this on a paddleboard with other women, doing exactly the same thing. He was just a little bit too good at this.

"So did you give Jillian lessons?" She immediately wished she could take the words back.

"No," he said, and she relaxed a little.

"Jillian doesn't need any lessons."

What was that supposed to mean?

"Besides," Ritchie said, his breath tickling her ear. "I'm only interested in teaching one woman new skills."

Every nerve tingled as she thought about the other new skills Ritchie could teach her.

"You'd be amazed the things people can do on a paddleboard."

"Like what?" Her heart was beating faster, and it wasn't from fear of flipping the board and landing in the water.

"Well, there's a group I've seen in Miami that go out on the bay every morning at sunrise to do yoga on their SUP's"

"SUP's?"

"Stand Up Paddleboards."

"They do yoga? They must have amazing balance."

"We can work on your balance." Ritchie gently removed the paddle and set it crosswise behind him. "Try moving a little."

"I don't know any yoga poses." She paused. "But I did take ballet when I was a kid." Free classes at the community center.

"See if you can stretch your leg out behind you." His hands were on both her sides just under her ribs, his fingers spanning her waist.

"Don't blame me if we both end up in the water."

"You know how to swim, don't you?"

She shifted on her left foot and extended her right leg slowly behind her. She knew Ritchie was stabilizing the board and helping her keep her balance, but still she was surprised at how steady she felt. She raised her leg higher, extending her body forward and stretching her arms out to the sides.

"That's it," Ritchie said. "Close your eyes. You just have to let yourself go."

Amazingly, once she closed her eyes, it was actually easier to balance. And her other senses seemed suddenly heightened. She could feel

THE MILLIONAIRE'S
Convenient ARRANGEMENT

the warm breeze, the slight ripples of the water under the board, the texture of the grip under her feet. She moved slowly through a series of half-remembered dance moves, from a time when everything had been so much simpler. Her movements became surer, her balance more certain. And every way she leaned she could feel Ritchie, shifting with her, as if he was part of her dance.

As his fingers trailed along the back of her knee, her breath caught in her throat. "Are you seducing me?"

"Is it working?"

Instead of answering, she lowered her leg slowly until both feet were back on the board then pivoted so she was facing him, less than an inch between them. The sun was beating down, but the heat she felt seemed to be from his body to hers.

Maria raised up on her toes and pressed her lips on his. She ruled the kiss, her tongue tangling with his, her body pressing closer. She could feel the muscles of his chest against her wet body, felt the heat spreading from her core, her nipples tingling as they hardened and pressed against the thin fabric on her bikini that kept them from being completely skin to skin. She felt powerful, and in control, for the first time in a long time. There was nothing in the world she wanted more that to keep on kissing him right now, in this moment.

Then the balance shifted, so subtly she didn't realize it at first, until she felt herself going under. She was out of her depth, and she didn't care. Because Ritchie was there to hold onto as a thousand electric bolts seemed to shoot through her body, leaving her weak and strong at the same time.

He lowered her onto the board and she felt the hard surface warm against her back, her feet dangling over the side in the cool water. She kept her eyes on his as he knelt between her legs, bracing his hands near her shoulders. The sun glistened off the water, and on his wet skin. And then he was kissing her again. Softly this time. Kisses that grazed her lips and left her wanting so much more. There was no one around. Even the sea birds seemed to have gone silent. She held her breath as he lifted one hand from the board, stared into his eyes as he stroked the side of her face. Then felt his hand move slowly down to her neck, over her collarbone, then between her breasts, where he tugged on the bow that held her bikini top together.

He shifted his gaze lower as the fabric slipped away from her body, and she was startled by the raw need she saw in his eyes. She gripped the sides of the board with both hands as he cupped first one breast and then the other, running his fingers over her as the sun shown on her skin. She reached her arms back slowly, trailing her fingers through the water, and arched her back toward him. He slid lower, his lips closing over her nipple and the pleasure of it was almost unbearable.

She felt a sudden spike of panic. What if someone saw them? It was indecent. It was...intoxicating.

Ritchie stretched out full length over her, their bodies pressed so tightly together that she was no longer sure where her body ended and his began. He raised his head and her body arched uncontrollably, her breast yearning for the touch of his lips and tongue. She looked into his eyes and saw her own desire reflected there. He slid his hand down her body and over the curve of her hip, shifting his weight to the side.

"Wait! No – " She felt the board tilt and then they were underwater. The cool water hit her heated skin with a shock as she went completely under, her legs still wrapped around Ritchie's. She came back to the surface sputtering, his strong arms holding her up until she caught her breath.

Maria glanced down at her breasts, visible just below the surface of the water.

"Oh my God, I'm topless."

Ritchie gave her a wicked smile. "I'm not complaining."

"Ritchie, come on."

She watched as he swam a few yards away to retrieve the board and sighed in relief when he pulled his hand out of the water to reveal her bikini top.

She retied it quickly and then climbed back onto the paddleboard, scanning the surrounding water until she spotted the paddle floating some distance off and pointed it out to Ritchie, who swam off the retrieve it. His powerful strokes cut through the water, and she imagined him leaning over her in his bed instead of on a paddleboard drifting on the water. But there'd be no shock of cold water to bring her to her senses. Nowhere to fall but into Ritchie's arms. No turning back. As he turned, swimming back toward her with the paddle in tow, she wanted him with a yearning that made her chest ache.

Ritchie pulled himself up onto the board in a smooth motion. Maria sat cross-legged, facing him, as he paddled them back to the dock.

She stepped up onto the wooden platform and waited while he stowed the paddleboard. When she turned toward the house he stepped in front of her, blocking her way. She could feel her heart pounding.

"I told Joey he could sleep in the boat tonight."

"I know, he's really excited." Maria had come up with the idea so she could put Joey's gifts out without him sneaking out of bed to watch her. Sure, he was way past the age of believing in Santa Claus, but she'd worked hard to keep the magic of Christmas alive. And waking up to find the gifts under the tree was a tradition she wasn't ready to put aside.

"I'll help you put the gifts out," Ritchie said.

"Ok, um, great." Why was he looking at her so intensely?

"Then you'll spend the night in my bed." He tilted her chin up. "It's about time we finished what we started."

He reached out and touched the side of her face, and she felt her pulse pounding.

"So if that's not what you want, tell me now."

"It's what I want," she said softly.

Chapter Nineteen

The Christmas Eve dinner was probably spectacular, but it might as well have been crackers and tea for all Maria tasted it. Her mouth felt dry despite the glass of wine she was sipping, and her thoughts kept turning to what she and Ritchie would be doing once Joey was tucked into the cuddy cabin on the boat for the night. At any rate, there'd be plenty of leftovers tomorrow.

"Eat," Ritchie said. "You need to keep your energy up." He gave her a slow smile, and she felt the color creeping into her cheeks.

"That's right," Joey said. "I bet you have lots of presents to put under the tree tonight. You'll probably be up really late."

There *would* be lots of presents for him under the tree this year. She was still paying the rent on her now-empty apartment, but thanks to Ritchie insisting on footing the bill for their food and all of Joey's other necessities, she'd had enough expendable income to go a little crazy with Christmas shopping. Joey wasn't going to be a kid much longer, and although she'd done her best since their mom died, the holidays had still been a bit sparse.

"This stuff is great!" Joey said, helping himself to another big serving of the seafood and pasta medley Jillian had said would reheat really well or could be served cold tomorrow.

"Hey," Joey continued, "Jillian said she saw you guys out there on the paddleboard."

Maria's fork clattered onto the table. "What did she say?"

Joey shrugged. "Just that you looked like you were having a good time."

She wanted to reach across the table and wipe the smirk off Ritchie's face. Joey went on, oblivious.

"Jillian said she'll be back before New Years because she has this big catering job. She said maybe I can go out paddleboarding with her and her partner sometime." Joey was beaming.

"She has a partner in her catering business? I've only seen Jillian here by herself."

"Not a business partner," Ritchie said, eyes twinkling.

"Yeah," Joey piped in. "You don't have to be jealous of Jillian, Sis, 'cause she has a girlfriend."

"I am not the least bit jealous of Jillian," Maria said.

"Right," Joey said. "Sis, you're so busted."

Maria gave him a stern look. "Do I have to remind you again what day this is?"

"You're the best sister in the whole world," Joey proclaimed, recovering nicely.

"Um hmm. We'll see," Maria said, but what she was thinking was, *Jillian is gay?* She supposed Ritchie thought he was pretty funny with all those comments about Jillian this and Jillian that.

She gave him a hard look, but when she caught the grin on his face, she had to break out laughing. Suddenly, Jillian's seafood salad tasted a lot better. But her nerves still kept her from really enjoying the meal. The last time she and Ritchie had been in a bed together, he was the one who put on the brakes. For good reasons. The thing was, she didn't think any of those reasons had really changed. Sure, she no longer looked at him as the one-dimensional ambitious young prosecutor who had counted her brother as just another notch on his career path. But the fact remained, he had been ruthless in his prosecution of not only the gang members but also anyone who – like Tito – had been even peripherally involved in drug and weapons cases.

It was like Ritchie was two different people. The man she had come to know over recent months could at times seem both arrogant and de-

THE MILLIONAIRE'S
Convenient ARRANGEMENT

manding — he had taken over their lives, uprooting them from their apartment and controlling every aspect of Joey's daily life. In the process, he'd swept her up into a completely different world.

But he had put Joey back onto the right path – something she herself had been unable to do. His kindness and generosity shown through his charitable work at St. Theresa's, the time he spent with Joey, and his close relationship with his own family. That part of him drew her despite herself. There was no use pretending that her pulse didn't take off like crazy whenever she was near him, and that she didn't lie awake in bed each night wondering what it would be like to make love with him. This time, tonight, he wasn't going to stop at foreplay. He wasn't going to show the restraint he had each time before, and there wouldn't be a spill into brisk water to cool them off when things got too intense. He told her he was taking her to bed tonight, and he meant it. She knew that if she changed her mind, told him no, he'd respect that. But she also knew that from the moment he reached out and touched her tonight, she would be powerless to stop the desire coursing through her own body.

She knew there was a good chance she would regret sleeping with Ritchie tonight. She also knew she would regret it even more if she didn't.

As she cut generous pieces of the apple pie Jillian had baked and lifted them onto dessert plates, she could feel him watching her. Could he pick up on how nervous she was? Maybe he thought finally letting go of her virginity was what troubled her. But he'd be wrong. She'd been ready the first time Ritchie carried her up to bed. What she was truly afraid of was losing her heart to a man she could not, would not, allow herself to love.

• • •

After dinner they played board games and watched old Christmas movies until it was time for Joey to head out to the boat for the night. She got him settled in the cuddy, and reached over and ran her hand over his hair, then kissed him on his forehead. She knew there wouldn't be many more moments like this before he left the little boy part of him behind forever.

"Maria?"

"What, Joey?"

THE MILLIONAIRE'S
Convenient ARRANGEMENT

"I'm glad we came here for Christmas with Ritchie."

"Me too. Are you sure you're going to be okay sleeping out here?" Part of her wanted to put off the inevitable. If Joey decided to come back in the house and sleep in the room right down the hall from Ritchie's, there was no way she'd feel comfortable joining Ritchie in his bed tonight.

"I'm good. This is gonna be cool. I'll see you in the morning."

"Okay," she said softly.

By the time she walked back up to the house, Ritchie had already gotten all the packages for Joey out of the storage room built into the side of the house, and they were stacked in a jumble on the living room floor. He'd had them all brought over from Miami the day before they arrived.

"This looks like way more than I bought," Maria said, and Ritchie grinned.

"I picked up a few extra things."

It took an hour before everything was organized, and Ritchie had assembled and connected the drums and guitar for the Rock Band 4 Band-in-a-Box video game, and Maria had adorned it with a giant red bow.

She sat back on the couch and surveyed the array of brightly wrapped packages surrounding the tree. Joey was getting plenty of loot on Christmas morning, but she knew this gift was the one he had his heart set on.

"I can't believe you bought another game console just so he could play this on Christmas morning."

"We'll be rocking out all day tomorrow," Ritchie said, and Maria felt a warm glow spread through her heart as she thought about how much it would mean to Joey for Ritchie to play with him in the video band. Ritchie was the closest thing Joey had ever really had to a father. He'd been so young when his dad died that he barely remembered him.

Ritchie walked deliberately toward her, and at first she thought he was going to join her on the couch. Instead, he pulled her to her feet. In an instant, the mood in the room shifted. Their bodies were close together, almost touching, and the air between them felt charged with electricity. She'd worn a soft deep-green halter dress for Christmas Eve dinner. The high strappy sandals she'd started with had been discarded during the package assembly. She wished she had the extra height now. Her face was level with his chest, and she had to tilt her head back to look up at him. He then lifted her as if she weighed nothing at all.

"Wrap your legs around me, Maria."

She held onto his shoulders as he kissed her. The kiss started out gentle, easy, then quickly moved beyond her control. All she could do was hang on. His hand was under her skirt, against her skin, supporting her weight while her legs tightened around him, and she pressed herself as close to him as she could. His other hand was splayed across her bare back, moving up and down, caressing her skin. Everywhere he touched her felt like she was on fire. The heat was building so quickly inside her she thought she might explode.

"Oh, God Ritchie, hurry."

She heard his low laugh. His breath was warm on her ear.

"We've waited this long, Maria," he said, as he carried toward the staircase. His voice was low and sexy. "The one thing I can promise you is, it's not going to be fast."

• • •

He set her down slowly in the bedroom, letting her slide down his body. Her lips were already swollen from kissing. He ran his fingertips slowly up and down the front of her dress. She was incredibly responsive to his touch, and he felt himself go rock hard as he took her nipples between his thumbs and fingers, manipulating the soft cloth to increase the friction. Her eyes glaze over with pleasure.

"Ritchie, please, I can't take anymore."

"You have no idea how much more you can take." He paused. "But I'll show you."

He continued exploring her breasts through the thin silk as he trailed his mouth along the side of her jaw, down into the little hollow on the side of her neck that he already knew made her tremble. The skin on her back was silky smooth, and she smelled like an exotic flower.

He moved his other hand up her back, following the line of her spine, until he reached the single button that held up her dress, and undid it. The dress slipped free, sliding down her body. It landed in a soft cascade around her bare feet, and she was wearing nothing but a pair of lacey dark green panties that matched the color of her dress.

She looked suddenly self-conscious and started to cover her breasts with her arms. He caught her hands and held them at her sides.

"Don't do that. I want to look at you."

He ran his hands up and down the outside of her arms and let his eyes move over her. Those perfect breasts were slightly flushed, her nipples even more aroused after the attention he'd given them through the silk.

He raised his eyes to her face. "God, you're beautiful."

Her lips parted slightly, and she ran the tip of her tongue nervously across her teeth. "Ritchie."

He scooped her up in his arms and laid her on the bed, her dark hair fanning out on the pillow. "So beautiful."

He saw the surprise register on her face when, instead of sliding in next to her, he moved to the bottom of the bed and lifted one of her delicate feet in the palm of his hand, moving his lips over the arch while keeping his eyes on her face. He took his time with each foot, and felt her shiver when he used his lips to explore the inside of her ankle. Her hands gripped the soft comforter on the bed as her whole body tensed, then relaxed. And he wondered why he'd waited so long, when this was exactly what they both wanted.

After tonight, she would just have to put the past in the past. Because Ritchie had no intention of letting the mistakes her brother made ruin the future the two of them could have together.

But right now, he had more interesting things to focus on. Like that soft sound she made when he put his mouth on the back of her knee.

"Ritchie."

Her hands fluttered and she grasped his hair, tried to urge him up the length of her body, but he was planning on taking his time.

"What's your hurry?" He nipped the inside of her thigh lightly and heard her gasp. When he traced both hands up those long, silky legs, hooked two fingers in the sides of the lacy panties and slid them all the way down, she moaned, soft and sweet.

"That's it. Right there," he said, as he trailed slow kisses up the inside of her thigh, pressing his hand against her other thigh to keep her legs apart and give him full access. Then he bent her knees, slid his hand under her hips to lift her slightly, and used his mouth on her. She came apart instantly, straining to clamp her legs around him as he held her firmly in place, reaching up her body with his free hand to tease her nipple and draw out her orgasm.

While she was still trembling with the aftershocks, he leaned forward over her, his legs straddling hers, and closed his mouth over her nipple, circling the tip with his tongue. She arched her back, her head falling to one side as she sighed.

"Don't close your eyes. I want you looking at me when you go over. Every time."

She turned her head back, those dark, expressive eyes looking straight into his.

"Every...time?"

"Every time."

"How many...Ohhh." Her words ended on a moan as he turned his attention back to her breast, sucking harder on one nipple as he pinched the other one. The taste of her was still on his lips, and it mingled with the sweet scent of her skin. He was glad he still had his pants on, or he'd have entered her by now, and he wanted to take her over at least two more times before he let himself take her completely. Once he was inside her, he wasn't sure how long he'd be able to maintain control. Already the friction of his jeans against her soft skin was almost too much to bear.

"Oh, God, Ritchie, I can't take anymore." Her face was flushed, and her skin damp.

"Take more," he said, and she grabbed the front of his shirt with both hands, ripping the buttons open as he took her over again. As her hands ran over his chest he closed his eyes for a moment, maintaining control, then watched as Maria's eyes dilated and her breathing quickened.

"More," he said, reaching down with his hand to stroke her and then enter her with a finger until he felt her clench around him. He swallowed her startled cry with his mouth as he kissed her.

Hating to lose the physical contact for even a moment, he straightened, took a step back. She lay on the bed looking up at him with wide eyes as he dispensed with his clothes and quickly sheathed himself with a condom. Then he slipped back into the bed, positioning himself between her knees.

"Maria," he said, surprised there was a catch in his throat. He had never seen her as beautiful as she was at this moment, naked on the bed beneath him, her curly hair wildly disarrayed, her eyes filled with arousal and trust, her lips swollen, and her entire body shimmering with a fine sheen of perspiration. He lowered himself over her so that his chest grazed her breasts. The feel of her smooth skin and her firm nipples against his own skin was intoxicating.

She slipped her arms around his neck, and everything seemed to move in slow motion as he kissed her, gently at first then with increasing pressure as he felt her hands gripping him. He rocked against her slowly and she arched toward him. He felt her muscles tense for a moment as he entered her, then moved his mouth along her jawline to the side of her neck, speaking to her in a low voice, telling her how beautiful she was. Then he was kissing her lips again, bracing himself over her with his arms, as he felt her start to relax again. He lifted his head so he could look into her eyes, as in one smooth stroke he filled her. He could feel her heart pounding, heard her sudden intake of breath, and then she was moving under him, slowly at first and then faster.

"That's it, that's right. My beautiful Maria."

"Oh, God, Ritchie. Ritchie!"

He adjusted his angle then, and began moving inside her, setting a slow easy pace at first, and then with more determined strokes, holding onto his control until her body moved frantically under his, until she tightened her arms around his neck, and he felt the sharp prick of her teeth on his shoulder. Then he let go of his control, thrusting harder, faster, touching her everywhere just as she was touching him. He felt her legs clasp around his waist, and he changed the angle again until their bodies were moving as one. He reached down between them, added his hand to the friction already rubbing her sensitive nub as she jerked and writhed under him. She sobbed out his name, her inner muscles clenching and contracting, and her entire body tensed as her fingers gripped his back. He quickened his thrusts even more, driving her through the orgasm as he felt himself come, hard and intense.

Then he groaned and rolled over, still inside her, pulling her with him, until he was flat on his back and she was splayed across him, limp and satisfied.

He ran his hand lightly up and down her back and she shuddered then lifted her head up slightly to look at him.

"I may never move again." She looked as sated as a cat that just drank a bowl of cream, but within moments, he saw a flicker of doubt cross her eyes, and she shifted slightly to the side as if she wanted to retreat under the covers. He planted a hand on that cute, round bottom and held her in place.

"Don't do that."

"What?"

"Don't even think about covering yourself up or feeling embarrassed."

"I wasn't."

He lifted his hand and gave her a playful smack across her bottom.

"Hey! What was that for?"

"Lying in bed."

"Huh?"

"Telling lies in bed," he amended.

He massaged her bottom, and she wisely didn't contradict him.

"And you're wondering if you did okay. If it was good for me."

"I'm –"

He lifted his hand slightly. "No lies, remember?"

She turned her head to the side. "So, was it?"

"I wouldn't say it was good..." He chuckled as she struggled to get up. Now she was looking at him, and there was fire in her eyes, just the way he liked her.

"Are you laughing at me? You let me up right now, Ritchie."

He had his hand clamped over her bottom again, and the way she was wiggling on top of him had him starting to go hard again already. She must have felt him growing inside her, because she stopped moving and looked at him, her eyes round.

"It wasn't good," he said, then paused. "It was great." He reached up and brushed the damp hair back from her forehead with his hand. "You were amazing."

"You mean that?"

"No lying in bed, remember?"

"Ok, because I could smack your butt, too, you know."

"I've got a better idea." He put his both hands on her hips and lifted her, leaning her back against his knees while he dealt with the used condom. He then quickly unwrapped another one.

"Let me do that."

He leaned back with his hands behind his head while she dealt with it, getting more and more aroused as her fingers fumbled slightly, rolling it down his shaft. Then he lifted her by her hips again and slowly eased her into place.

"We'll take it easy this time," he promised her. He knew she had to be sore.

"I don't want to take it easy," she said as she began riding him, awkwardly at first, then with growing confidence. "I want to take it all." When he reached up with the palms of both hands and began rhythmically caressing her breasts, she started moving faster and faster. He adjusted her to give her a better angle, and she braced her hands on his shoulders, her hips moving faster and faster while he kept stroking her breasts, moving his hips to kept pace with the wild tempo she was setting.

He hadn't lied to her when he said the first time was great, and this time was even better. As soon as she started to come, he let himself go as well. Maria threw her head back and gasped his name – her eyes glazed and her face flushed with pleasure.

When she collapsed on top of him this time, he pulled the thick comforter over them and just held her close until she fell asleep.

Chapter Twenty

Maria stretched languidly and blinked at the first rays of sunlight coming in the window. She was lying on her side, her head inches from Ritchie's, their legs tangled together. He opened his eyes, and she felt a shiver of excitement run through her as she watched his mouth curve in a slow smile.

She was just too happy to let it be awkward.

"Hey."

"Hey yourself."

He brushed the hair back from her forehead. "Merry Christmas."

"Merry – oh my gosh! Joey! He'll be up any minute."

He gave her a wicked grin. "Then we better hit the shower right now."

He scooped her up and carried her, naked, into the bathroom. Hot water from multiple showerheads flowed over her body, the stream of tiny pellets awakening every nerve ending. She'd been worried she might feel regrets, but instead, she was filled with so much joy her body couldn't contain it. No matter what the future might hold, making love with Ritchie couldn't have been a mistake. Nothing that made her feel so good could be wrong. She refused to think about the future. For right now, being here with Ritchie was enough.

Ritchie poured shampoo over her head, worked her hair into a lather, then slid his soapy hands down over her neck and shoulders. When he began soaping her breasts she had to hold onto his shoulders for support. Ritchie turned her around, positioning her with the palms of her hands braced against the tile wall.

She smelled the fresh citrus scent of her body wash and then, moments later, it filled her senses as Ritchie lathered her back and shoulders with one of the luxurious washcloths. She wondered what the thread count was as the soft cloth moved over her skin. Then she stopped thinking at all as he pressed closer to her and used the washcloth on her breasts. He added more body wash, and she felt drunk on the aroma, lost in the sensations of the soapy cloth over her breasts, the friction of the cotton on her nipples almost unbearably arousing.

She felt him nudge her legs apart with his knee, and the washcloth moved lower. He slipped the cloth between her legs and moved it back and forth in a slow rhythm. The more intense the sensations, the more firmly he held her in place, and squirming to try to ease the pressure that was building inside her only increased the delicious friction. He kept her legs apart as she went over, continuing to move the washcloth against her in its slow rhythm all the way through her shuddering orgasm.

Then the washcloth was gone and his hands were exploring her, every nerve in her body acutely sensitized to his touch. She struggled to catch her breath, tried to turn around to face him, but he pressed her hands back against the tile again.

"I not done with you yet, Maria."

He nudged her legs farther apart, positioned her hips, and she realized he was going to take her, right there in the shower, while the steamy water sluiced over them both in rivulets.

"Ritchie, we don't have time . . ."

She was wet and slick from the soap and the water and her already quickening arousal, and he entered her in one quick, hard stroke.

"Then you better come fast for me," he said, thrusting harder and deeper.

Her orgasm while he used the washcloth on her had left her shattered. Her body responded to him now, and she realized she wanted more. Craved more. Where had this wanton woman come from?

The sound of his wet skin slapping against hers made her crazy with need. This was nothing – *nothing* – like the slow, easy lovemaking from the night before. It felt wild and dangerous and reckless.

Ritchie braced one hand beside hers on the tile wall, his other arm circling her body and supporting her with steely muscles while his fingers rubbed over her slick and swollen nipples. Then, incredibly, he was moving even harder and faster, taking her to a place she hadn't even imagined, as her senses spun out of control. Her body was moving on its own, rocking with his, matching each thrust, her inner muscles clenching around him. Her orgasm broke through her in sharp-edged waves.

Afterward, she would have slid down the tile wall into a puddle if he hadn't supported her. She turned into his arms, her head against his chest and he just held her while the aftershocks of good, hard sex went though her body. She barely noticed the water hitting her in her face until he shifted their bodies, protecting her from the spray.

The front door slammed. "Hey! Wake up you guys!" Joey's voice echoed from downstairs.

"Oh my gosh, Joey!" Maria scrambled to get out of the shower, but Ritchie loped an arm around her and pulled her back in.

"Relax, I can get down there a lot faster." He took a step back, but then grinned and yanked her hard against him and kissed her. Then he was out of the shower, wrapping a towel around his waist, and calling out to Joey that he'd be right down.

Maria leaned back against the tiles a few moments and waited for her breathing to come back under control. Making love with Ritchie was so much more than she had imagined it would be. She was going to have to be very, very careful not to get too comfortable being in his bed, being in his life. But for now, what harm could there be in just enjoying the moment? He made her feel full of life and full of hope – things she hadn't felt since that last magical summer in Italy.

If she could put her worries and responsibilities aside, just for a little while, didn't she deserve it?

By the time she got downstairs, Joey was poised to hurl himself at her.

"You got it! You got me Rock Band!" He flew across the room and tackled her in a hug that almost knocked her off her feet. "You're the best sister in the whole world."

She'd filled stockings for the three of them as well, mostly with candy, a few gag gifts for Ritchie and Joey, and some gaming gift cards for Joey. But her own stocking seemed to be bulging with much more that it had when she'd left it there last night.

She sat on the couch and started slowly pulling items out, while Joey dumped his on the floor.

"What did you guys do?" she asked, as she slowly pulled the bow on a small, brightly wrapped box.

Joey looked up from where he was sitting on the floor, searching through his own bounty.

"That one's from me," he said. "Me and Ritchie went shopping last week, but I paid for it myself."

She opened the box and found a beautiful bracelet made of finely polished shells.

"Do you like it?" Joey's face was eager, and she went over and hugged him.

"I love it," Maria said, and slipped it onto her wrist, fastening the delicate clasp. "It's perfect."

"Now open the other one," Joey said. "It's from Ritchie."

"Okay, okay." Her fingers felt nervous as she slipped the bow off the box. This one was squarer and smaller than the one that had held the bracelet. Inside was a jeweler's box. She lifted the lid to reveal an exquisite pair of pearl earrings.

She looked up at Ritchie. "They're beautiful."

"They're vintage natural pearls. Beautiful and rare."

She lifted them out of the box and put them on, her hands trembling a little. What must these have cost?

"I knew they'd be perfect," Ritchie said. He reached over, brushed her hair behind her ear, and grazed his fingers gently on her neck for a moment. "Beautiful and rare," he said, and suddenly, she wasn't sure he was talking about the pearls.

Joey smiled at her and Ritchie, satisfied that they were having a good Christmas, and then dove back into his own gifts, crawling under the tree to search out more, until the floor was littered with wrapping paper, bows, videogames, and clothes. For a kid who would have turned his nose up at getting clothes for Christmas just a few years ago, Joey was amazingly excited at the trendy t-shirts and board shorts. She almost

THE MILLIONAIRE'S
Convenient ARRANGEMENT

laughed at the look he shot Ritchie when he opened the bottle of men's cologne and said, "Dude, thanks, this is cool," then proceeded to practically bathe himself in it.

Ritchie had also bought him the latest iPhone upgrade, and that one had him jumping up and down and shouting. Until everything but Rock Band was eclipsed by the shiny iPad Joey pulled out of a brightly wrapped box.

His jaw fell open, and he stared at Ritchie. "Dude, really? This is for me?"

"I thought you'd like having one of your own," Ritchie said.

"You spent too much," Maria said.

Ritchie shrugged and glanced over at the happy look on Joey's face. "It's Christmas," he said.

Joey reached farther back under the tree, pulled out a package he'd wrapped himself just the night before, and handed it to Ritchie.

"Hey," he said, trying to act casual. "This one's for you."

Joey had gone online and ordered a gamer t-shirt for Ritchie that had some saying on it that Maria didn't recognize. She'd tried to talk Joey into getting Ritchie something sensible, like a tie – he was a lawyer, after all, and wore ties every day – but Joey would have none of it. She watched nervously as Ritchie opened the clumsily-wrapped gift and then realized she needn't have worried at all. Ritchie pulled the shirt out of the box and held it up for a moment. All while Joey watched him. Then he lowered the shirt and looked at Joey and said, "This is seriously cool."

"I told you!" Joey shouted gleefully at Maria. "I told you he'd like it."

When Ritchie matter-of-factly peeled off his own shirt and put on the new one, Maria thought Joey's face would explode from pure joy.

"Here!" Joey said, dragging a bulky package out from behind the tree. "Open the one from Maria!"

She felt suddenly nervous. She reached up self-consciously and touched one of the pearl earrings he'd given her. They were expensive and tasteful. Personal but impersonal at the same time. What if her own gift gave away too much of herself?

After he opened it, he stared at it for a few moments, saying nothing, and her heart pounded in her chest. Finally, he looked at her.

THE MILLIONAIRE'S
Convenient ARRANGEMENT

"How did you know?"

"How did I know?"

"Vivienne must have seen my reaction to it when I stopped by the studio."

"No." He'd been by the studio? "Vivienne never told me you stopped by."

He frowned. "But then, how did you know I'd been there? To that exact spot. To that same café, in Florence."

"I didn't. I just...I wanted to give you something of the feeling I had when I was in Italy, and I remembered that perfect day. So I painted it for you."

"You painted this specifically for me?"

"I know it isn't perfect, I just —"

"Stop it," he said, his tone a little harsh. "It's a brilliant piece of work. You have to know that."

"So," Joey said, looking from one to the other, seeming to pick up on the tension that had suddenly cut through the air, "do you like it or what?"

"I like it very much," he answered Joey, but his eyes were on Maria's face. "In fact, I can't think of anything you could have given me that I would appreciate more."

"Cool," Joey said. "So, can we eat?"

"Not just yet," Ritchie said, leaning his painting carefully against the wall. "I have one more present for each of you."

He went outside for about a minute then called them to follow him. He was standing on the pathway by the porch with a paddleboard leaning on each side of him, both adorned with giant red bows.

"Holy shit! For real?"

"Joey! Watch your language," Maria said. Secretly, she was grateful for the distraction, because she couldn't look at the paddleboard without thinking about how close she and Ritchie had come to making love on his. He gave her a long heated look, and she felt her skin warming. He was obviously remembering the same thing she was.

"We'll spend some time later today practicing," Ritchie said, his eyes still on Maria.

"Cool!" Joey said. "So, let's go eat and get out on the water!"

THE MILLIONAIRE'S
Convenient ARRANGEMENT

Ritchie rubbed his hand affectionately through Joey's hair, and the two of them took the new paddleboards down to lean them against the railing on the dock. Maria heard her cell phone ringing, and she rushed back in, locating it under a pile of torn wrapping paper.

"Vivienne," she said, as she answered the phone. "Merry Christmas!"

• • •

When Ritchie and Joey came back into the house, Maria had the orange juice out and was opening a bottle of champagne.

"Someone's feeling festive," Ritchie said, grinning at her as he walked into the kitchen to help Joey drag out the platters and bowls of food Jillian had left in the fridge. Ritchie and Joey loaded up the table. Ritchie felt his stomach rumble as he sat down in front of the spread of bagels, smoked salmon, cream cheese, chopped onions and tomatoes, capers, and a variety of cold salads, fruits and pies. And, of course, Maria's homemade chocolate chip cookies.

Maria poured mimosas for herself and Ritchie and topped off Joey's orange juice with ginger ale, raising her glass in a toast.

"To the best Christmas ever!" Joey broke in before she could speak.

"I'll second that," Ritchie said, sending Maria a look that made her blush all over again. He loved watching the slight flush on her skin and knowing that wanting him was what put it there. He was already thinking of ideas to occupy Joey after they spent some time on the water later that afternoon. He had a sudden image of Maria lying across his bed wearing nothing but the pearl earrings, smiling up at him, and he wanted to make that image a reality as soon as possible.

"I can't remember when I've had a more memorable Christmas," Ritchie said.

"Now I have news that makes it even better," Maria said, her face lighting up with excitement. She took a long breath and let it out slowly. "Vivienne called to say that a local developer is interested in commissioning some of my paintings for a condo building downtown!"

One look at her face and Ritchie knew the phone call he'd made to an acquaintance on the Arts and Business Council had been well worth it.

"What do you mean?" Joey asked.

THE MILLIONAIRE'S
Convenient ARRANGEMENT

"It means," Ritchie said, "that your sister's paintings are going to be hanging in the lobby and new condos that are up for sale in a fancy building downtown."

"You've heard about this kind of thing?"

More than she realized. But Ritchie was keeping that bit of information to himself. "There's been a long time marriage between real estate and art for high-end Miami development. I think extending it to some of the more mid-priced condo buildings is new."

"I'm just so excited! I don't know how this developer even found out about me. I guess Vivienne must know someone who had a connection."

Ritchie had a pretty good idea that Maria wouldn't appreciate knowing that he'd made a few phone calls on her behalf. It was a good idea. His visit to Vivienne's studio had made him think about it in the first place. But that didn't mean he was interfering. However, considering the way Maria balked when he tried to get her to cut back on working so hard, and her continued insistence that she contribute financially toward her and Joey's living expenses, he didn't want to take any chances on what her reaction would be if she found out he had anything to do with this opportunity coming her way.

"Well," Ritchie said, raising his glass, "however it happened, congratulations."

"The only problem," Maria said, frowning, "is that the turnaround time is really fast." She spread cream cheese on a bagel and then added small amounts of the other toppings.

"You have a number of pieces done already, don't you?" Ritchie asked, thinking about the canvasses he'd seen leaning against the wall at Vivienne's studio.

She nodded. "Not enough, though. Vivienne will give me time off to pull everything together, but this time of year is when things really pick up at the restaurant."

Joey looked from one to the other. "So why don't you just quit?"

"It's called making a living," Maria said, and Joey shrugged.

"What's the big deal? Ritchie will take care of us."

"*I* take care of us," Maria said, turning toward Ritchie. "It's not that I don't appreciate everything you do for us, but it's really important for me to make my own way."

THE MILLIONAIRE'S
Convenient ARRANGEMENT

Ritchie took a deep breath and spoke evenly.

"It seems to me that if you're focusing on the future for you and Joey, meeting the deadline for the developer would be a lot more productive in the long run than holding onto a job waiting tables. Do you understand what an opportunity like this really means?"

"I'm not stupid. Of course, I know what it means. I also know that plenty of people have thrown away their future by giving up a secure job to take a risk on something that might not even work out."

That's what it was really about. Taking risks.

Ritchie leaned back in his chair. "You're afraid."

"Well, of course I am. There's no guarantee that they'll buy any specific number of my pieces, or that the condo buyers are going to – "

"No, that's not what I mean. You're afraid your work isn't good enough." When she didn't answer, he continued. "Because there's no risk when it's all hidden away in the upstairs loft at Vivienne's studio. You can tell yourself you don't have the time to follow your dream of being an artist. When maybe the truth is, you're just too scared to take the leap."

Maria stood up, her face flushed.

"How can you say that? That's not true at all. For years, I've done everything I can to provide a safe, secure life for Joey and me, to keep food on the table, to pay the rent. The only reason I've put off seriously pursuing my art is because we needed to have that security."

"So prove it."

"What?"

"Prove it, Maria. If you think you're good enough to make it as an artist, take your shot. You're not going to get another opportunity like this." He picked up a half bagel and spread cream cheese on it while she stood there, fuming. "Or you can stop pretending to be an artist and just be a waitress the rest of your life."

"No way," Joey said. "Tell him, Maria. Tell him you're going to quit the job at the restaurant. You're an artist."

"It's not like it's one or the other," Maria said. "If I hold onto my job while I see how this opportunity works out – "

"You'll end up getting no sleep and spending all your spare time at Vivienne's studio, instead of . . ."*Instead of with me*, he almost said.

Christ, what was wrong with him? "Instead of with Joey," he finished. "Is that what you want?"

"No," she said, slowly settling back down into her chair. "You might be right. If this is my shot, I should probably take it, no holds barred."

"Way to go, Sis!" Joey reached over to give Maria a high five, and she smiled at him, but the smile didn't reach her eyes. Ritchie realized she was very worried about what was going to happen next.

THE MILLIONAIRE'S
Convenient ARRANGEMENT

Chapter Twenty-One

Ever since they got back from Bimini, Maria felt like she was living in a fairy tale. Never more so than tonight, sitting in the back of the sleek limo with Ritchie, wearing a gown that had cost more than she'd earned at the restaurant in three months. Quitting her job there had been a big step. But now that it was done, there was no turning back.

When she was with Ritchie, everything was so easy. It was only when she was away from him that the doubts took over. What was she thinking? Tito still refused to even consider the possibility of staying in Miami, and really, how did she think that would work even if he did? Did she really think she'd be spending cozy family holidays sitting around the dining room table with her brother the ex-con and the man who put him away for eight long years? Eight long years that would have been ten, if the time hadn't been shortened for good behavior.

Tito was the other half of her soul. Allowing him to just leave the state and slip out of their lives was something she couldn't even imagine. When the time came, and she had to choose between Ritchie and Tito, there was only one decision she could make. Tito deserved a fresh start, away from Miami. He also deserved to have his family there with him, even if he didn't realize it yet. If Maria's art career was going to happen, she could paint anywhere. And if not, well, she certainly could get a job as a waitress anywhere. Still, a little voice inside her whispered that maybe tomorrow when she visited Tito and told him about the success she'd finally achieved with her art, and the pride she had felt putting one of her own paintings in the silent auction tonight, just maybe he would change his mind and decide to stay. She wanted to be there for Tito, whatever his plans were. But she also wanted to build on the great start Joey had made in his new school, with his new friends. And she wanted, oh so much, to stay here in Miami with Ritchie. Maybe she just wanted the impossible.

The limo pulled up to the curb, and the driver opened the door for her, taking her hand and helping her out. People were snapping photographs, hoping for a glimpse of Miami's elite. She hesitated then felt Ritchie move behind her, slipping his arm around her waist, guiding her through the crowd and into the ballroom.

Like Vivienne, Maria had donated a piece of artwork for the auction. While Vivienne's donation was a coup for the event, she knew very well that the reason Ritchie had asked for her donation was to advance her own career. The kind of publicity she was receiving at being a featured artist was invaluable and would boost the developer who was showcasing her art in his new construction. She just hoped she wouldn't be totally humiliated by a lack of bids on her painting – and shuddered at the thought that Ritchie might actually have to buy it himself to save her the embarrassment.

They stopped abruptly, and she realized they were standing in front of her painting. She looked down at the silent auction sheet and gasped when she saw the numbers. The painting was one of her favorites, of a sleek sailboat cutting across Biscayne Bay. She'd sat by the water with her sketchbook one crisp clear day a year ago and had made dozens of sketches until she got it just right. She'd frozen the image in her mind in vivid color. The exact shade of the sky. The clear surface of the water and the boat that cut through it. The wind in its sails. The bright splash of red on the bow –the jacket of the man who sailed it. Then she'd brought it to life back in Vivienne's studio.

She turned to Ritchie, suddenly suspicious. "Those aren't all your bidding numbers, are they?"

He laughed. "No, but I bet– " He stopped talking as his partner Jonathon came up behind them.

"Not trying to outbid me, are you, buddy?"

Ritchie slapped him on the back. "I wouldn't think of it."

Jonathon turned to Maria. "When Ritchie mentioned this painting, I knew I had to have it."

"If I'd known you were interested, I could have sold it to you separately and donated something else to the auction. I'm afraid you'll end up paying a lot more for it here."

"Oh, he can afford it," Ritchie said. "And it's for a good cause."

Jonathon smiled. "I'm sure you encouraged Maria to donate this particular piece. You knew I'd pay whatever it took to have it hanging on my wall."

"What are friends for?" Ritchie said, grinning.

Jonathon leaned over, studied the bid sheet, then entered a bid number that had appeared several times before. "Time to get serious," he said and added a dollar amount that upped the bid by an additional decimal point, winked at her, and strolled off.

"That's *fifteen thousand dollars*," Maria said in a hushed voice. "Why is he doing this?"

She'd expected that Ritchie might try to overbid on her painting just to make her look good, but why was Jonathon paying that much?

"You really don't know, do you?"

"Know what?"

"Don't worry, he's happy to make a charity purchase tonight for something he actually wants. People will be paying ridiculous amounts of money tonight for things of little or no value. Your painting – and the sculpture Vivienne donated, of course – will be the exception to that."

"Thank you for including me, darling." Vivienne put her hand on Ritchie's shoulder briefly then turned and embraced Maria.

"Why didn't you tell me you were coming? You hate these things." Vivienne might be generous with her donations, but she was anything but generous with her time. Especially at society functions she considered both pretentious and frivolous.

"And miss seeing one of your paintings on display for the first time? How could I do that?"

Maria noticed Vivienne glancing over surreptitiously at the bid sheet and nodding in satisfaction, and the realization dawned.

"You came here to make sure there were enough bids," Maria accused. "And if there weren't, you'd have placed one yourself."

"Nonsense," Vivienne scoffed, but her eyes twinkled. "I'm here to embarrass all the self-proclaimed art patrons into donating a respectable sum to acquire my sculpture."

"Where are you sitting?"

"At your table, of course. Where else would I be?"

As they walked back to the table, Maria was surprised to pass by Jonathon and his date – a local socialite who had recently become famous for her appearance on a reality show.

"Are they a couple?" she whispered to Ritchie.

"Doubt it," Ritchie said. "Jonathon dates someone new about every week. Ever since he got on that most eligible bachelor list . . ."

"Well, you should be on that list," Maria said, and then blushed when she realized he probably *was* on the list.

"That's just what my mom says," Ritchie whispered, his lips grazing her earlobe, sending shivers through her whole body.

"Why aren't Jonathon and his date at our table?"

"We try to spread it around a little, as sponsors. Especially since Sam and Camilla opted out of attending."

Maria had been glad to hear that. Not that she didn't trust Joey these days, but still, she'd asked him to check in with Sam and Camilla every so often, since it was unusual for her and Ritchie to leave him at home, unsupervised. Joey had balked when she'd suggested he go over to Sam and Camilla's for the evening, insisting he just wanted to play some video games and watch a series on Netflix that everybody at school had been talking about.

Maria let herself relax and just enjoy the event. The drinks were flowing, the food was exquisite, and she'd never seen anyone look as good in a tux as Ritchie did. When Vivienne's sculpture broke the record for the highest bid during the live auction, Maria thought there couldn't be a more perfect evening. And when Ritchie slipped his hand under the table and stroked the side of her leg, she realized it was actually going to get better when they got back in the limo.

Everything ahead of her was so bright. If she could be successful as an artist, then maybe she could make a real difference in Tito's life when

THE MILLIONAIRE'S
Convenient ARRANGEMENT

he was finally released in a few months. She allowed herself to think for the first time that there might actually be a future for her and Ritchie.

After the silent auction closed, she walked over with Ritchie to congratulate Jonathon. A distinguished looking man was sitting at Jonathon's table beside a thin expensively dressed woman Maria recognized from the society pages as his wife. She felt the color drain from her face, and she forced herself to smile while Ritchie congratulated Jonathon on his winning bid.

Jonathon made introductions around the table, and Maria nodded numbly, wondering why it had never occurred to her that *he* might be here. Bradford Thornton. Partner at one of the most elite law firms in Miami. After all, this was his world, not hers.

Maria managed to maintain her composure as she assured Jonathon she'd be happy to help him decide the best spot to hang his new painting, then she excused herself. Yes, she should have known he might be at an event like this. But seeing him sitting at Jonathon's table was just too much.

Maria stood at the long marble counter in the ladies room, took several deep breaths, opened her small black clutch, and then freshened her lipstick. It was fine. No big deal. She'd just go back out to the table, find Ritchie, and put it out of her mind.

She stepped out of the restroom and felt a hand take her elbow.

"I need to speak with you."

It was *him*. Of course, he had followed her, waited for her.

"I have nothing to say to you. I had no idea you would be sitting at Jonathon's table."

"Really?" His grip tightened. "I don't believe in coincidences. What kind of a game are you playing?"

"Nothing. I'm not playing games. Just leave me alone."

"No, you leave me alone. It's bad enough you've ingratiated yourself into this event, and the Arts and Business Council project, by sleeping with Ritchie Perez.

"Oh, yes, I know all about that. How he called one of his friends on the council and set up a deal for his little plaything. No one on the council had ever even heard of you. Of course, I had to go along with it. Did you know I was a member when you convinced your lover to call in his favors for you? Or was that just a coincidence too?"

"What are you talking about? Ritchie didn't have anything to do with me getting that position." But even as she said the words, she realized they weren't true. Ritchie just hadn't *told* her.

"You're such a liar. And I suppose it's just another coincidence that Perez' partner paid a ridiculous amount for that painting of yours."

His gaze swept over her, and suddenly the dress she'd worn so proudly seemed cheap. She felt cheap.

"It's not that I don't know what Perez sees in you. You look exactly the same."

"Don't even go there."

"No, I'll tell you where you don't go. You leave *my* wife and *my* family alone. You'd be smart to avoid the kinds of events you could expect us to attend. I won't have you causing embarrassment to her." She just stared at him, and he added. "Oh, yes she knows all about you. You and that degenerate brother of yours. He's still in prison, isn't he?" He shook his head. "Pathetic.

"I told my wife about the…situation…years ago, and she understands that it was an indiscretion on my part. And something that should have been taken care of at the time."

"Taken care of? That's a horrible thing to say."

"It's a fact. A word of advice. Ritchie Perez has made a name for himself in this community. You get yourself pregnant in the hopes of latching onto a wealthy husband, and he'll toss you aside."

"Not everyone is as cruel as you."

"Or as naïve as you, apparently. Listen, you stay out of my life, and I don't care what little games you play with Perez. But you try to play games with me, and you'll be very sorry."

She felt a movement behind her.

"There you are. I thought you were having trouble finding your way back from the restroom." Ritchie looked from Maria to Thornton. "I wasn't aware you two knew each other."

"We've met before," Maria said. "If you'll excuse me." She had to get out of here. She walked toward the door, trying to pull her thoughts together.

In seconds, Ritchie was beside her, but she shrugged him off.

"Maria, what's the matter?"

"I have to leave."

"Maria, I'm sponsoring this event. It would be awkward for me to just leave before the evening is over."

"Well, I wouldn't want you to do anything awkward." She stepped through the doors and into the lobby. If Ritchie wouldn't leave, fine, she'd get a cab. Right now, Ritchie was the last person she wanted to be with anyway.

Bradford Thornton was right. She didn't belong here. She'd just been fooling herself. She thought she'd made this huge breakthrough in her art, seized this wonderful opportunity, but it wasn't real. All of it was just because of Ritchie. And he hadn't even had the decency to tell her. The clock was about to strike midnight and, like Cinderella's carriage, Maria was going to turn back into a pumpkin.

She ran out through the front doors, desperate for a breath of fresh air.

• • •

Ritchie caught up with her standing on the sidewalk, looking around for a cab. He grabbed her arm and spun her around.

"Would you tell me what's wrong?"

Her eyes were bright. "What's wrong? I'll tell you what's wrong. You let me think Vivienne arranged the opportunity with the Arts and Business Council. But it was you."

He sighed. Damn that Thornton. The man had always been an ass, but what motivation he would have had for discussing Ritchie's suggestion to his friend on the Arts and Business Council was beyond him. Some people just couldn't keep their nose out of other people's business.

Thornton was one of those old money snobs that Ritchie abhorred. Guys who made their money by inheriting it, and looked down on people who became successful because of honest hard work. His partner Jonathon came from the same kind of old money background. One of the things Ritchie admired about him most, however, was that he'd taken a different path from generations of Berringtons, moved from the exclusive Northeast enclave where he'd been raised, and made a name for himself in Miami on his own merits.

Ritchie knew Thornton considered him inferior because of his own

THE MILLIONAIRE'S
Convenient ARRANGEMENT

humble beginnings, and resented the influence Ritchie had developed with groups like the Arts and Business Council. He supposed that's why he'd apparently taken this opportunity to get in a few digs at Maria. He cursed himself for not just telling her in the first place, because it really wasn't a big deal.

"Look, I was just trying to – "

"I know what you were trying to do. Did it ever occur to you to ask me first?"

She was livid, and for the first time, Ritchie felt a twinge of fear. When the idea had occurred to him in Vivienne's studio, he'd just acted on it. And when Vivienne had called her in Bimini, Maria had been so thrilled about the whole deal that there was no need to tell her he'd had a hand in it.

"Look, come back inside. Then as soon as we get home tonight, we'll talk this all out."

"Home? You mean, your home. It's not my home. You talked me into quitting my job. For this opportunity that, it turns out, isn't even real."

"Of course it's real. You're being ridiculous."

"You set it up! Did the developer even come out and *look* at any of my pieces before he agreed? I'm betting not. Now you think I'm being ridiculous? Because I don't just fall in with your plans? Because it wasn't worth bothering to even ask me before you arranged everything? You've arranged Joey's life, and now you're arranging mine. Maybe you ought to try minding your own business."

"It's not like that," he said, but there was no stopping her.

"And another thing. I don't appreciate you getting your partner to pay a ridiculous amount for the painting I donated – that you convinced me to donate, because I didn't even choose the painting, did I? I'm spending the night at my apartment. Mine. You have a problem with that? Too bad. You don't get to arrange everything, Ritchie. You made a fool of me. It's obvious now that everyone here thinks the only reason I'm getting either of these opportunities is because I'm sleeping with you. Well, I've had enough."

Why couldn't she see that there was nothing wrong with using a few connections? No one was going to think less of her for it – except maybe that ass Thornton. Besides, anyone who looked at her paintings and

THE MILLIONAIRE'S
Convenient ARRANGEMENT

didn't know instantly that they belonged in a gallery was an idiot. Her sheer talent humbled him.

"Maria, I'm sorry. I should have talked to you first. And listen, about the painting – " But he could tell she wasn't hearing anything he said.

She turned back to the street. "Dammit, how hard is it to get a taxi around here!"

She looked like she was about to cry, and it broke his heart. How could he have gone so wrong when he was just trying to help her? What the hell was Thornton doing sticking his nose into Ritchie's private business?

More importantly, how the hell did that guy even know Maria? The conversation he'd interrupted had obviously been personal. It was clear she'd had some kind of relationship with him. She'd been a virgin the first time she slept with Ritchie, so at least Bradford Thornton wasn't an ex-lover. But the idea of any sort of sordid relationship between Maria and a man Ritchie considered a pompous ass turned his stomach. If he found out that asshole had sexually harassed Maria, Ritchie was going to clean his clock. But the first order of business was to get Maria out of here, give her a chance to calm down.

"Take the limo," he said, and signaled the driver.

"I told you, I'm not going back – "

"The driver will take you wherever you want. But Maria," he said, lifting her chin and forcing her to look him in the eye. "This conversation isn't over."

He opened the door and watched her slip into the back of the limo. This was a far cry from how he had expected this evening to end.

He tapped on the window and she rolled it down.

"You still didn't tell me how you know Thornton."

"Didn't I?" The look on her face was one of pure disgust. "He's my father."

Ritchie stared after the limo as it pulled away. For once in his life, he was utterly speechless.

Chapter Twenty-Two

It was strange walking back into her apartment. She didn't feel like the same person who had left it just a few short months ago. *This is your life, Maria,* she told herself. Not mansions on the water and charity galas and beach houses in Bimini. She didn't fit in Ritchie's world, and she'd been a fool to think she ever could.

And she didn't want to live in his world. Not when it was populated by people like the father who had never acknowledged her. People who were going to look at her and see just what he saw. On what should have been the most amazing night of her life, instead, she found out it was all an illusion. She'd thought she was donating her talent to support Ritchie's charity. But it turned out *she* was the charity case.

She walked into the bedroom that didn't feel like hers any more, and rummaged through the few remaining possessions in her drawers to find something to sleep in. At least she hadn't moved everything into Ritchie's house. She slipped out of the sleek black dress and pushed aside thoughts of how she'd imagined Ritchie would be peeling it off her after Joey was asleep in his room. She pulled on a pair of comfy boxers and an oversize t-shirt and texted Joey that she was staying at their old apartment tonight just to check up on things. There would be time enough tomorrow to figure out what to do. Then she crawled under the covers and shut out the world.

• • •

The next morning Maria woke up to sunlight streaming in the window. Her first thought was that this was the day she was supposed to visit Tito. Her second thought was how was she going to get from her apartment to Ritchie's house to pick up her car?

She went to the small kitchen to start the coffee then noticed something shoved under the door. She unfolded the piece of paper and found her car key inside. The note, in Ritchie's handwriting, said: *Call me. We have to talk.*

He must have dropped her car off sometime during the night. Sure enough, it was sitting right outside the building, in her old parking space. She didn't know what she was going to say to Ritchie. So as hard as it was going to be to put on a happy face and visit Tito, she was glad that commitment at least gave her a little time before she had to deal with a conversation with Ritchie that was probably going to break her heart.

At least, she no longer felt conflicted about her decision to follow Tito when he was released. She knew now that there just wasn't any future for her and Richie.

• • •

Unfortunately, Tito didn't like the idea of her and Joey coming with him anymore than he liked the idea of him staying in Miami.

She sat down across from him at the table in the visiting area and told the only person who would understand.

"I saw him yesterday."

"Who?"

"Our father. He was at the charity thing. I guess I should have expected it."

"Don't ever use that word to describe him. Our father was the man who raised us from age ten. That bastard was nothing but a sperm donor."

"You're right."

"That's what's got you so upset? Don't even pretend you're not. I knew the second you sat down something was bothering you."

"No. It's not that."

"So what's the matter?" His eyes narrowed. "It's Perez, isn't it?"

"Yeah."

Tito slapped his palm on the table, and a guard looked over. He took a deep breath and lowered his voice.

THE MILLIONAIRE'S
Convenient ARRANGEMENT

"What did he do?"

"Oh, God, Tito, I fell in love with him."

He leaned back in his chair. "And you're worried what I'm going to think about that? Look, it's your life. I'm over blaming him for putting me here."

"Since when?"

He shrugged. "You know how sometimes you tell yourself something so long you actually start to believe it?"

She shook her head. "But Ritchie Perez did put you in here. He's the one who refused to even consider a plea deal."

"Enough," Tito said. "I'm the one that put me in here, Maria. Me. Nobody else."

"You were just at the wrong place at the wrong time."

"Just stop it." He raised his voice, then glanced over at the guard and lowered it again. "I lied to myself, I lied to Mom, I lied to you, all these years. Because it was just easier. I knew about the drugs, I knew about the guns, I was part of all of it, Sis. Everything I was headed for was bad. Hell, by locking me up, Ritchie Perez probably saved my life." He drummed his fingers on the table.

"I'm a different man, now. And damned if I'm going to walk out of these doors carrying with me all that self-pitying, victim crap that's been weighing me down for the past eight years."

"What happened to you?"

"I finally grew up," he said simply. "For some of us it takes a little longer than for others." He shook his head. "Hearing how Joey was starting down that same path was a wake-up call. No way I want our little brother to ever end up in a place like this. I've wasted a lot of time blaming other people, including Perez, for my own stupid mistakes."

"I don't know what to think anymore."

"Well, think this: If it's guilt about me that's keeping you from building a life with the man you love, then you need to just let it go. We can't change the past, Maria. God knows I've lain awake enough nights wishing I could.

"If you want to be with Perez, you've got my blessing."

"It's not that easy. I found out some things he did behind my back."

His face hardened. "If he's cheating on you, then get the hell out of his house. I don't care how much he's helped Joey, you don't have to take that shit."

"No, it's nothing like that."

"So what is it?"

She sighed. "I thought I had this great opportunity with the Arts and Business Council to feature my paintings in a new condo development downtown, but it turns out it was a total set up. Ritchie arranged the whole thing, came up with idea of using an artist, and got them to pick me."

Tito stared at her. "Are you nuts?"

"What do you mean?"

"So, um, this is a *bad* thing he did? Helping you get the kind of opportunity you've always dreamed of?"

"He should have talked to me first," Maria said, frustrated that she couldn't get Tito to understand. "It's important to me to do things on my own."

Tito shrugged again. "Don't let your pride stop you from going after what you want."

If only things were that simple, Maria thought as she drove away from the prison. It was a good thing that Tito was taking responsibility for his actions. She'd read articles that said that was an important step in turning a life around for people in the criminal justice system. But she was having a hard time wrapping her mind around the fact that everything she'd believed about his arrest, his trial, his conviction had been so colored by her mother's absolute belief in Tito's innocence. And nothing Tito had ever said to her before today had changed that.

She still thought that there could have been a fairer outcome, that Ritchie should have offered a plea deal, that having a better defense lawyer might have made a difference. But if Tito had found peace with letting all those thoughts and issues go, then shouldn't she be able to do the same?

None of that, though, changed the fact that Ritchie had gone behind her back and set up the Arts and Business Council deal without ever consulting her. That he had let her believe it was Vivienne who led someone on the committee to discover her paintings and open the door for her to work with the developer. Tito might think it was no big deal, but, to her,

THE MILLIONAIRE'S
Convenient ARRANGEMENT

it mattered a lot.

And it didn't change the fact that Ritchie had gotten his partner to bid on her painting because he apparently didn't think a legitimate buyer would place a high enough bid. The bottom line was he didn't trust her to succeed on her own. How could she even consider having a relationship with a man who had so little faith in her?

Everything she'd achieved before this had been on her own. The art scholarship to Temple University had been the result of hundreds of hours of work building a winning portfolio. And later, supporting her mother through her illness. Convincing Vivienne to hire her on part-time, and then talking her way into a job at an exclusive South Beach restaurant when she had no experience at all as a server. Taking on responsibility for Joey, moving them out of the old neighborhood, earning the money to pay for the apartment and support the two of them.

She didn't have much to show for herself but her pride, and because of that, her pride meant everything to her. Not once had she asked for a handout. It was humiliating to have Ritchie just snap his fingers and take over her life, making decisions for her, putting her in a position where Bradford Thornton could look down his nose at her and make her feel so cheap and dirty.

Maybe she couldn't change the fact that she had fallen in love with Ritchie. But she could take back control of her life and Joey's. And if that meant things between her and Ritchie were over, then that's just the way it would have to be.

• • •

When she walked into the house, Ritchie was waiting for her.

"Look," he said, "I know we have a lot to talk about, but something's going on with Joey." He jerked his head toward the family room, where Joey was sitting staring at cartoons on the big screen TV.

Ritchie walked over and shut it off.

"All right, kid," he said. "We're both here now. What's the deal?"

Joey shifted his stare to Maria. "Where were you?"

"You know where I was – this is the Sunday I go visit Tito."

"Right." He clenched and unclenched his fists, then looked away from both of them and asked in a quiet voice, "Is it true?"

"Is what true?"

THE MILLIONAIRE'S
Convenient ARRANGEMENT

He shifted on the couch. "I knew you guys were going to be out late last night. I decided to go by the old neighborhood."

"Joey, I told you never to go back there."

"I saw some of the guys. I guess I was bragging some, about how I'm living now and shit." He looked at Ritchie. "And my friend Angel said he recognized your name, that you were some kind of a prosecutor. I told him he was crazy, you did accidents and stuff, and I knew that 'cause I got a job at your office.

"But Angel told me his brother said the prosecutor who put Tito away was named Ritchie Perez.

"I told him it has to be a different guy, right? I mean, there has to be a lot of lawyers named Perez."

He looked down. "But then I got thinking how when I had to go to court, it was like, everybody knew you and stuff. But then I just figured you're a big important lawyer, a partner at a fancy law firm. Of course, other lawyers and judges know you.

"So, it's not you, right? Just tell me you didn't put my brother in jail."

The combination of hope and fear in his eyes made Maria want to cry. She looked over at Ritchie.

"I'm sorry, kid. I used to work in the State Attorney's office. I prosecuted hundreds of gang members on drug and weapons charges. Your brother, Tito was one of them."

"No!" Joey yelled. "No! I don't believe it." Hot tears ran down his flushed cheeks. "How could you do that?"

"Like I said, I prosecuted a lot of people. After you told me about your brother at the baseball game, I went back and looked it up."

"You had to look it up? You didn't even remember him? You ruined his life and you *don't even remember?*"

"I hoped it wasn't me. I didn't want it to be me, but I prosecuted a lot of people, Joey. People who were arrested for breaking the law. You're upset, and I understand that."

"You don't understand anything."

"Your brother broke the law, and he went to prison for it. That's how things work. I wish it wasn't true, but it is."

"You're a liar!" Joey screamed. "You lawyers are all liars! My mom

THE MILLIONAIRE'S
Convenient ARRANGEMENT

told me how she paid that lawyer all that money who was supposed to help Tito but he didn't, and it was because of you! You didn't give him a chance! But I'll make you pay, just wait and see. Liar! Liar! Liar!"

"Joey, stop." Maria took a step toward him, and he spun back toward her, his face incredulous.

"You're on his side?" He stared at her, and then his eyes went dark with anger. "You knew, didn't you? You knew what he did, and you let us move in here and you did it with him! I know you're sleeping with him," he choked out, "I'm not some stupid little kid. I've seen you go in his room at night when you thought I was asleep."

"Joey, it isn't what you think. It's complicated."

"It seems simple to me. You don't care about Tito. You just want to play with your paintings and quit your job, and you're just screwing him so he'll buy you stuff and you can live in this fancy house and go to fancy parties."

The accusation, coming from Joey, took her breath away. Her entire body went cold.

"Joey, that's not true."

"It is! You're just a lousy whore!"

Her hand flew out, and before she realized what was happening, she had slapped Joey across the face. He stood there in shock, his eyes wide, frozen.

"Joey, I – "

"I'm going to wait until Tito gets out of jail," he said, sobbing now, "and I'm going to live with him, and I'm never going to see either one of you again. And I meant what I said, Maria. Go ahead and hit me again. I don't care." He mouthed the word *whore* and stood there, defiantly.

Ritchie stepped toward him. "All right, Joey, that's it. Get up to your room and stay there until you can discuss this rationally. And you use that word to your sister one more time and you'll have me to deal with."

"It's not my room. It's not my house. It's not my anything. I don't have to listen to you and your stupid rules, Ritchie. I wish you were dead."

Joey ran up the stairs, and a few moments later, they heard the door to his room slam. Ritchie turned to Maria.

"Maria. It's my fault. I should have told him."

THE MILLIONAIRE'S
Convenient ARRANGEMENT

She sank down on the couch and put her head in her hands. "How did we not see this coming?" She looked up at Ritchie. "I can't believe I hit him. His whole life, I never laid a hand on him before. Not once."

"If I'd been the one standing next to him, he'd have landed on his ass."

"You're just saying that to make me feel better. You're the most controlled person I've ever met." She sighed. "I just wish he hadn't found out this way."

"Look, it was a long time ago. I always thought I'd have time to sit him down some day and explain it all. Since he doesn't visit Tito, who was going to tell him? We've been keeping such a tight leash on him, I didn't think he'd end up back in the old neighborhood. And the one time we cut him a little slack . . ."

"I saw Tito today." She paused. "We talked. Really talked. He doesn't blame you."

Before he could comment, she continued. "And before you say anything, I know you think of course it wasn't your fault, you were just doing your job, being tough on crime. But what you have to understand is that for all these years, I've really believed that Tito was just in the wrong place at the wrong time, and you railroaded him through." She took a deep breath. "Tito told me today that he wasn't so innocent after all, and that he's accepted responsibility for what put him there.

"I still think with that being his first offense and everything, he shouldn't have gone to prison, but if Tito is letting it go, then I guess I have to, as well."

"Come on," Ritchie said. "Let's sit out back. It's time for you to tell me."

"Tell you what?"

"About your...father."

She took a deep breath and let it out slowly. "Ok."

They walked out across the terrace and leaned against the railing, looking out over the water.

"My father – if you can really call him that – was a senior at a fancy prep school. My mom was there on scholarship because she was a talented artist."

"That's where you got your talent."

THE MILLIONAIRE'S
Convenient ARRANGEMENT

"That's right. Anyway, she met him and fell in love and thought he was in love with her too." Maria shrugged. "Maybe he was. He was young and was defying his parents to even date her. He took her to the prom her junior year. He got her pregnant. When she went to him, he said he'd marry her."

"But it didn't work out that way?"

"No. It didn't. Instead of a wedding ring, he gave her money for an abortion," Maria said bitterly. "She'd disgraced her family. But she was a good Catholic girl, and an abortion was out of the question. He promised he'd come back for her. Once he got out of his parent's house, went to college. He talked about a trust fund. How they'd be together."

"But it never happened."

"No. She waited a long time. She called him when she was going into labor. And later, after Tito and I were born. He never came."

Maria was quiet for a moment then continued. "She used to show me pictures of him when I was a little girl. In the society pages. She said it was important to know where I came from, even if he didn't acknowledge us. She only ever spoke to him once more. When Tito was arrested. She went to him for help. She thought he would hire a lawyer for Tito. He broke her heart all over again."

"I've had a few dealings with him. I've always thought he was a bastard."

"You were right."

"But you'd met him before tonight."

"Once. I went to him when my mother was very sick. There was medicine she needed and we couldn't afford it. He wrote a check and said he never wanted to see me again. He treated it like it was blackmail. All he thought about was how embarrassing it would be to him personally and professionally if anyone found out his son was a criminal."

"I don't know what to say."

Maria shrugged. "The only real father I ever knew was Joey's dad. We struggled when we were growing up. My grandparents never forgave her for getting pregnant. The only happiness she ever had was when she met my stepdad. They got married when Tito and I were ten, and he always treated us like we were his own kids. Once Joey was born, things just got better and better. But it didn't last. He died of a heart attack. He never saw it coming. None of us did. It all happened so fast."

"I'm sorry."

"When he died, it hurt Tito and me so much. I threw myself into my art. Tito..."

"Tito went in another direction."

"He started hanging out with the gang in our neighborhood. He became sullen, withdrawn, not the same person. Maybe if I'd been paying more attention, instead of being so caught up in my own grief."

"Maria, you can't blame yourself."

"But I can make sure I'm paying attention this time. I can make sure Joey doesn't end up the same way Tito did. I have to."

"And I'll help you."

"I'm sorry, Ritchie. Can't you see it's not going to work?"

"Maria, I know you're upset about this thing with Joey, but it will blow over. He's a kid, and he's going to have to get past this."

"It's not that I don't appreciate everything you've done for him. I just can't... Ritchie, I can't have someone controlling everything in my life. Tito's planning to go to Texas once he's released. I think the best thing is if Joey and I go with him."

"We need to talk about this."

"Not tonight, Ritchie. Besides, I've made up my mind."

She went back upstairs and stood outside the door to Joey's room. She thought she heard the muffled sounds of him crying, but when she knocked on the door he just said, "Go away."

• • •

The next morning Joey wasn't speaking to her, which she supposed was an improvement over screaming insults at her like the night before. He sat across the counter, staring sullenly into his cereal bowl and doing his best to ignore her.

She had to try.

"Joey, you may not be ready to listen to this yet, but there are things you have to know. I'm sorry I didn't tell you about Ritchie. I know finding out the way you did was a shock."

"When I first realized who Ritchie was, I hated him too."

Joey glanced up for a second then looked away again.

"Look, Mom never wanted to believe anything bad about Tito —"

"But you're happy to, right? Because if Ritchie says it then it's okay."

She sighed. "Look, I love Tito. I'll always be there for him. But I've been wrong all these years to keep blaming other people for what happened. Tito told me he takes responsibility for everything."

"You're lying. You just want me to tell you it's okay for you to be Ritchie's girlfriend, but it's not. It's not, okay? I have to go to school." He pushed his cereal bowl back and grabbed his backpack.

He didn't speak to Maria on the drive to school, and when they got there, he reached to open the door, but she grabbed his arm before he could get out and waited for him to look at her.

"What?"

"Just think about what Ritchie meant to you before you found this out, okay? He's still the same person. And so am I."

Joey yanked his arm free and got out of the car, walking into the school courtyard without looking back.

Chapter Twenty-Three

The man sitting across the table from him looked familiar, but Ritchie figured it was more likely due to his resemblance to Maria and Joey than any recollection Ritchie had of prosecuting him. There had been so many. All gang members, with the same look of being older than their years, the same smirk on their faces. Tito was just one in an endless chain of defendants who had gone through the court system.

But Tito wasn't smirking. His eyes were steady, his face impossible to read.

"I wasn't sure you'd see me," Ritchie said.

Tito gave him a level gaze. "Like I've got so many more interesting things to do with my time."

"Maria's told you we're involved."

"That's why you're here? I already told her I'm cool with that."

"That's only partly why I'm here." Ritchie wasn't sure he believed what he was about to say, but he was taking the leap for Maria. If they were going to have a future together, he was going to have to meet her half way. And that meant allowing for the possibility that he might have misjudged her brother.

"Look, if it makes any difference to you, I saw everything as black and white back then. But I'm thinking now sometimes things are a little gray. I'm thinking you did get a raw deal. I could have taken the time to meet with your lawyer, find out if there were extenuating circumstances."

"Yeah, well, what difference does it make now? Like I told Maria yesterday, I'm done with blaming other people for my mistakes. Did you take a hard line on my case? Yeah. But I'm the one who put myself in that courtroom. Look, I've missed out on every opportunity I could have had. I caused my mother so much sadness. And I couldn't even be there when she died. I left Maria stuck with all the responsibility for our mom and then for Joey.

"All I've done is hurt the people I love. When I get out of here, I'm going to get as far away from the two of them as I can. That's the best thing – the only thing – I can do to help them."

"Well, Maria says she's going with you."

Tito shook his head. "Not gonna happen."

He looked up. "Thanks for everything you're doing for Joey. It more than makes up for...anything else."

Ritchie nodded. "He's not too happy with me right now."

"Somebody finally told him you're the prosecutor?" Tito shook his head. "I told Maria she was crazy to think the kid was never going to figure that out."

"He's not too happy with her at the moment either."

Tito shrugged. "He'll get over it. Kid's got nobody else."

"That's not true."

"Shit, you think I'm a role model?"

"Depends on what you do with yourself once you get out of here."

"Like I told Maria, a guy I know has an uncle with an auto body shop in Texas who's willing to give me a chance."

"You'd get out earlier if you got into the work release program here in Miami. And you'd have a job waiting for you when you got out." Ritchie leaned back in his chair and studied Tito. "I checked your disciplinary record. You're totally clean. No question you'd qualify for work release."

"Yeah, well there's one big problem. Who the hell's gonna offer a guy like me a job?"

There wasn't any sound but the clock ticking on the wall. If he were wrong, he'd be putting his partners and his firm on the line, too.

"Me," Ritchie said.

• • •

Maria got off the elevator and stepped onto the polished floor of the law firm's lobby. She was hoping to catch Richie in the office, since her call had gone directly to voicemail. The least they could do was come up with a plan of action for when Joey got home from school today.

The receptionist looked up and smiled. "Miss Martinez, I'm sorry, Mr. Perez isn't in the office. Was he expecting you?"

Just then Jonathon walked past the large conference room behind the reception desk and saw her.

"Maria – come on back if you have a minute. I want to show you something."

She followed him down the hallway uncertainly. "I wanted to say thank you for placing that bid. It was way over the top." After all, it wasn't his fault Ritchie had pressured him to pay an outrageous sum for her painting. The least she could do was be gracious.

He glanced back over his shoulder. "Worth every penny. Here we are," he said, gesturing her into an office that was as spacious as Ritchie's, with an equally stunning view of the Miami skyline. But that's where the similarity ended. He came from old money, and she'd expected old-style elegance. Instead, everything was sleek and modern. The surface on his oval desk shown like polished ebony. She stepped in and turned and...there it was. It the midst of all the stylized furnishings and spectacular views, her painting was the focal point.

"I came in last night to hang it. I know the logical place would have been on the wall behind my desk. But I wanted to be about to look at it while I'm working."

"I'm..." *Speechless,* she thought.

"What, didn't you think I was going to put it up in here? Frankly, I spend more time at the office than at home, so this was the best place for it. And it reminds me what my reward is for working this hard."

"It reminds you?" She sounded like an idiot, parroting his words.

"That in ten minutes, I can be there," he said, gesturing to the painting. "On my boat."

"Oh." It was starting to become clearer to her now. "My painting reminds you of your boat. That's why you wanted it."

THE MILLIONAIRE'S
Convenient ARRANGEMENT

Jonathon looked at her and chuckled. "You seriously don't know?"

"Know what?"

"Maria, that painting doesn't *remind* me of my boat. It *is* my boat." He walked closer to the painting. "And that splash of color you captured in a red windbreaker at the helm is me."

What? It was actually Jonathon's boat? She made a conscious effort not to stare at him with her mouth hanging open.

"I had no idea. What are the odds that when I was sitting on the shoreline with my sketchpad, it would be your sailboat cutting across Biscayne Bay?"

He laughed again. "Pretty good odds, at least, if you listen to my partners. Sometimes they accuse me of spending more time on that boat than anything else."

"That's why you paid so much." And why Ritchie had looked like the cat that ate the canary when he suggested she contribute this particular piece – one of her favorites – to the charity auction.

"Well, I couldn't have anyone else walking out of there with it, now could I? Plus, it was a good cause, and I was planning on donating anyway. In return, I got something priceless."

"I think it looks perfect in here." Her phone buzzed, and she frowned then looked apologetically at Jonathon. "I'm sorry, I have to take this. It's Joey's school."

Within seconds, her day got a whole lot worse. She hung up the phone and turned to Jonathon.

"Sorry, I've gotta run."

"Is there a problem at Joey's school?"

"Joey's gone."

"He cut class?"

She nodded.

"Look, don't be too upset. Kids cut class all the time."

"No, you don't understand. He found out something…very upsetting last night, and he wouldn't even talk to me when I dropped him off. I've got to go find him." She started for the door, but Jonathon stepped in front of her, reached out and took hold of both her shoulders, and looked her in the eye. Her heart was pounding and she knew she looked like an idiot, getting this upset.

THE MILLIONAIRE'S
Convenient ARRANGEMENT

"I have to go now."

"Look, I don't know what's going on between you and Ritchie, but I don't think you should go running out of here by yourself." He picked up his phone, hit speed dial, shook his head, and then pressed end. "Still going straight to voicemail."

He turned back to Maria. "He said he had something to take care of this morning. Hard to imagine where he would go and shut off his phone.

"Where do you think Joey is?"

"I'm pretty sure he'll head back to the old neighborhood."

He nodded. "Well, then, let's go."

"Wait, you want to come with me?"

"From what I understand, that's a rough neighborhood."

"I grew up there."

"And you moved out because it changed, right?"

When she just nodded, he said. "I think the sooner we go find your brother and get him out of there, the better."

They checked Maria's apartment first, just in case, then headed over to the old neighborhood. As they drove up and down the streets, she realized she had no idea where Joey had hung out with his friends, where he'd ended up all those times he'd snuck out at night before she'd managed to sell the old house.

She pointed as they drove by, and Jonathon slowed down. "That's where I grew up."

It hurt to see her mother's flower garden already getting overgrown, the front porch paint starting to peel. The new owners didn't have the pride in the property that her mom had had. But no one else in the neighborhood did either, not anymore.

She saw someone she knew a few doors down. "Stop here. I went to high school with that guy. No, just wait," she said, as Jonathon pulled to a stop and started to open the door.

She slipped out of the sleek sports car and walked toward the stoop.

"Hey, Carlos."

"Nice ride, chica. You slummin' today?"

Carlos used to be a funny kid. She'd sat behind him in 10th grade algebra. Before he dropped out and started just hanging around the neighborhood, getting high, selling drugs. It looked like nothing much had changed in his life in the past ten years.

"I'm looking for Joey."

"Yeah, I saw him and that kid Angel around earlier with Angel's brother and some guys."

"Angel's brother? You mean Gino?" That wasn't good. Gino had been in and out of the system since he was just a kid. And he was part of the gang Tito had gotten involved with.

"Who else?"

"So you know where they went?"

Carlos shrugged and moved down the steps toward her. "I mind my own business. Nobody around here now, so how 'bout you come in and have a beer with me?"

"No, thanks."

"What, too good for the old neighborhood now? He reached out and grabbed her arm. "Come on in with me, and we'll wait and see if Joey shows up."

Maria jerked her arm free, just as she heard the car door open. Jonathon came up behind her. She glanced over and caught her breath. Jonathon didn't look like the laid back, rich lawyer he'd seemed before. There was steel in his look, and she saw something flicker in Carlos' eyes.

"You have a problem?" Jonathon asked, and Carlos took a step back.

"No problem, man." Carlos looked at Maria. "You come back some time without your fancy boyfriend, Maria. We'll talk about old times."

"Hey," he called after her as she got in the car. "Tell Tito to come around when he gets out."

Not likely, Maria thought.

As they drove away, Jonathon asked, "Did you find out anything?"

"Joey was here, but Carlos either didn't know where he went, or just wasn't saying. I don't know where to look next."

"You think he might have gone back to Ritchie's?"

"I don't know what to think. Joey doesn't answer his phone. Ritchie doesn't answer his phone. I don't know where to look."

"It'll all work out."

"No, it won't. I never should have gotten involved with Ritchie."

"Are you kidding me? You and that kid are the best thing that ever

THE MILLIONAIRE'S
Convenient ARRANGEMENT

happened to him." Jonathon's phone rang.

He handed his phone to her. "It's Ritchie."

What he told her made her stomach clench.

"Oh my God. We're on the way." She hung up the phone. "Take me to Ritchie's house."

"You got it." The sports car accelerated, and they were there in minutes.

Jonathon touched her arm as he turned the car toward the driveway. "You want me to come with you?"

"No, I . . . thanks, but Ritchie said I should just come in, at least until the police leave."

He nodded. 'Okay."

The car had barely come to a stop before she flew out of the door and ran past the police cars to find Ritchie.

She stepped in the front door. Ritchie was standing in the kitchen talking to one of the policemen. The house was trashed. And Joey was nowhere in sight.

Maria started forward to ask about Joey, but Ritchie caught her eye and shook his head. She took a deep breath. Ritchie knew something and whatever it was, he didn't want the police to know.

She went into the living room and sat down on the couch and waited. It seemed like forever before the police left, promising to contact Ritchie if they got any leads.

Finally, Ritchie walked over to her.

"Seems like Joey and his 'friends' had a little party here that got out of hand. He called me. I told him to get out and stay out until the police were gone.

"But where is he?"

The door opened to the terrace and Joey walked into the room.

Chapter Twenty-Four

"I didn't mean to do it." Joey was crying. "I'm sorry, Maria. I'm sorry, Ritchie. It's all my fault."

The kid looked terrified. Good, Ritchie thought. Because what he'd done was enough to land him in a juvenile detention center. If Joey had been here when the police arrived, he'd have been back in front of the same judge who'd only reluctantly released him into Ritchie's custody in the first place.

The second Joey called, Ritchie hadn't thought twice; he'd just told him to get out of there and stay out until the police left. Then Ritchie had called 911 and gotten there as fast as he could.

Ritchie's house was trashed, and the breakage and theft ran into tens of thousands of dollars. But that wasn't the worst of it.

"I tried to stop them, I swear I did." Joey was staring at the floor.

"Look at me." Ritchie's voice didn't allow any room for disobedience, and Joey looked up.

"Do you realize what might have happened to your sister if she came home alone and those gangbangers had still been here?"

Joey swallowed, and looked back down at the floor. He still hadn't looked at Maria.

"Answer me!"

"Yes, sir. I know."

Ritchie nodded. "I guess you do."

Maria got up from the couch, started over, but Ritchie waved her back. "Let me handle this."

"He's my brother."

"And he'd be your brother if you were lying there on the floor, raped and maybe dead."

Her face paled, but she stood her ground.

"He's my brother," she repeated.

Ritchie turned to face her. "Maria, you have to trust me here. Now, sit down there on the couch and let me handle this. Please."

"I'm sorry, Ritchie," Joey said again.

"I know you're sorry, kid. But the thing is, I have to decide what to do about this." And he knew in that moment that he'd do whatever it took to protect him. Joey was a good kid. A good kid who had made a bad mistake. And he'd made that mistake despite all the sports and supervision and Ritchie's own influence. Because sometimes kids made the wrong choice. If they were lucky, they didn't end up paying for that choice for the rest of their lives.

"I'll tell," Joey said. "I'll make a list of names to give to the cops when they get here."

"The police already left, Joey," Ritchie said.

"I'll do the right thing. Like you told me before, I have to tell the truth."

Ritchie squatted down in front of him. "Here's the thing, Joey. You know and I know those guys are part of a gang from your old neighborhood."

Joey nodded. "Yes sir."

"And since they were already out of here when the police arrived, and apparently nobody in the neighborhood saw anything that would identify them, if you give their names to the police they're going know it was you."

"I know."

"What do you think happens to you then?"

"Somebody's gonna stick me with a knife when I'm in juvie." Joey's lower lip trembled, but he was making a visible effort to hold back the tears.

"You aren't going to juvie."

"But –"

THE MILLIONAIRE'S
Convenient ARRANGEMENT

"Stop talking and sit down, and I'll tell you what's going to happen."

Ritchie could hear Maria crying quietly over on the couch, but his focus was on Joey.

"First, as much as I hate to let these guys get away with this, we're not going to make you a target, so that's that. We'll change the security here at the house, and I'll ask some guys I know on the police force to keep an eye on our street for awhile until we're sure those guys aren't coming back."

Joey jumped up. "You're just gonna let them get away with it?"

"You don't want to push me right now, Joey. I told you to sit down and keep your mouth shut, and I'm not going to tell you again."

"Yes sir." Joey sank back down onto the chair. He look scared shitless. And he should be.

"They may trip up fencing some of that stuff, or maybe they'll just go down for some other crime. That's not what I care about."

He gave Joey a look that had him shriveling up in the chair.

"Which brings me to you."

The kid stared back at him with hound-dog eyes, looking like he thought he was about to be sentenced to death.

"First of all, you are grounded a month. In fact, I'll take your cell phone right now." Ritchie held out his hand. Joey stared at him, looking confused, and Ritchie realized the kid had assumed Ritchie was going to throw him out.

"Now," Ritchie ordered, and Joey scrambled to get the phone out of his pocket and handed it over.

"When you get it back, all your old contacts are going to be gone. And you're not going to have any more communications with anyone from your old neighborhood. Ever. Do I make myself clear?"

Joey nodded.

"I would take away your video game systems and your laptop, but your former friends seem to have already solved that problem by cleaning out every piece of electronics in the house."

"They weren't my friends," Joey muttered then apparently remembered he wasn't supposed to be talking, and he quickly clamped his hand over his mouth, looking up at Ritchie with big eyes.

"That's right," Ritchie said. "They weren't your friends. From now on, I approve your friends. And if I get a bad vibe about anyone you're even thinking about hanging out with, you cut it off right there. Understand?"

"Yes sir."

"That won't be a problem for the next month because you won't be having any friends over here, and you won't be going anywhere except to school, and to my office, where you will either be doing your homework or doing whatever job anybody in my office asks you to do. Got that?"

"Yes sir." The kid looked like he wanted the chair to open up and swallow him. Sure, he'd been terrified of going to juvenile detention and having to face the same judge who'd warned him to stay out of trouble. But he was probably almost as upset at the prospect of living under the authority of the man who'd sent his brother to prison. The kid would just have to get used to the idea. Because Ritchie wasn't going anywhere.

"You've made it clear by your words and your actions, Joey, what you think about me. Too bad. That's your problem."

Joey opened his mouth, but Ritchie held up his hand.

"I'm not done talking." Ritchie paused. "I don't think I have to tell you how disappointed I am with the way you behaved. But at least you called me when you realized how out of hand things had gotten. I don't plan to continue with this temporary quasi-official guardianship over you that the Judge appointed me to," Ritchie said, and he saw a panicked look cross Joey's eyes and realized Joey thought this meant Ritchie was done with him. Not by a long shot.

"Since I intend to marry your sister as soon as she'll have me, and since she's already your legal guardian, the simplest thing would be for me to just adopt you." He heard Maria make a strangled noise, but kept his eyes on the kid.

Joey stared at him, the shock plain on his face.

"You want to...be my dad?"

"I love Maria, and I love you, and no boneheaded idiotic stunt like you just pulled is going to change that. Having a hardass like me as a father may be your worst nightmare right now, but –"

"It's not! It's not!" Joey yelled, jumping up out of the chair. "I want you to be my dad. I love you, Ritchie! I got so mad 'cause I didn't want it to be true, but I didn't mean all that stuff I said. I didn't mean it, Ritchie." Joey took a few steps toward Ritchie, and then stood there like he didn't know what to do. Ritchie solved it by closing the gap between them and pulling the kid into a hug. Joey's arms tightened around him, and something in Ritchie's chest felt like it was going to explode. The adoption was just a formality. Joey was already his son in every way that mattered. They stood there, just hugging really hard and not saying anything until Maria's voice broke in coolly from across the room.

"Is that what you consider a marriage proposal, Ritchie? Because I think we have a few things to talk about."

• • •

Maria took a deep breath and tried to battle through the mixture of gratitude, shock, and frustration that had her senses reeling. Ritchie released a teary-eyed Joey, then walked a few steps to the side of the room and leaned against the kitchen island, watching her.

"Before you say anything, I want to thank you for what you just did for Joey. I can never repay you for everything you've done for both of us."

"Dammit, Maria!" Richie slammed the palm of his hand down on the counter. He looked over at Joey, who was staring at him with wide eyes. "You. Up to your room. Now."

"Yes, sir," Joey said, and headed up the stairs. But Maria was pretty sure he'd be listening to everything from the landing.

"I know you think you have to do everything for yourself. You're pissed off at me for contacting the Arts and Business Council. Well, that's just too bad."

"You didn't have any right – "

"Any right to what?" he asked, cutting her off. "Any right to walk into Vivienne's loft and be absolutely blown away by the talent I saw leaning against the wall, just waiting to be discovered? Maria, what difference did it make if it was me or some patron of Vivienne's who walked in there? Anyone would have had the same reaction. And I'd just been to one of the high-end condos I've invested in downtown and saw some prominent artists' work displayed there and the idea hit me – why not team up-and-coming artists with the developers of more moderately priced condominiums? So I made a phone call. The Arts and Business

Council went for it."

"You should have asked me."

He sat down in a chair across from Maria and rubbed his hands through his hair.

"I'm so used to just doing things." He took a deep breath. "You're right. I should have asked you. I'm sorry."

He looked over at her. "When I see a way to help someone I love, I tend to take action. And I know you think I was behind Jonathon buying that painting, but – "

"I already talked to him today. I know it's his boat."

"And I admit, I should have explained that to you. I can't help it. I want to fix things for you. For both of you."

"I don't want you to make things easy for me. I want you to respect me."

"My God, you actually think I don't respect you? You gave up everything you'd worked so hard for, every dream you had, to come home and take care of your mother, and then you built a life around caring for your little brother. You've done an amazing job with Joey."

"Yeah, right," she said, gesturing at the trashed living room. "Here's the evidence of what a great stand-in mom I've been."

"Stop it. Joey made a bad decision and let his anger take the place of good judgment. But when it came right down to it – when he realized how out-of-control things were getting – he made the *right* decision and called me. He's a good kid. And he got that from you."

She could feel tears burning behind her eyes.

"Listen, Maria, I get that you want to do everything yourself. I get that your background makes you feel like you've got something to prove. Hell, I'm the same way. Which is even more the reason why I want to do things for you. I'm not used to having to explain myself, Maria.

"And I'm not used to admitting when I'm wrong." He got up, paced across the room, and then stood a few feet away, facing her.

"So I'm going to start now. I was wrong not to mention anything to you about the Arts and Business Council deal. I put you in a position where that scumbag Thornton could make you feel cheap. And I'm sorry for that."

"Ritchie – "

THE MILLIONAIRE'S
Convenient ARRANGEMENT

He held up his hand. "I've been wrong about a few other things, too. I was wrong to treat every gang member I prosecuted like they were all the same, not to take the time to consider whether, for a few of them, there was a better solution than locking them up for the maximum sentence. I was wrong about your brother Tito."

She gave a short laugh. "No, I was wrong. I love my brother, but I've been blind for years to the fact that Tito made choices that led to prison. I went to see him yesterday, and he told me he's taken responsibility for his mistakes. And he has nobody to blame but himself."

"Well, I went to see him this morning, and I think he deserves another chance."

"You went to see Tito? Why?"

"I didn't give him the chance eight years ago that I'd want someone to give my own brother, my own son, if he ended up on the wrong path." He lowered his voice, looked her in the eye. "I didn't give Tito the chance I'd want someone to give Joey."

Ritchie paused. "But I'm giving him that chance now."

"What do you mean?"

"He's eligible for a work release program if he has a job right here in Miami. Tito's willing to give it a shot, and I've offered him a job at my firm, working on client intake. It's not much, but it gives him a chance to stay here in Miami, maybe even go back to school, get a degree."

"You did that for me?"

"I thought I was doing it for you, for us, so we could be together. But I realized a few moments ago that I'm doing it because it's what's right. And it would be the right thing to do even if I'd never met you.

"Now, before you start yelling at me for jumping into this without talking it over with you first, I just want to say – "

Maria flew across the room and into his arms, laughing and crying at the same time. "I don't know how I can stay mad at you Ritchie Perez when everything you go about doing in the wrong way turns out to be exactly right."

"Well, there's one thing I want to do in the right way, starting now." He got down on one knee in front of her and pulled a jeweler's box out of his pocket. "I had this with me Saturday night, but things didn't turn out the way I expected."

THE MILLIONAIRE'S
Convenient ARRANGEMENT

"Ritchie, I – "

"Don't say anything yet. Maria, I'm hardheaded, opinionated, and stubborn. When I see something that needs fixed, I don't spend time talking about it, I just do it. I see a lot of things in black and white that maybe I should take a closer look at. I have a lot of faults, and nobody could point them out better than you.

"But in my whole life, I have never met a woman that mattered the way you do. I've never met another person I loved so much that being apart from them was like not breathing. When you said you couldn't be with someone who controlled things without discussing it first, I decided I'd have to change the way I do things."

"And your idea of changing the way you do things was to go see Tito and –"

"Okay, so change isn't easy, but I promise I'll try harder. And I need you to help me see that life isn't always black and white. That people *can* change. I need you because I love you, and I can't imagine my life without you and Joey in it. You are my pearl of great value, the love of my life. Maria, please, marry me."

He opened the small box, lifted out the sparkling ring, a vintage pearl ring surrounded by diamonds, in a setting that had withstood the test of time.

"Say yes!" Joey yelled from the staircase.

Maria looked into Ritchie's eyes, and suddenly, all the mistakes he'd made just pushing ahead and making decisions didn't seem so much like an attempt to control her. It was his way of trying to make her happy. And since she knew she was just as stubborn as he was, well, it seemed clear that both of them had met their match.

"I'll marry you, Ritchie, because as aggravating and frustrating as you make me feel sometimes, I can't imagine my life–and Joey's – without you in it. I love you, Ritchie. I want to spend the rest of my life with you. So, yes, I'll marry you."

Ritchie slipped the ring onto her finger, stood up, pressed her against him, and kissed her.

"It's about time!" Joey yelled as he flew down the steps and threw his arms around both of them.

Ritchie looked around the cluttered room. "Come on," he said. "Let's go out and get some dinner. Maybe stay in a hotel tonight until I can get a cleaning crew in here to put this place back together."

"Wait, I thought I was grounded," Joey said.

"Oh, you're grounded, kid," Maria said. "Starting tomorrow. Tonight, we celebrate."

Epilogue

Maria watched as Ritchie and Tito carried not one but two giant turkey platters in from the kitchen, setting up carving stations at both ends of the formal dining room. The table was already overflowing with every holiday dish imaginable. A year ago, she would never have believed it was possible that her brother and the man who put him in prison would be laughing and joking and sharing a meal together on Thanksgiving, surrounded by friends and family.

Ritchie's mom had caved to the pressure and brought the celebration to Ritchie and Maria's house, recognizing that there was no way to fit more than thirty people around her own dining room table. And she'd probably felt she owed them one, after nixing their plans for a simple wedding in Bimini in favor of a formal wedding at St. Theresa's and a huge reception. Maria had never been prouder than when Tito walked her down the aisle. And never happier than she was today, having all their family and friends together for Thanksgiving.

Even in Ritchie and Maria's expansive dining room, they'd had to spill over into the living room with a foldout table. But Maria had been more than happy to let Mama G rule the kitchen. Particularly since, at five months pregnant, she still had the occasional bout of morning sickness.

Olivia and Joey walked in just as everyone was getting ready to sit down to dinner.

"It's about time," Maria said, as JD and the various nieces and nephews swarmed Joey.

"Sorry," Olivia said. "You wouldn't believe how many people were there."

Maria had been surprised when Joey offered to help serve the noon Thanksgiving dinner at St. Theresa's. It hadn't been all that long ago that she'd had to practically drag him kicking and screaming every Wednesday night to volunteer feeding the homeless. That fact that he now not only went willingly, but that it was his own idea just showed how far he had come in the past year.

"Olivia," Maria said, "I saved you a seat right here in front of the tofu turkey. Joey, don't you dare turn on the Xbox, we're about to sit down to eat!"

After Joey's month of being grounded was over, Ritchie had replaced all the electronics that had been stolen or destroyed. Now, in the evenings, Maria and Richie would often relax by the pool, listening to the sounds of loud video games and shouting boys coming from the family room. Maria remembered how not so very long ago, she'd envisioned just such a scene – but it had been in her cramped apartment, and she'd been a single mom trying to raise Joey on her own.

Everyone sat down and held hands, connecting the two tables, as Ritchie's dad gave the blessing.

Maria was finishing her art degree right here in Miami, and would be graduating soon. Tito had settled in at Ritchie's firm and was fast becoming one of their most valuable employees. He'd taken over the lease on Maria's apartment, and had enrolled in a program at a local community college, taking evening classes and working on a degree in psychology that he hoped would help him realize his new dream – establishing a nonprofit diversion program for at-risk juvenile offenders. Ritchie and his partners had already committed to a significant financial contribution to help get the program off the ground, and they'd been surprised by a large check from an anonymous donor.

Maria's work with the downtown condo developer had been such a success that the Arts and Business Council had recommended her for additional projects, and her first showing at Vivienne's had received promising reviews. Ever since they'd found out she was pregnant, Ritchie had been almost obsessively pampering her. Vivienne wasn't any better, and she'd had to beg her to go ahead with the showing rather than postpone it until after her due date. Maria expected that she'd have a lot less time on her hands – and a lot less sleep – once the baby was born.

Vivienne smiled at her from across the table. "What are you thinking, darling?"

"Just how happy I am to be here with all of you, sharing Thanksgiving together."

"Well, cheers to that," Sam said, raising his glass, while deftly keeping it from being grabbed and spilled by Sophia, who would be turning two in just a few months, and was in her usual spot, perched on her Dad's lap.

"Let's hope this is the beginning of a long tradition of spending the holidays together," Ritchie added, grinning as his parents' bulldog poked a cautious head out from under the table, looking for a handout.

The only one who was missing was Jonathon, who'd decided to take advantage of the slow-down in work at the office over Thanksgiving to take his sailboat on a jaunt through the Caribbean.

Later that evening, when dinner was over and everyone had gone home, Ritchie stretched out on the wide chaise beside her, and they both looked out at the sunset.

"Who would have believed such a stubborn, independent, opinionated woman would ever fall in love with me?" he asked, as he gently kissed the side of her neck and rested his hand over her swollen belly.

Maria laughed. "Probably anyone who would have believed such a stubborn, hardheaded, opinionated man would fall in love with me."

She leaned her head against his shoulder and sighed. "I wouldn't have it any other way."

Turn the page for an excerpt from Book No. 1 in the *Miami Lawyers* series, *The Millionaire's Unexpected Proposal* (available now from Entangled Publishing), and following that, an excerpt from Book No. 3, *The Millionaire's Intriguing Offer*, coming in 2017 from Mr. Media Books.

One night together will change his life forever...

THE MILLIONAIRE'S
unexpected
PROPOSAL

a Miami Lawyers novel

Jane Peden

Prologue: The Millionaire's Unexpected Proposal

Sam Flanagan was on top of the world. Two weeks ago he'd won his biggest jury trial ever, defending a multimillion-dollar product liability case.

Five days after the jury returned its verdict for the defense, he cashed his bonus check and turned in his resignation. Now he was spending three glorious weeks in Las Vegas. When he returned, the new office in one of Miami's high-rises would be decorated, furnished, and staffed, and the law firm of Flanagan, Berrington & Perez would officially open its doors for business.

But for now, Sam deserved to cut loose and have a little fun.

He took the elevator from his luxury suite to the lobby of the casino hotel and walked into the lounge. He took one quick look at the cool blonde seated alone at the bar and complimented himself on making the right decision.

The answer to how he was going to spend his first evening in Vegas was sitting right there at the bar. Short skirt, long legs, silky sleeveless blouse, and an air of class about her that made a man look twice and wonder if he could get lucky. And know that it would be well worth the effort.

She glanced around the room, her classically beautiful face expectant, not as if she were waiting for someone in particular but rather as if she were waiting for something interesting to happen. Her hair was cut in a sleek style just past her chin. She reached up and tucked a few strands behind her ear, revealing the long and lovely line of her neck, before she turned back to her drink and said something to the bartender.

Sam slid onto the barstool next to her. He ordered a beer, turned to her, and smiled.

"I'm wondering if you could help me out?"

She angled her chin toward him and raised an eyebrow, her expression cool. She had to be wearing contacts. No one's eyes were that blue.

"I'm sorry, have we met?" Her voice was as cool as her demeanor, and it made him want her more.

"Sam Flanagan," he said, and reached out his hand.

She hesitated, then put her hand in his. Her grip was firm but her skin was soft. He held her hand a second longer than necessary, then released it.

"May I ask your name?"

She hesitated again, then said, "Camilla."

"Just Camilla?"

"I don't give my last name to men I meet in bars. Not even in Vegas."

Maybe that explained the trace of nerves he was sensing. He prided himself on being able to read people, and this was a woman who, despite her cool exterior, had just a hint of strain beneath the surface. Instead of flashing warning signals, it intrigued him.

He put some money on the bar, waved away the glass, and took a long drink from the icy cold bottle.

"Well, you know what they say about Vegas."

"What happens here stays here?" she asked, and he nodded.

"I'm counting on it," she said.

Now that was interesting. Was she running away from something? And he questioned again why such a sophisticated and beautiful woman was alone in a hotel bar. She definitely had his interest now. He leaned in a little closer.

"So will you help me?"

She shifted on the stool, crossing those long, elegant legs. When she raised her gaze to meet his, he was struck again by the beauty of her electric blue eyes. And the sudden heat that seemed to fill the small space between them. He knew she felt it, too. And was almost as good as him at masking her reaction.

"What exactly is your problem?" Her voice was still cool, but she broke eye contact and reached for her wineglass, running her fingers down the stem for a moment before lifting it slowly to her lips.

"My friends have both canceled. Which means I'll be eating dinner alone."

"You don't like your own company?"

He extended his hands, palms up. "It's just that they always give a lone diner the worst table."

She looked him over. "I'm sure you've never been put at a bad table in your life."

You'd be surprised, he thought, but his answer was smooth to his own ears. "Wouldn't it be terrible if I started tonight? Especially when I was supposed to be celebrating." He gave her his best "innocence tinged with sadness" look.

"Okay, I'll bite. What are you celebrating?"

"Fresh starts."

That seemed to get her attention.

"Really." She gave him a look that reminded him of 1940s movie stars, sultry and icy at the same time. She had a restrained sensuality Sam couldn't wait to unleash.

"Really. And what are you doing here, alone?"

"Actually, I'm on the run."

He glanced around the room. "Should I get my gun?"

"Do you have one?"

"No." He leaned closer. "What are you running from?"

She laughed. "At the moment, the spa where I've spent the last three days."

"So an army of spa workers is searching the Strip for you?"

Her eyes narrowed. "How do I know you aren't a deranged killer? You could be wondering how much time you have."

He pulled out his wallet and extracted his driver's license and a newly printed business card, pausing to write *Camilla is safe with me* and signing his name and the date on the back of the card before setting them both on the table in front of her. She picked them up, read the back of the card and smiled, then handed him back his license.

THE MILLIONAIRE'S
Convenient ARRANGEMENT

"Looks legit. What happens if I call the number on the card?"

"The answering service will tell you we open for business in three weeks."

"Good thing I don't have a pressing need for legal services."

She tapped the business card against the smooth wood on the surface of the bar.

"I gave my treatment schedule to a willing victim. No one will even know I'm gone." She grinned. "Slap enough mud and seaweed on naked female bodies, and it's pretty hard to tell any of us apart."

He held his finger up so she'd pause. "Sorry, just needed a moment to process that image."

She laughed, the sound bubbling out of her, sweet and fresh, and suddenly she looked like a girl barely out of her teens. He'd pegged her in her midtwenties, close to his age, when he'd first spotted her at the bar. Now he wasn't so sure.

Time to close the deal. "You're alone. I'm alone. We could have dinner at two separate tables. Pitied by waiters. Or we could enjoy the evening together. It's as simple as that."

"How do you know I'm not waiting for someone?"

"Maybe you were waiting for me."

She laughed and shook her head. "That's a really bad line."

"Have dinner with me and I promise to do better."

He could almost see her mind working, considering. Could read in her eyes that she was weakening, the same way he could always read a jury.

"It's just dinner," he prompted.

"I'm not leaving the hotel with you," she said, and he knew he had her. It was only a matter of time until she was in his suite.

"We'll have dinner right here at the hotel," he assured her.

He took her hand to help her off the barstool, then rested his palm lightly for a moment on the smooth silk on the back of her shoulder as he guided her out of the lounge and toward the nearby restaurant. Las Vegas was a town that was built on luck. And Sam was feeling lucky.

THE MILLIONAIRE'S *Convenient* ARRANGEMENT

Chapter One: The Millionaire's Unexpected Proposal

Five years later

The hot Miami sun beat down on Camilla as she shaded her eyes with her hand and looked up at the towering building. She stepped through the revolving door onto the marble floor and breathed in the crisp air-conditioning. She would never have come here if she had any other choice. *Desperate times call for desperate measures*, she thought, squaring her shoulders and steeling herself. It was, after all, the story of her life. And Danny—the man she'd married for all the wrong reasons and ended up loving for all the right ones—was hardly going to swoop in and save her this time. Or ever again.

The elevator whooshed her soundlessly to the fortieth floor, its doors opening directly into the impressive lobby of the firm. Camilla hesitated for a moment, then ruthlessly suppressed the urge to ride back down to the lobby. Her heels clicked as she walked across the polished wood floor toward the reception area.

The receptionist was a middle-aged woman, impeccably groomed and tastefully formidable.

"May I help you?"

"Yes, I'd like to see Sam Flanagan."

She frowned slightly. "And you are?"

"Camilla Winthrop."

THE MILLIONAIRE'S
Convenient ARRANGEMENT

She looked at her computer screen, then back at Camilla.

"I'm sorry. I don't seem to have you listed on Mr. Flanagan's schedule. Let me call his assistant. Jennifer will be happy to set up an appointment for later this week."

"No."

The woman looked up, hand poised over the phone, and raised one perfectly arched eyebrow.

"It's urgent I see him today." *Before I lose my nerve.*

"I'm sure Mr. Flanagan's assistant will—"

"Just tell him…it's Camilla from Las Vegas."

"Camilla from Las Vegas."

"Yes." She reached into the pocket of her jacket and pulled out a card. "And give him this."

The receptionist frowned at the business card, flipped it over, then looked back at Camilla.

"Please take a seat and I'll check with Mr. Flanagan," she said finally.

Camilla was too nervous to sit. She walked to the window overlooking a view of the Miami skyline and wondered if she was crazy to just show up here, at his office, unannounced. The two weeks they'd spent together in Las Vegas seemed like a lifetime ago. What had started out as a casual fling had quickly meant so much more, at least to her. But obviously not to Sam. The memory of how coldly he'd ended things still stung.

By the time she'd realized she was pregnant she had already married Danny, going through with the plans that ensured that her younger sister would get the expensive medical care she needed. Still, she'd tried to contact Sam. When he didn't even bother to return her phone calls she knew that staying with Danny was the right decision, the *only* decision, for her sister and for her baby.

• • •

Sam was pacing in his office, fine-tuning the closing argument he would give to the jury when the case reconvened the next morning. His secretary's voice came through the intercom, jarring him back into the present.

"Mr. Flanagan? I'm sorry to interrupt you, but—"

THE MILLIONAIRE'S
Convenient ARRANGEMENT

It better be important. "Jen, I asked you to hold all my calls."

"I know but—" She lowered her voice. "Can I come in?"

"Sure." Whatever crisis it was now, he'd just have to get past it.

Jen slipped into the office and shut the door firmly behind her.

"There's a woman in the reception area who is insisting that she see you today."

"What's her name?"

"Camilla Winthrop."

He frowned. "I don't recall anyone by that name."

"She says she's from Las Vegas. And she had one of your cards. But it looks like the old ones."

He held out his hand, flipped the card over, read the inscription. The fact that his expression didn't change was a testament to his finely honed ability to hold a poker face whenever damaging evidence was presented by the other side at trial.

"Send her in."

He walked over to the window, frowning as he gazed out at the panoramic view of Miami afforded by his corner office. They were in the same office tower where they'd started out five years ago. But now, instead of a suite of offices they'd sublet from another tenant, their firm had taken over the entire floor. He flipped the card idly between his fingers.

Camilla. Camilla Winthrop. He realized with a start that he hadn't even known her last name. He'd spent the most amazing two weeks of his life with her. Had actually thought he might be falling for her. And then realized it was time to back off fast. The last thing he'd needed before starting his new firm was to be distracted by an entanglement with a woman he met in a bar in Las Vegas. So he'd cut his trip short. He winced when he remembered their awkward last breakfast, in the dining room of the resort hotel, overlooking the glitter of Vegas. The way she looked when he said it was probably better if they just said good-bye. He'd watched the warmth fade from her eyes, replaced by the cool reserve that had first drawn him to her in the bar. *That's fine, Sam,* she'd said. *As it happens I have plans of my own.*

For a while he'd regretted leaving so abruptly and had hoped she'd contact him. She had his business card, but he didn't have a clue where

THE MILLIONAIRE'S
Convenient ARRANGEMENT

she was from. It was only afterward that he realized that when they weren't making love, they'd talked about *his* plans, *his* future. Maybe the fact that she'd been such a complete mystery had added to the way the memory of those two weeks still haunted him.

He shook his head. He'd certainly never expected to hear from her five years later. Obviously, she was in some kind of trouble. And he didn't need this kind of distraction, regardless of how strong the pull of curiosity was.

He turned, sensing a movement in the doorway.

"Hello, Sam." His assistant retreated discreetly, closing the door behind her.

His first thought when Camilla walked across his office toward him was that she was even more stunning than he remembered. He felt, suddenly, as if someone had punched him in the gut. There was a large diamond on her left hand, and her clothes reflected understated elegance. Whatever her problems were, it didn't look like they were financial.

"Camilla." He kept his tone even.

He gestured to a visitor's chair and sat down behind his desk. She was still the picture of cool sophistication and class, even more so than the first time he'd ever seen her. He had a sudden flashback of her sleek blond hair mussed as he ran his fingers through it, those long legs tangled in the silky sheets, her porcelain skin flushed, her quick little intake of breath right before she...*Get a grip, Sam*, he told himself, and kept his face carefully without expression. There was some reason she'd shown up here today, and he doubted if it was to reminisce about ancient history.

"I didn't expect to ever see you again."

"You've done well for yourself," she said, looking around the office.

He was annoyed by his own reaction to her, and his words came out harsher than he intended.

"What are you doing here, Camilla?"

She shifted slightly in the chair. "It's a little hard to explain."

"Look, I don't have time for small talk. So why don't you get to the point." He sat back, ready to digest whatever legal problem was on her mind. He'd help her if he could, but only because he still felt bad about the way he'd ended it in Vegas.

THE MILLIONAIRE'S
Convenient ARRANGEMENT

"Fine." She crossed her legs and leaned forward, looking him straight in the eye. "I'm here," she said, "because I need you to marry me."

• • •

The look he gave her made her feel like a witness being questioned in one of his trials. She'd gotten his attention, but the interested and slightly amused look had been replaced by eyes so hard that she felt as if his stare were physically pinning her to the chair. The last five years had transformed any lingering traces of boyish charm into chiseled good looks with a slightly dangerous edge. His gray eyes appraised her coolly. She could remember a time when they had darkened with passion. Eyes like storm clouds that reflected the swirling passions he'd aroused in her during that brief escape from the most desperate time in her life. His thick black hair, so perfectly in place now, had been wildly unruly and she resisted the impulse to reach out now, to lean across his desk and see if it still had the texture of silk as it slipped through her fingers. Rekindling an old romance was not what she was here for.

"Is this a joke?" There was no warmth in his voice.

"No."

"I spent two weeks with you in Las Vegas five years ago. I've regretted ending things the way I did." He paused and glanced pointedly at her ring finger. "But apparently you moved on."

The nerve of him. He was the one who dumped her, before she even had a chance to explain what was going on in her life, how badly she wished things were different. She hadn't gone to Vegas intending to meet a man who'd turn her emotions upside down. But she'd felt a connection to Sam. She remembered how they'd strolled through shops on the Strip the last evening they spent together, and how sweet he'd been when she spotted a simple silver chain in a jeweler's case, with two interlocking hearts. He'd bought it for her, fastening it around her neck, and she had felt like she could at least carry with her this one perfect memory. But the clasp must have broken sometime that night, because when she reached to touch the hearts as she lay in bed thinking about her future, the necklace was gone.

After a sleepless night, she'd decided to tell Sam everything and ask for his advice. She had foolishly believed he might help her think of another solution. But before she'd been able to confide in him about her plans, plans she desperately wanted *not* to go through with, he'd cut her off, discarded her like a stray poker chip left on a table by a vacation gambler returning to his real life. So she'd married Danny, completing her end of what began as nothing more than a business proposition.

"As a matter of fact, I got married a week after you left," she said, meeting his eye and lifting her chin. She was not going to feel guilty when he was the one who had walked away from her. And when the decision she'd made had been to put her sister, Olivia, above all else.

"Well. Then it seems you already have a husband."

"Not anymore. That's why I'm here."

"I don't handle divorces."

This wasn't going at all the way she'd planned. To be honest, she hadn't really had a plan. She'd headed for his office and thought she'd just figure out the best approach once she got there. But the man sitting across the desk from her wasn't the same man at all that she had known in Las Vegas. That Sam had had been cocky and sure of himself, but approachable. This Sam, measuring her with steely eyes, exuded power and control. It would be much harder than she'd expected to get him to understand and to agree with her proposal. "I don't need a divorce lawyer, Sam." She leaned forward. "What I need is for you—"

He cut her off. "To marry you. So you said."

"For you to listen," she finished.

"Camilla, it was…interesting…seeing you again, but unless you have a serious legal matter to consult me on, you need to leave. Now."

He was looking at her like he thought she'd lost her mind, and she realized it probably seemed that way.

"Look," he said, "if you had called and made an appointment—"

"I didn't think you'd take my call. Why would it be any different than last time?"

He looked genuinely perplexed. "I don't know what you're talking about."

He didn't even *remember* not returning her phone calls? It had been more than four years since she'd last tried to contact him. But Camilla remembered it very clearly.

She took a deep breath. "I'm here now. Just let me explain."

THE MILLIONAIRE'S
Convenient ARRANGEMENT

He glanced at his watch. "You have two minutes. I'm finishing a trial tomorrow, and I don't have time for games."

"Meet me tomorrow then. After you get out of court."

"Why should I do that?"

He was so formidable. She searched his face for a trace of the warmth she'd been drawn to five years ago, but couldn't find it. She just saw someone who got what he wanted through ruthless determination. She felt herself shudder.

"I can't—it's too much to explain. Have dinner with me tomorrow night, and I'll explain everything."

He seemed to consider for a few moments and she held her breath. In the sleepless nights she'd spent deciding whether or not to come see him, the one thing she'd never considered was that he might dismiss her without even hearing her out.

Finally, he nodded. "All right. Give me your number and I'll call you when I get out of court. It may be late."

She let her breath out slowly.

"That's fine. I'm not going anywhere."

• • •

If there was one thing Sam was good at, it was compartmentalizing his life, locking problems away to be dealt with later, so that he could focus clearly on the matter at hand. It had gotten him through a rocky childhood and served him well in his chosen career.

When he faced the jury, no other thought intruded on his impassioned plea for justice for his client—now a paraplegic thanks to a reckless driver who'd been too busy drinking coffee and texting at fifty miles per hour to notice the red light. Or the compact car coming through the intersection, and the promising high school basketball player in the passenger seat who was now never going to walk again. The driver herself didn't have any money, but the insurance company was sure as hell going to pay every penny of the policy limits. His client's mother sobbed quietly in the background as Sam wrapped up his closing argument.

But when he sat in an empty room in the courthouse, waiting for the jury to return, he let his thoughts entertain the puzzle of Camilla Winthrop showing up at his office. Clearly the woman had lost her mind. It was a pity, because she was even more attractive than he remembered.

THE MILLIONAIRE'S
Convenient ARRANGEMENT

He'd been surprised at how strong the impulse had been to walk around the desk and take her into his arms to find out if the chemistry between them was really as strong as he remembered. Fortunately, reason prevailed. He was not going to take any chances with a woman who obviously had delusions about marrying him.

She had to be running some sort of scam, but he couldn't figure out what her angle was. The sugardaddy she'd latched onto after Sam returned to Miami had apparently left her high and dry, and she'd decided to find out what had happened to that young lawyer she met once upon a time. Sam wasn't that same kid anymore. He cringed when he remembered how he'd let his guard down, opened up to her, shared his plans and dreams. And apparently Camilla had found out he'd actually surpassed his own expectations.

When he'd started the firm with Jon and Ritchie, he'd expected to be successful. He just hadn't imagined *how* successful they would be. It had been his idea, which was why his name was first on the door. But it hadn't taken much to talk his law school buddy Jonathon Berrington, an associate at another of Miami's major insurance defense firms, into trading in the long hours and associate's salary for a chance to own their own firm and bring in million-dollar verdicts for plaintiffs. They would change people's lives and make themselves rich in the process. As the plan began to take form, they'd added Ritchie Perez, a hotshot young prosecutor in the state attorney's office, whose handling of high-profile drug and gang violence cases had catapulted him into the public eye as the champion of the underdog, a man who got justice for the little guy. It was exactly the image they wanted.

The three of them had agreed from the beginning that there would be no fender benders, no dog bites, no slip-and-fall cases handled by the law firm of Flanagan, Berrington & Perez. And no clients with dubious claims, no scammers in neck braces faking injuries. They weren't ambulance chasers, and they wouldn't take a case for a client who didn't deserve to win. They would be the ones who stood up for the innocent victims of drunk drivers and of unscrupulous companies that ignored the warnings in their own product safety tests and caused needless suffering. They would specialize in wrongful death, serious bodily injury, and million-dollar verdicts.

THE MILLIONAIRE'S
Convenient ARRANGEMENT

And that's exactly what they'd done.

"The jury's in."

Sam looked up, nodded to the bailiff, and went into the courtroom.

• • •

"You mean you didn't tell him?" Camilla's sister stared at her. "How could you not tell him?"

"He's different now." Camilla paced across the room, stopped, and looked out the window at the Atlantic Ocean.

"Well, duh," Olivia said, stretching her long limbs and leaning back on the bed. To all appearances, she was the typical 15-year-old, obsessing over the latest pop star, the coolest fashions, the hottest boys in school. Thank God, Camilla thought. She would never let a single day go by without remembering to be thankful. If this had been the only thing Danny had given her, it would have been enough.

"So what did you say?"

"That I wanted him to marry me."

He sister stared at her, mouth gaping. "Well, that's an original opening."

Camilla shrugged. "It bought me a meeting with him. Dinner. Tonight." She looked at her watch.

"So where's he meeting you?"

"Here."

"*Here?*" Olivia glanced at the closed door across the suite. "What about JD?"

"Well, since JD's the whole point…"

"Look," Olivia said, her brilliantly blue eyes turning a deeper shade with intensity. "Let's just leave now. We can go anyplace. There's enough money—you don't have to do this. We'll just…we'll go live in Italy!"

Camilla shook her head. "We're not going to start running." Arguably the only thing of value her mother had passed on to her and her sister was dual citizenship in Italy, a result of her mother's paternal grandfather, who immigrated to the United States in the 1930s, dying a few years later without ever having renounced his Italian citizenship. It seemed to Camilla to be a tenuous link, but her mother had investigated it and obtained dual citizenship for herself and both her daughters, claiming it gave them "an international flair." Camilla, however, had no desire to live in exile from the only country she considered her home. Compared to that, a marriage of convenience to the father of her child seemed like not such a big sacrifice at all.

"Trust me, Liv. This is the only answer. It'll be fine."

"He'll hate you."

"Probably. It'll only be for a year at most. Then we really will be able to start over."

"Promise?"

"Absolutely."

Olivia didn't look convinced.

"Listen," Camilla said. "I better get downstairs. I'm supposed to meet him at the restaurant, and he's probably on his way here now."

There was a knock at the door and they both jumped guiltily.

"Do you think..."

Camilla shook her head. "He doesn't know what room we're in." She peeked through the eyehole in the door, then looked at Olivia. "I guess he found out."

Camilla opened the door and tried to slip out into the hallway, but Sam blocked the door from closing.

"Aren't you going to invite me in, Camilla?"

"No, I'm ready to go down..." Even with heels on, she had to tilt her head up to look in his eyes. She'd forgotten how tall he was. His shoulders seem broader now that she was so close to him, and he had an air of confidence that bordered on arrogance. He exuded a kind of casual power that seemed just as intimidating standing in a hotel hallway as it had been sitting behind the desk in his opulent office.

"Who's in the room with you?" He took hold of her elbow lightly. "Your lover? I want to know exactly what's going on here, and I don't think you want to have this conversation in the hallway."

She stepped back and let him in the door.

• • •

Whatever he'd been expecting, it wasn't to see a teenage girl sitting on the bed.

"This is my sister, Olivia. Livvy, this is Sam Flanagan."

"Hi."

THE MILLIONAIRE'S
Convenient ARRANGEMENT

Sam felt a little foolish.

The girl was staring at him like he was some sort of fascinating other species. She looked over at Camilla. "Oh my God, Cam. You didn't tell me he looked exactly like—"

"Liv!"

"Sorry." She silently studied Sam another ten seconds or so, then shrugged.

"Are you satisfied? Can we go to dinner now?" Camilla started toward the door.

Olivia looked back down at her book, something ghoulish with vampires on the cover from what Sam could see of it, and gave every appearance of tuning the adults out.

"Maybe it would be better to talk in the restaurant," Sam allowed.

"Yes, let's do that."

They were almost out the door when another voice interrupted them.

"*Mommy?*"

Sam jerked his head around. The connecting door opened and a small boy walked out, rubbing his eyes and clutching a tattered teddy bear.

"I thought you were asleep, honey," Camilla said, hurrying over and bending down to give him a hug. She brushed a wavy lock of black hair back from his forehead, and Sam felt something clench in his gut. The little boy looked up then, staring at him with Camilla's brilliantly blue eyes.

"Who are you?"

"That's Sam, honey. He's an…old friend of Mommy's." She looked over at Sam. "Sam, this is my son, JD."

Sam just stared. Was it possible? Of course it was. But for the eyes, he was staring at a mirror image of himself as a child.

"I'm sorry, just let me get JD settled back into bed."

"Not quite yet," Sam said, walking over and crouching down in front of the boy, who leaned back against his mother, but kept his eyes on Sam's face.

"Where's your daddy, JD?" Sam asked softly, then regretted the question when the little boy's lower lip began to tremble.

"Daddy had to go away," JD said.

"That's enough," Camilla said sharply, looking at Sam as she pulled the little boy toward the other room. "JD, let's get you back into bed."

The little boy rubbed his eyes and held Camilla's hand, walking with her back toward the bedroom. He paused when he got to the door and turned back to look at Sam.

"Daddy can't live with us anymore. God needs him up in heaven," he said solemnly, and Sam heard Camilla catch her breath before she looked back over her shoulder and gave Sam a look that said she wished *he* was the one who was dead.

THE MILLIONAIRE'S
Convenient ARRANGEMENT

The Millionaire's Unexpected Proposal available now.

Praise for *The Millionaire's Unexpected Proposal*

"Jane Peden gives readers exactly what they want – plenty of sass, sizzle, and surprises on every page!" – Roxanne St. Claire, *New York Times* and *USA Today* Bestselling Author

"The conflict here is rich and deep. There's no greater grist for the gut than two scarred lovers trying to find a way back into each other's arms." – Julie Leto, *New York Times* and *USA Today* Bestselling Author

Chapter One: The Millionaire's Intriguing Offer

(Coming in 2017 from Mr. Media Books, *The Millionaire's Intriguing Offer*, Book No. 3 in the *Miami Lawyers* series.)

Jonathon glanced in the mirror in the lobby of the law firm as he adjusted the bow tie on his tux, while his two partners smirked in the background.

"I can't believe I let you two talk me into this." It wasn't enough that the firm bought a premium table and wrote a substantial check to help underwrite the event. No. Sam and Ritchie had also volunteered him as one of the featured bachelors at the charity bachelor auction. So he was off to an evening of being paraded across the stage while giggling tipsy women placed bets to try to win "The Date of a Lifetime" with him.

"I'm sure you'll have a great time," Sam said. Jonathon turned and stared at him.

"Right," Ritchie piped in. "How bad could it be?"

Then they both started laughing. Probably remembering the time shortly after they opened their office when all three of them had been listed in a magazine among Miami's most eligible bachelors, and they'd all done the bachelor auction thing for another worthwhile charity. Ritchie had ended up at the opera with a society matron who kept putting her hand on his knee and talking about May-December romances, and Jonathon had endured a painfully awkward evening with a rebel debutante

THE MILLIONAIRE'S
Convenient ARRANGEMENT

whose mother was trying to push her into a good match. The date went so well that the girl eloped later that evening with her "unsuitable" boyfriend, the lead singer in a local band. Sam had actually had a nice time and dated the woman who "bought" him at the auction a few times after that, then broke it off before things got serious.

Back then Sam had been a confirmed bachelor, just like Jonathon and Ritchie. But all that changed two years ago, when Sam found out he had a son. Now six-year-old JD was the pride of his life, he was reunited with Camilla, the woman he'd loved and lost, and they were happily married with a second child – one-year-old Sophia. Rounding out the family was Camilla's 17-year-old sister, Olivia, who had become a fixture here in the office working part-time after school and dreaming about the day she'd go to law school and follow in Sam's footsteps.

And last year Ritchie, who had been a prosecutor with the state attorney's office before the three of them started their successful personal injury law firm seven years ago, had fallen for Maria, a woman with a huge heart who volunteered at the soup kitchen at Ritchie's church, and was single-handedly raising her younger brother, Joey. As it turned out, Maria was also the twin sister of a man Ritchie had prosecuted and sent to prison for drug and gang related crimes almost a decade ago. But they'd worked through everything, and Maria's brother Tito, recently released from prison, was now working at the law firm doing new case intake, and had been instrumental in launching an organization that provided opportunities for a fresh start to juvenile offenders. The very same organization that was benefitting from the bachelor auction tonight. So really, how could Jonathon say no?

He just hoped whoever placed the winning bid tonight was up for a bit of adventure. Because what Jonathon had planned for their "Date of a Lifetime" was a lot different from the typical fancy dinner and night out on the town.

• • •

Bailey Reid smoothed the borrowed dress and glanced over at her friend Mitsy. "I still can't believe you talked me into attending this."

"Well, with Trip stuck working on some real estate deal, did you really expect me to come alone?"

"We could have stayed home and made caramel popcorn and binge-watched old Parks and Rec episodes." Which was exactly how Bailey had planned on spending the evening on her own, while Mitsy and Trip went to the fancy benefit.

"Hey," Mitsy said. "We paid $1500 a plate for this. You wanted me to let it go to waste?"

"Fifteen hundred..." Bailey shook her head.

"Besides, it's for that charity I told you about. The one with the job opening for someone with a masters in social work." Mitsy nudged her and winked.

Mitsy had been trying for years to get her to move to Miami, but this visit was a full-on onslaught. From the day they first met at freshman orientation at Brown University, they'd become the unlikeliest of best friends. Mitsy came from a long line of Miami debutantes who had all attended Brown. Bailey was there on a full-ride academic scholarship, and was, as far as she knew, the first one in her family to ever go to college.

Thanks to Mitsy, studious, focused, goal-oriented Bailey had learned to relax and have fun. And when Mitsy found out freshman year that Bailey planned to stay in Providence over the Christmas break rather than exhaust her meager savings on a plane ticket to visit her adoptive parents in the mid-west, she'd insisted on taking Bailey home with her to Miami. Bailey had been adamant that she didn't want her new friend paying for the trip, but somehow she'd wound up anyway sitting next to Mitsy in first class, leaving snow-clad and wind-swept Rhode Island behind and headed for bright sun, city lights, and Florida beaches. It was the first of many occasions where Mitsy just swept aside Bailey's objections and got her own way.

Look, Mitsy had said, *you're the one who will be doing me a favor by coming. I think it would be mean of you to keep me from spending the holidays with my best friend, just because of money.* Mitsy had grinned. *What's the point of being born filthy rich if my best friend is going to be all stuck up about me paying?*

Do you always get your own way? Bailey had asked, scowling.

Absolutely, Mitsy had said, grinning infectiously.

And although Bailey had been sure she wouldn't fit in with Mitsy's debutante friends or her blue blood family, it had never been a problem.

THE MILLIONAIRE'S
Convenient ARRANGEMENT

After college, Mitsy returned to Miami and took a part-time job as a docent in a local museum because, as she said, it seemed a waste not to use her art history degree for something. But her condo in the trendy art deco section of South Beach had come courtesy of her trust fund rather than her paycheck. She'd given that up, though, when she married Trip and they settled into a more traditional – and even more expensive – condo spanning an entire floor in one of the toney highrise buildings on Brickell Avenue in downtown Miami.

After graduation from Brown, Bailey went on to Boston University for her MSW, then took a job working for a small nonprofit that helped obtain benefits for developmentally disabled children and adults. But while the work was satisfying – and her salary helped her chip away at the student loans she'd had to take on to get through graduate school – it wasn't what she wanted to do with her life.

She had to admit – the job Mitsy had told her about, and convinced her to apply for, was intriguing. It was a foundation run by a man named Tito Martinez – a convicted felon who had turned his own life around – dedicated to providing diversion for juvenile offenders. But it went further than typical programs, engaging the young offenders in activities like sailing and team sports, tutoring them, and partnering with local businesses to provide paid internships and mentoring. Although the program had only been around a few years, the success rate so far was impressive.

Misty propelled her into the ballroom, then pulled her along when she stopped to look at the display about the charity.

"Come on, you've already practically memorized their website," Mitsy said. "Let's check out the bachelor auction."

"What are you doing looking at a bachelor auction?"

"Just because I'm married doesn't mean I can't still enjoy looking at a good looking man. Besides, *you're* still single."

"And planning to stay that way." Bailey liked having control of her own life. Where she lived. Where she worked. Who her friends were. She'd spent her childhood with very little control over her own life, until she wound up at 15 with the foster family who later adopted her, and everything changed for the better. Before that, the only semblance of stability in her life had been the precious two years she'd spent living with

THE MILLIONAIRE'S
Convenient ARRANGEMENT

her grandfather before he died.

"Is this for real?" Bailey studied the photo of a cover-model worthy man in a tux. "*Fly to Paris for the weekend on my private jet. Enjoy an evening of fine dining, visit the Paris night life, and wake up in a luxurious suite at the Four Seasons Hotel Georges V in time for a marvelous brunch by the Eiffel Tower before we board the jet for the return trip.*" Bailey pretended to consider it. "So what do you think the bidding will be on that one?"

"Whatever it is, it's not worth it," Mitsy laughed. "Believe me, you would not want to spend the weekend in Paris – or anywhere else – with that guy."

"That bad, huh?"

"Worse."

They browsed through the other photos and descriptions on the display. Most of them were fairly predictable, ranging, on the high end, from dinner and a Broadway show in New York, to meals in exclusive Miami restaurants, followed by a night of VIP clubbing.

Then she turned to the last display and froze. *What was he doing in Miami?* Jack stared back at her from the glossy framed photograph. The jaw was squarer, the face older, but there was no doubt it was him. She didn't need to look at the name on the bio to know it was Jonathon Berrington. To her, just Jack.

"Oh, hey, that's a good one. Jonathon Berrington. Nice guy, but a total player. Let's see what he's offering." Mitsy leaned closer to read the display. "Well I'm not surprised."

"What?"

"*Sail with me to my cottage in Bimini, where we'll enjoy fresh local seafood prepared by my private chef, then continue the next morning to the Florida Keys, exploring the reefs and enjoying the tropical nights.*" Mitsy grinned. "I bet. From what I've heard, a night with Jonathon Berrington is something worth experiencing."

"Mitsy, you *are* married now."

"And I wouldn't trade Trip for anything. But a girl can still use her imagination," Mitsy said, sighing.

"Come on," Bailey said. "Let's go find our table." But she allowed herself one lingering look back at Jack's photo before following Mitsy

THE MILLIONAIRE'S
Convenient ARRANGEMENT

into the main ballroom.

By the time the cocktails and mingling were over and the guest were being gently herded to their tables, the distinguished crowd was already pretty well lubricated. Except for Bailey, who didn't drink. Ever. She liked to joke with Mitsy that the real reason they'd become best friends was because Bailey had been the designated driver-partier-and all around trouble stopper, using her clear head to make sure Mitsy got home safely from every college bash, bar and after hours club in Providence, New York, or wherever else Mitsy's spur of the moment jaunts took them. The adrenaline rush had been more than enough for Bailey. And she had her own reasons for avoiding alcohol and any other potentially addictive substances.

The dinner was delicious, but Bailey figured that for $1,500 a plate it had better be. The champagne was flowing freely at the tables too, and it was apparent – once the bachelor auction began – that some of the bachelors had already overindulged, if their performance on stage was any indication. But they were not to be outdone by the succession of tipsy women who went on stage for a photo opp for their winning bid. Which in some cases involved a bit of extravagant flirting while audience members whistled and cheered. Bailey knew it was supposed to be a fun event, but she still felt things got a little out of hand. She hoped Jack was not going to get up there and make a fool of himself.

She turned back to Mitsy. "So do you actually know Jonathon Berrington?"

"Hmmm, I thought I saw you paying attention to his photo. Quite the hottie, isn't he? Want me to introduce you?"

"No, don't be ridiculous. You said he was a player, right?"

"That's his reputation. He's already dated most of the eligible single girls I grew up with."

A sudden thought occurred to her. "Did you ever . . .?"

"No, I was already with Trip before I met Jonathon. But I've heard plenty of stories. He's one of those guys who makes it clear right up front that he has no intention of anything getting serious. But he sure knows how to show a girl a good time." She leaned closer. "Danielle Branson told me he was so good in bed he absolutely ruined her for other men."

THE MILLIONAIRE'S
Convenient ARRANGEMENT

"Isn't Danielle the one who's dating the state senator who's 25 years older than her?"

"She thinks he has a real future in politics."

"Right."

"Anyway, Jonathon has a reputation for being a complete gentleman. And some kind of an incredible lover. Not to mention a brilliant lawyer. Trip says if he had to trust anyone with a sticky legal issue, it would be Jonathon Berrington."

Bailey thought back to the boy she'd know, his gangly adolescent legs dangling from the dock beside hers as they looked out over the water. How earnest he'd sounded when he said there was no way he was going to fall in line with the plans his parents had for him. Well, it hadn't stopped him from going to an Ivy League law school, obviously. So maybe living in Miami was his small rebellion.

"I wouldn't be surprised if he ends up one of these days with some blue blood fiancé from another old Boston family, and then he'll probably say goodbye to Miami for good."

It didn't make any difference to her now.

"Ok, that's enough about Jonathon Berrington. Let's talk about-"

"Oh, I don't think so," Mitsy said.

"What?"

She tapped her program then gestured toward the stage. "There he comes now."

The MC read the bio and described Jonathon's "Date of a Lifetime" while he walked out onto the stage. Bailey didn't really pay attention to the words. She was transfixed, studying the man her childhood best friend had become. She'd met him when she was eleven. And worshipped him for two summers with the level of devotion only an adolescent girl could bestow on an older boy who paid attention to her. Who treated her with kindness. Kindness had been something Bailey had just been beginning to believe in. Of course, her name hadn't been Bailey then. And before long the bottom had fallen out of the world she'd only started to discover.

There was a flurry of excited laughter through the crowd as the bidding began. In less than two minutes the number was well over the price paid for any of the other bachelors auctioned off so far. And no wonder,

THE MILLIONAIRE'S
Convenient ARRANGEMENT

Bailey thought. The stunning photo she'd seen in the lobby didn't even begin to do him justice. He had the square jaw and clear blue eyes that marked him as part of the Berrington line. And even from out here at her table in the crowded ballroom she could see the cleft in his chin that had been more of a dimple when he was a boy.

"What are you doing?" Bailey hissed when Mitsy raised her paddle and the auctioneer pointed in their direction, announcing her bid.

"I have to bid on something. Especially since I lost out on those last two items," Mitsy said, still pouting about the antique ladies' Rolex and the couples' deluxe spa weekend she'd been outbid on by last-minute write-ins on the silent auction.

"Do I have to remind you that you're *married*? What's Trip going to say if you come home with an eligible bachelor?"

"Oh, he's not for me."

Bailey felt her eyes widen in horror. "You better not be buying him for me," she hissed.

Mitsy just grinned wickedly and raised the bet another $500.

"Stop it," Bailey said, kicking her under the table.

"No," Mitsy said. "I think this is exactly what you need. Jonathon Berrington will treat you to a first class weekend. Who knows, you might even get laid. Besides, I saw you looking at his profile. Don't tell me you're not interested."

"I'm not interested."

"Um-hmmm. Just keeping saying that, girlfriend."

He was dressed in a tux that must have been custom made for him, and he strolled across the stage as if he owned it. Some of the earlier bachelors had made a bit of a spectacle of themselves, gyrating their hips to the music to the delight of the women in the crowd, doing little dance moves, even engaging in some banter with the crowd. Jack simply turned when he reached the center of the stage and pivoted slightly to face the audience. He slipped his hands into his pockets and held a pose that could have been right off the cover of GQ Magazine.

When the bids hit $10,000 he took off his jacket, and the crowd went wild. His shirt was a perfect fit, tapered to the lines of his well-defined body. And it looked crisp and pressed. Everything about him looked . . . perfect. And Bailey wondered if any part of the boy she'd known was

THE MILLIONAIRE'S
Convenient ARRANGEMENT

still there underneath the veneer of casual sophistication. She would rather have just remembered him the way he used to be. Back when he was just Jack and she was Sparrow and the sleek little sailboat he taught her to sail was a pirate ship, setting out across the Caribbean to unknown lands in search of treasure and adventure. She really didn't want to think of Jack as some stuffy lawyer pushing papers all day and negotiating deals that helped the rich get richer. Being exactly what his parents had planned for him. Exactly what he'd said he would never become.

Mitsy upped the bet again and Bailey sank further down into her chair. Obviously Mitsy had seen her lingering at Jack's photo and had mistaken her curiosity about someone she used to know for interest in a hot bachelor. And why not? Mitsy didn't know anything really about Bailey's life before she went to live with the Reids. Her past wasn't something Bailey liked to remember, much less talk about to a friend who, despite her kind heart and best intentions, simply would never understand.

Maybe if she stopped protesting so much, Mitsy would just let it drop. Especially if the bidding kept escalating.

Mitsy didn't let it drop.

"Going, going, gone! To one of the lovely ladies at Table 19!" The celebrity auctioneer swung the spotlight to their table, where Mitsy pointed at Bailey and the audience clapped. "We have a new record, " the auctioneer continued. "That's $18,000 for Jonathon Berrington. Come on up here young lady and claim your prize."

She had no choice but to get up out of her chair and step forward.. Her heart was beating so strongly she was afraid it would jump right out of her chest as she went up the few steps onto the stage. Then she was standing there, directly in front of him. She had to tilt her head back to look directly into those clear eyes. Eyes that had once been the mirrors to her own hopes and dreams.

Hello Jack. The words were on the tip of her tongue but she couldn't say them. She waited for the sudden recognition to come over his face. But it didn't come. Of course he didn't remember her. What did she expect?

• • •

About halfway through the bidding Jonathon had noticed Mitsy

THE MILLIONAIRE'S
Convenient ARRANGEMENT

Hamilton was one of the bidders. And wondered what Trip's wife was up to. His interest was definitely caught when Mitsy won the bidding and the woman sitting next to her got up somewhat reluctantly and walked toward the stage to claim him as her prize.

Reluctance was not something he was accustomed to when dealing with the opposite sex. Women orchestrated elaborate "accidental" meetings in the hopes of dating him, and lied about their pasts to try to interest him. When you were not only a successful and sometimes controversial trial lawyer but also hailed from one of the wealthiest families in New England, interesting propositions from women came with the territory. But he couldn't recall any of them ever approaching him looking like the thought of a date with him was making them physically ill.

She gave her name to the auctioneer as he took her hand to assist her onto the stage, then she was standing there in front of Jonathon, looking up at him coolly. There was something both forced and tentative about her smile, though, and he wondered why she'd allowed her friend to place bids on her behalf when apparently she'd rather be just about anywhere else than standing there on the stage with him.

Her dress – obviously a couture original – hugged the slim curve of her body perfectly. But it was her eyes that caught and held his attention. Golden brown, the color of light amber, and as clear as a precious stone. He'd known someone with eyes like that once, a very long time ago. Whatever had become of her, it was a sure bet that she hadn't ended up wearing a ten thousand dollar dress and going to a bachelor auction in Miami. He smiled. This evening was everything Sparrow would have hated. And he found himself hoping that wherever she'd ended up, she hadn't changed. But the quick memory made him look a little more indulgently at the golden-eyed beauty standing uncertainly in front of him.

"All right, everyone," the auctioneer said, "let's give it up for Bailey Reid, the winner of a Date of a Lifetime with prominent local attorney Jonathon Berrington!"

Jonathon took her hand and turned them both to face the audience. She looked so damned uncomfortable that, on impulse he put a hand around her waist and pulled her toward him, dipping her dramatically and kissing her, to the loud delight of the crowd.

"Well, well, let's keep this G-rated," the auctioneer said, laughing.

THE MILLIONAIRE'S
Convenient ARRANGEMENT

But for a few second the crowds disappeared, the sounds of the audience and the auctioneer fading to white noise, as Jonathon felt her startled lips part under his. What he'd meant as a playful gesture, playing to the crowd and maybe getting his nervous date to relax and lighten up a bit, shot through his system like a bolt of electricity. Fascinated and more than a surprised, he dipped her lower, lingered a little longer sampling the taste of her before setting her back on her feet and grinning sheepishly at the crowd.

Judging by the stunned look on her face, she'd been as affected as he was. And he was starting to think of this whole Date of a Lifetime thing as less of a chore and more of an intriguing interlude that he might actually enjoy.

Acknowledgments

It was so much fun writing about Ritchie and Maria, and I hope the readers who asked for Ritchie's story, after meeting him in Book #1 (*The Millionaire's Unexpected Proposal*), were not disappointed. Thank you so much to publisher Bob Andelman at Mr. Media Books for publishing the next book in the *Miami Lawyers* series.

Special thanks to my agent Elizabeth Winick Rubinstein for her support and encouragement. And thank you to my editor Bev Katz Rosenbaum and copy editor Rebecca Cartee for helping me make this book the best it could be. Kudos to cover designer Lori Parsells for capturing exactly the look that was needed.

Thank you to Dani Barclay and Cameron Yeager at Barclay Publicity for their wonderful work promoting this book and the series.

I'm also grateful to my beta readers Cheryl Mansfield and Mary Ann Strozak Efron for reading the early draft of this book, and sharing their always helpful comments and insights. And to Cheryl for all those hours spent at our local Starbucks, writing and drinking way too much coffee.

Thank you to my family – my husband Dave, son Tom, and daughter Megan – for putting up with me disappearing to Starbucks with Cheryl for so many long Saturdays of writing, and spending lots of time at home as well distracted by the characters having conversations in my head.

And most of all, thank you to all the readers of the Miami Lawyers series. Please stop by my website (www.janepeden.com) and visit my Facebook page for more information on the rest of this series, and other books about lawyers and love in the Florida sun.

About The Author

Jane Peden is a Florida trial attorney who writes sexy contemporary romances set in the exciting South Florida city of Miami, where millionaire lawyers live extravagant lifestyles and find love when they least expect it. When Jane isn't in court, you can find her at the beach with her laptop, dreaming up stories about successful, confident men who know what they want and how to get it, and smart, sexy women who demand love on their own terms. Jane lives on the Gulf Coast of Florida with her husband, two kids, two dogs, and a fish.

THE MILLIONAIRE'S
Convenient ARRANGEMENT

*Get to know romance novelist **JANE PEDEN**, author of **THE MILLIONAIRE'S UNEXPECTED PROPOSAL** and **THE MILLIONAIRE'S CONVENIENT ARRANGEMENT**, in this Mr. Media® interview*
https://youtu.be/4tKM2x-1VzA

What is Mr. Media® Interviews? The calm of Charlie Rose, the curiosity of Terry Gross and the unpredictability of Howard Stern! Since February 2007, more than 1,000 exclusive Hollywood, celebrity, pop culture video and audio comedy podcast interviews by Mr. Media®, a.k.a., Bob Andelman, with newsmakers in TV, radio, movies, music, magazines, newspapers, books, websites, social media, politics, sports, graphic novels, and comics!

For more interviews like this one: http://MrMedia.com

Made in the USA
Charleston, SC
27 October 2016